BLOOD
OF
TEXAS

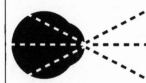This Large Print Book carries the
Seal of Approval of N.A.V.H.

BLOOD OF TEXAS

Will Camp

G.K. Hall & Co.
Thorndike, Maine

Published in 1996 by arrangement with HarperCollins Publishers, Inc.

G.K. Hall Large Print Western Collection.

The text of this Large Print edition is unabridged.
Other aspects of the book may vary from the original edition.

Set in 16 pt. Plantin.

Printed in the United States on permanent paper.

Library of Congress Cataloging in Publication Data

Camp, Will.
    Blood of Texas / Will Camp.
      p.   cm.
    ISBN 0-7838-8209-2 (lg. print : hc : alk. paper)
    1. Large type books. I. Title.
  [PS3562.E964B58   1997]
  813′.54—dc21   97-13076

For Mom and Dad
who first took me to Goliad, San Jacinto,
and The Alamo

San Antonio de Bexar, September 16, 1835

"Viva la independencia! Viva Mexico!" shouted the nighttime throng crowding upon the Main Plaza at the foot of the Church of San Fernando. Tejanos, dressed in their finest clothes, filled the square and celebrated Mexican Independence Day to the strains of lively music. Tejanos, so called for they lived in Mexico's farthest province, and mestizos, named for the mixed blood of their ancestors — themselves fathered by the Spanish conquistadors, in the loins of Indian mothers — meandered through the plaza laughing, singing, and dancing. They sipped wines and liquors, drank chocolate and tasted the delicacies that vendors displayed on makeshift tables or woolen blankets spread upon the ground.

The vendors, many animated by liquor, sold tamales, goat meat, frijoles wrapped in tortillas, and candies like *nueces dulce* — a sweet concoction of sugar, cinnamon, and pecans — or *queso de tuna,* a sweetmeat made from the fruit of the prickly pear cactus. Scattered across the plaza like walnuts dropped from a great tree, musicians played their guitars, mandolins, violins, and flutes. And they sang, the Spanish flowing softly from their tongues with each ballad.

Everywhere there was music, and wherever there was music, people danced and laughed, their smiles white slashes in their brown faces. A few curious Indians gathered on the perimeter to watch the festivities, and a smattering of Anglos, primarily men but occasionally women and children, wandered through the crowd of mestizos.

The plaza was lit by torches with flames burning as hot as the talk of revolution, particularly among the Anglos. Blazing against a black sky, the torches threw off dark shadows that danced step for step with every person moving among the celebrating multitude. The shadows were as fleeting as the rumors of rebellion that had consumed San Antonio de Bexar in the previous weeks.

Rubio Portillo strolled among the revelers, his arm entwined with that of his betrothed, Angelita Sanchez. The flat brim of his wide hat shaded his dark eyes from the flaring light of the torches. He regretted leaving his rancho, for much work remained for him and his brother, Tomas, to complete before winter. The chores seemed endless after their father's death during the winter. Tomas, he knew, would have come to Bexar anyway, for his brother never missed a celebration or fandango, nor avoided a young lady, save his bride-to-be, Angelita.

Though Rubio longed to see Angelita, he felt he should have stayed at the rancho to manage chores, in spite of her missive insisting that he come. He gave in to her request, which was certainly reasonable, though not as practical as working. But as he meandered around the plaza with Angelita on his arm, he wished he had remained on the rancho.

He didn't feel like celebrating because the responsibility of running the rancho weighed heavily upon him. Or maybe, he thought, it was the guilt he carried for listening to Angelita instead of his common sense. Then, perhaps it was the whisper of revolution in the air that seemed to hover above everything else. Or maybe it was his marriage, planned for Christmas. At thirty years old, he had long been of marrying age. Despite his age, the notion of marriage gave him pause.

Already the Tejanos of San Antonio de Bexar were talking of the marriage, because the fair-skinned Angelita was the only child of the town's wealthiest merchant, though her aged father was no longer as prosperous as he'd once been. Many said Angelita was the prettiest young lady in all of Texas, and Rubio found no reason to argue with that. As for himself, Rubio was proud to be considered one of the best horsemen between Nacogdoches on the east and the Rio Grande on the west. With his father's death, he now ran one of the largest ranchos on the San Antonio River. Some men had even suggested that one day he might be the Texas representative to the Coahuila legislature, though Rubio believed, like many Anglos, that Texas should have its own legislature more responsive to Texas's needs than distant Coahuila.

He felt Angelita's fingers squeeze his arm and he looked down into her dark eyes. She smiled, and he consumed her beauty as others around him drank wine. Her dark hair was parted in the middle and tied in back with a red silk ribbon. As he looked at her, Angelita let her lace rebozo slide from her shoulder down her arm so he could see the cut of her dress. The tan flesh of her shoulders disappeared beneath the red silk and mounded into her heaving bosom. Her slender hips were layered with white lace that billowed out and brushed against his trousers as they walked. She lifted the fallen shawl to her shoulders and leaned against him.

"Why are you quiet tonight, Rubio?"

"I am worried for us, and for Texas."

Angelita cooed. "Once we marry, we shall have nothing to worry about except our children at our feet and our fortune."

"If war comes to Texas, Angelita, we could lose both."

"It is only the talk of the Anglos," she scoffed. "Most of them don't even speak our language."

"But I speak theirs and cannot help but hear their words."

"Their words mean nothing to me."

"Even when they're true?"

Angelita jerked her arm from Rubio's and lifted her rebozo until it covered her hair. "How can you say that?"

"It's true. Santa Anna himself ignores the constitution. The government will not recognize Texas as a state so that all of us — Anglo and Tejano — have representation. Texas is more than a province of Coahuila. Texas is destined for greatness."

Angelita stamped her foot, then planted her balled hands on her hips. "I'll hear no more of this. You're spoiling the celebration. You are too serious." She turned her head away. "Some say that I should marry Juan Paz instead of you."

Rubio gritted his teeth and shoved his thumbs in the red sash tied around his waist. He knew most men in Bexar, and liked or tolerated all save one: Juan Paz. It mattered not that Juan Paz once had courted Angelita. Rubio knew he would have hated him anyway, for his cruelty. An industrious *arriero*, or ox and mule driver, Paz had started freighting with a yoke of oxen and a *carreta* he had built at age seventeen. Now, fifteen years later, he had two dozen men working for him, freighting in supplies from the towns on the Rio Grande and from the primitive Mexican ports that dotted the Texas coastline. Paz never took a fair price for the goods he carted in, not when he could charge an exorbitant one. Rubio could tell a lot about a man by the way he treated his stock: Paz beat his.

Now, Rubio said, "Paz would be as mean to you as he is to his oxen."

Angelita's eyes flashed with anger. With both hands she jerked the rebozo tighter around her head, then lifted a forefinger at Rubio's nose.

11

"Maybe the others are right."

"The Anglos?" Rubio answered as he glimpsed his brother approaching, a girl on each arm.

"No, those who say I should marry Juan Paz."

"I prefer the Anglos to Paz."

"At least Juan wanted to be here tonight," she huffed. "He even brought fireworks to celebrate Mexico's independence."

Rubio smiled. "I brought you. That's fireworks enough."

Angelita grabbed her skirt with both hands and stormed away, almost colliding with Tomas and his two companions.

Tomas grinned wildly as she blew past, then turned to Rubio. "I have an extra senorita. Take your choice. They are tame, and either would be better for you than that heifer."

Both young ladies giggled.

"No, no, Tomas. The wilder the mare, the better the ride."

"That mare's not worth the ride." Tomas strolled away, pulling his two companions closer.

Rubio shook his head as his brother disappeared into the crowd. Tomas's fun-loving spirit appealed to women, but by morning Tomas wouldn't remember these two, though they would think fondly of him. As Rubio strolled among the throng, he greeted acquaintances, several asking about Angelita's absence. Answering that they had gotten separated in the crowd, he explained he was trying to find her. And he would find her, he knew, after her hot blood cooled.

He ambled around a circle of couples dancing at the feet of a guitarist and violinist. In the swirling crowd he saw Tomas in the arms of yet another senorita. He laughed and moved on, then heard the crisp command of a soldier and turned to see Colonel Domingo Ugartechea, military commander at Bexar, leading a company of soldiers past the revelers to the end of the plaza, where other soldiers waited at two cannons.

Rubio followed the soldiers, certain the colonel would make patriotic remarks and then shoot the cannons. If Angelita were correct, then Juan Paz's fireworks would follow. Rubio didn't care for the cannon blasts or the fireworks, but he was curious if the colonel would mention talk of rebellion among the Anglos.

The troops marched down the street, trying to keep their rows straight, but it was impossible with so many revelers crowding them. In the torchlight, the troopers' uniforms looked new, but Rubio had seen the soldiers in daylight and knew their outfits were tattered and patched, another indication of how little support the Mexican government gave to Texas. The soldiers wore dark blue coats with red collars and cuffs, and gray britches with a red stripe down the outside seam. Their flat-brimmed hats sported wide bands that covered all but an inch of the crown. Their swords hung from white belts and pinged against the wide-roweled spurs on their dull boots.

At the cannons, the colonel halted his men, then called out to the revelers. Few paid him any mind, and finally Ugartechea began to yell to those who watched and listened.

"We celebrate a great day for Mexico and a great day for Texas," he cried. *"Viva la independencia! Viva Mexico!"*

A few echoed his call as a tall Anglo dressed in buckskin leggings, blouse, and moccasins stepped beside Rubio. Glancing to his side, Rubio nodded at the frontiersman, who stood ramrod straight.

"Before us awaits a grand future for Mexico and for Texas," the colonel continued, "but some among us would harm Mexico and Texas by their treasonous talk. Texas is part of Mexico and will remain so always. *Viva la independencia! Viva Mexico!* The steel of our swords, the iron of our cannon, and the bravery of our soldiers stand ready to smite any who would take arms against our young country."

Rubio listened. It was a serious matter to take arms against one's country, he knew, but what if that country did nothing to give the people a voice in its government?

"Tonight we celebrate independence with the voice of our cannons. They sing a pretty song in praise of Mexico, but their music will turn mean against any who turn against Mexico. And shortly, all the cannons in Texas will be in the hands of the army, to defend against those who would harm Mexico and its citizens."

14

Rubio recalled a small cannon having been sent to Gonzales a few years previous to ward off Indians, but it was a little cannon, no more than two feet long, with a bore barely bigger than a man's thumb. Surely, that cannon could not have been what the colonel referred to?

As the colonel finished his speech, the tall man to Rubio's side tapped him on the shoulder. "Senor, my Spanish is not too good. Do you speak English?"

Rubio nodded.

"What was it, then, the fine colonel said about cannons?"

"He said the cannons sing for Mexico tonight but their music will turn mean. . . ."

"No, no, not that, but about all the cannons in Texas."

"It was something like one day, all the cannons in Texas would be in the control of the army."

As the frontiersman nodded, Rubio studied his gaunt, angular face, covered with an unruly beard. The man seemed taller than he because he wore the head of a mountain lion for a cap. The head, missing the lower jaw and having its eye slits sewn shut, sat as a fearsome crown upon the frontiersman's head. The tawny skin draped the man's head and back, giving him a fearsome appearance in the flickering torchlight.

"All of the cannons in Texas will be in the army's control," he mumbled. "*Gracias, amigo.* Now I'll have a drink." The man spun around, and Rubio saw a petite female, who had been

15

standing at the man's side, shielded from his view.

A cannon exploded, then another, bringing a sudden hush over the revelers. The young woman screeched and grabbed Rubio's arm in fright. Then in unison the crowd began to yell. *"Viva la independencia! Viva Mexico!"*

Rubio smiled at the young woman holding onto his arm. She was dark-skinned, likely with Indian blood in her, and comely. She hesitated, then released his arm and nodded shyly. "The noise scared me."

Before Rubio could answer, the frontiersman grabbed the young woman's arm and pulled her with him. "Come along, Mary, don't be getting friendly with any Tejanos."

Rubio thought he saw embarrassment in the young woman's eyes, and as the pungent odor of burnt gunpowder settled upon the plaza, he watched her and the man vanish among the crowd. Behind him, Rubio heard a popping, and he turned to see an eerie light coming from the openings in the arched steeple of the church. He caught the shapes of men and possibly a woman throwing lit objects into the sky. The missiles exploded, sending sparks of red and yellow in all directions. The crowd cheered at the spectacle, but Rubio turned away. He didn't care to see Juan Paz's fireworks.

After five minutes the fireworks stopped, then the church bells began to peal. No sooner did they end than music and laughter picked up.

Many would dance through the night. Others would stagger home drunk. Some would throw blankets down and sleep around the plaza, though Rubio questioned how they could doze through so much noise. Towns were always noisy. He preferred the quiet of his rancho, and as he wandered through the crowd, looking for her, he wondered how Angelita would adjust to life there. He did know, however, that she would still be too angry to dance with him. He finally spotted her in front of a vendor and strode toward her side before realizing that Juan Paz escorted her.

"There you are," he said, offering her his hand.

Angelita refused it. "Juan Paz has agreed to see me home."

Paz, with his hawklike nose, narrow eyes, and thin mustache, twisted his thin lips into a snarl. "Angelita says you are siding with the Anglo dogs who are snapping at the heels of Mexico."

"My only side is with what's right."

"I saw you from the steeple with that dog Calder, the one that wears a lionskin cap. He's a treasonous dog that should be shot."

Rubio looked from Paz to the drunk woman vendor before him. Paz squatted and grabbed a handful of the *nueces dulce* candies. He offered them to Angelita and she took two. Paz turned around, took Angelita by the arm and stepped away.

"You forgot to pay the senora," Rubio reminded him.

"She won't know the difference," Paz replied.

"But you should."

Paz mumbled under his breath, then steered Angelita away.

Rubio reached into his pocket and pulled out a coin. He squatted and pressed the money into the old woman's hand. She grunted as Rubio folded her fingers around the coin. As Rubio stood up, he realized his anger at Angelita. She had a habit of galling a man unless she got her way. She knew how he felt about Juan Paz, yet ran to Paz whenever Rubio did other than she wished.

She was a headstrong woman, no doubt, but her bloodlines were good. She would be the mother of fine, handsome children. For a moment Rubio considered buying a bottle of wine, but he knew he would drink too much if he did, and he needed to remain sober to help Tomas home after sunrise. He snugged his hat down to reduce the chances that he might be recognized by people who would ask him about Angelita's absence. With nothing else to do, he wandered around the plaza watching the merriment, but not sharing in it.

Mary Calder followed her father around the plaza, uncertain why he disliked the Tejanos. They were a decent and fun-loving people. They cared for their young no less than he had cared for her since her mother's death. Maybe something from his past explained it, but he was a man who shared few of his thoughts. Donley

Calder had been one of the first Anglos to trespass upon Spanish Texas. He had trapped for hides, captured mustangs to sell in Natchez, traded with the many Indian tribes, including the Apaches, and had failed to find rich minerals. He'd found an Apache woman for his wife, and she bore him Mary — twenty years ago, when he was thirty-four. Now, he was almost fifty-five, and nine years removed from his wife's death. The years of hard Texas life had worn him down, yet he still provided game for his daughter to prepare, and gave her fine pelts for her to barter for clothes and what small luxuries she wanted.

Mary Calder knew all this, but was puzzled as to why her father had chosen to attend the Mexican celebration. Still, she was thrilled to accompany him and to enjoy so much merriment and music. She did not know the dances the Tejanos performed, but they looked like fun and she wanted to join in. Her father overruled her, however, and she would not go against him, no matter how great the urge.

She struggled to keep up with her father's long strides. But even if they got separated, Donley Calder stood a head taller than most of the Tejanos he moved among, and she could easily spot him. She was embarrassed that he'd worn the lionskin cap. He wanted to scare the Tejanos, was how he put it. Mary supposed he was fearsome to those who didn't know him, for he had survived the early years in Texas intact, but to her, he was just her father, the only man she'd ever really known. Sometimes he could be rude, like to the man who had translated the colonel's words for him. Mary didn't know why her father had inquired, because he knew Spanish and English and a half-dozen Indian languages.

Nor did she know what her father sought on the plaza until he stopped at one of the vendors beneath a dying torch. The peddler had a half-dozen jugs of liquor arrayed before him. Mary shook her head. Her father didn't drink much, but when he did, he drank enough to make up for the rest of the time. He bought two jugs and ambled toward one of the low stone buildings bordering the plaza.

"Shouldn't we be going home?" Mary asked.

"I'm keeping an eye on the Tejanos. They can't be trusted."

"You can't be trusted when you've taken to drink."

Calder grinned. "I intend to celebrate Mexican independence. *Viva la independencia.*"

Calder backed up to the stone wall, then slid down until he was sitting on the ground, watching the festivities. He laughed. "You want to watch the fun, maybe even dance with a young buck. If I'm drinking, I won't be stopping you."

Mary walked away, uncertain whether she should be angry or pleased with her father. She moved among the crowd, finding herself laughing often at the merriment. She stopped for half an hour just to watch the dancers, hoping some young man would ask her to join him. Though a few pointed at her, she could not tell if they were laughing at her or merely enjoying themselves. Maybe they didn't care for her Apache blood. Or maybe they hadn't even given her a second thought. She did not know which would be worse.

When she finally realized how long she'd been watching the dancers, she turned around and bolted across the plaza. She was relieved to find her father where she left him, though he was sprawled across the ground, singing a ribald song. Both jugs were overturned and the air reeked of cheap liquor.

"Papa, it is time to go home," she said, embarrassed for passersby to see him drunk.

"It is indeed," he replied, windmilling his arms in an effort to rise. "I've got an anvil around my neck."

Mary bent over him to assist, but the more she struggled, the more he tried to help and the worse it got. She was entangled in his arms and angry when a voice from behind startled her.

"You need help?"

Turning with a start, Mary touched her hand to her mouth. She recognized the man whose arm she had grabbed when the cannons were fired. She felt embarrassed about that now.

"I am Rubio Portillo," he said. "Can I help you?"

"I am Mary Calder and I want to get my father home."

"Do you live far from here?"

"Less than a mile." Mary straightened her

blouse as she looked at Rubio Portillo. He was a handsome man with solid features that were partially obscured by the darkness.

"Then I shall help."

He bent over her father, put a hand under each arm and pulled him up to his feet. Mary lifted her father's arm over Rubio's shoulder, then picked up his lionskin cap and positioned herself under his other arm. She pointed the way toward her jacal, a small house of sticks chinked with mud and covered with a thatched roof.

"Where are we going?" Donley Calder demanded.

"Home," Mary replied.

"I've got to warn Gonzales," he answered.

"Who's Gonzales?" Mary asked.

"I can't say," he replied. "I don't want the Tejanos to hear."

Mary felt embarrassed as she looked at Rubio. "I'm sorry."

Rubio nodded, but said nothing.

All the way to his house, Calder kept mumbling. "Gonzales. I've got to warn Gonzales."

2

Rubio Portillo gave the sign of the cross as he passed the ruins of Mission San Francisco de la Espada south of Bexar. His Rancho el Espiritu Toro had been mission land until abandoned by the church in 1794, and his father had secured the title. The rancho was watered on the west by the San Antonio River and on the east by Cibolo Creek. The grass was good and the water dependable.

His father had named the ranch for a legendary bull said to be the ghost of the first bull brought to Texas by missionaries. Rubio had never seen the ghost, but he'd never known his father to lie, and his father said he had seen the bull twice. His father had been a brave man, but his voice trembled when he spoke of sighting the bellowing bull on the horizon one stormy night. The next day, he learned of the rebellion against Spain. And after Texas had learned of Mexican independence, his father saw the bull once more, leading a herd of cows onto the ranch. Rubio's father had ridden to inspect the herd, but as he drew close, the bull vanished. The cows and their calves had been real and many and strong, becoming the core of the Portillo herd.

Though Rubio could never fully believe the legend of the bull, he had never scoffed at it, like his brother. Tomas laughed at the tales, asking his father how much wine he'd consumed before his vision. On this warm morning, though, as the brothers passed the remains of the mission, Tomas was not laughing at anything. His head drooped until his chin rested on his chest, and his eyes were locked shut to block out the bright morning sun. Periodically he moaned as his chestnut gelding stepped hard upon the rutted road.

"We are passing the mission," Rubio said softly.

Tomas feebly signed the cross over his chest. "Do not yell."

"It is the wine that is yelling this morning, not me."

Tomas grimaced and covered his ears. "You are cruel as a Comanche to make me ride so early in the morning."

"We've work to do."

Tomas shook his head and lifted his arms. "I'll promise to work later if you'll promise to talk later."

"*Si.*" Rubio shook his reins, and his black stallion pranced ahead.

The gelding darted forward until Tomas pulled back on the reins and mumbled his disgust. "Keep your stallion at a walk." He grimaced at the sound of his own voice.

Reining in his stallion, Rubio smiled. He

would quit toying with his brother, for he had more to consider than just the chores at the rancho. Though he thought much about Angelita, Rubio remembered even more about Mary Calder. She had been grateful for his help in getting her father to their modest jacal. After lighting a candle and helping him ease her father onto his straw mattress, Mary had offered him chocolate to drink. Though tempted to accept, he had declined, thinking it unwise to be seen in the home of a young woman so pretty when he was betrothed to Angelita. Mary thanked him many times, first in English, then in Spanish, as he left her home.

Even as he departed, her father was still repeating that he must warn Gonzales. Rubio knew Donley Calder was thinking of alerting the town of Gonzales. If the men of Gonzales hated the soldiers as much as Donley Calder detested Tejanos, he thought, then trouble lay ahead for all of Texas. It was much more pleasant to think of Angelita. Rubio smiled. Or of Mary Calder. He smiled again.

As he rode he studied the countryside. Everywhere, the grass was yellow from too much sun and too little rain. Where the road paralleled the San Antonio River, he saw that the water was running at its lowest point of the year. But at least water remained. Many of the lesser streams had dropped to a trickle or dried up totally. Only the San Antonio River and Cibolo Creek kept a flow throughout the year. Fortunately, those two water

25

courses ran on either end of his rancho, so his cattle would always find water.

When he finally rode onto Portillo land, Rubio whistled shrilly, flushing a covey of quail from a clump of prickly pear.

Tomas groaned. "Must you always do that every time we return?"

"It is our land, Tomas. The best in all of Texas. Our bulls are stronger, our cows fatter, our horses faster."

"Our brothers louder." Tomas pried his eyes open and stretched his arms. He stifled a yawn, then managed a trace of a grin.

Rubio could only shake his head. "You enjoyed the celebration?"

Tomas scratched his head. "What I remember of it."

"You were squiring two young ladies about."

"Fine-looking ladies, I hope."

Rubio laughed. "You really don't remember."

Tomas held his hand to his head. "Already I have forgotten their faces and their names."

"Why dance with women whose names you can't remember?"

"It's not their names I'm after." Tomas abruptly reined up his horse. "But why should you care? You are betrothed."

"I care because you are my brother, but you drink too much."

"When you are married you will drink more to forget Angelita."

"Why do you say these things, Tomas? You

26

don't know her like I do. She is fiery, *si*, but that is strength."

"I know women. In her, it is a weakness."

Rubio shrugged. "You are not one to marry. You cannot know."

Tomas laughed, then pinched the bridge of his nose. "You are not as wise as you think, my brother, especially about Angelita."

Rubio rode on. "You do not make sense."

"You may not listen to me, but one day you will listen to your stomach." Tomas guided his chestnut beside Rubio's stallion.

"The drink has gone to your head. My stomach doesn't talk."

"One day it will. It will growl in anger."

"At what?"

"Her tortillas. More fire burns in her than will ever burn in her hearth. She cannot cook. She will not cook, not even for you. Her father has spoiled her, even her mother agrees. The fires of greed, not love, burn within her."

"You are wrong, Tomas."

"No, my brother, it is you who is deceived. Though I was drunk, I know that when you angered her, she danced with Juan Paz many times through the night."

Rubio's cheeks burned. He could not deny the truth. "We have talked enough."

"Now it is you who does not want a sound. Did you drink too much? My head aches from wine, but a thousand times the pain I had will befall you if you marry that woman."

Rubio spurred his stallion ahead until he could see the long, walled rancho compound, built during the mission era. The limestone walls stood ten feet tall and formed an uneven pentagon. Round bastions stood guard at three corners. In the far corner rose the walls of a chapel with a cross atop it. It was the biggest building inside the compound, and Rubio wished to store implements or feed within it, but he could not desecrate the holy building.

His and Tomas's quarters abutted the side of the chapel and the back wall. They were spacious for the two brothers, though Rubio was uncertain they would be adequate for Angelita. For a time he had worried that he must ask Tomas to abandon their house and bunk in smaller quarters within the compound, but he hadn't realized that Tomas would leave the ranch when he wed Angelita.

It was a fine place, his ranch, and it made his heart swell with pride whenever he looked upon it. One day, he thought, Angelita would come to love it as much as he did, especially when their children were learning of the land's riches. He was still thinking of his dream when Tomas caught up.

"Let's talk no more of my drinking or your betrothed. Both are painful to me."

Rubio nodded. "I have many worries, but neither your drinking nor Angelita's temper are among them."

"The chores we must do, right, Rubio?"

"No, talk of the government. The centralists want to give us no say in our lives. It can lead to nothing but trouble."

"You've been listening to too many Anglos, Rubio."

"But their ideas are good. The common man should have a voice in his government."

Tomas threw back his arms and stood in his stirrups. "Look around you Rubio. We are lords of all we see. The government does not tell us what to do."

"Not until the tax collectors come around," Rubio answered.

"Some things we cannot control, my brother. Let the Anglos complain, the soldiers will take care of them. As for us, we should worry about seeing the rancho through the winter. We should have a grand crop of calves in the spring. That is what we should worry about, not the foolish Anglos or our sullen government."

Rubio let out a slow breath. "It could come to war."

Tomas laughed. "Father said he never saw a soldier when Mexico rebelled against Spain. It will be no different for us. All father saw was the bull ghost, and we will not even see that."

"If it comes to war, you will have to pick a side."

Tomas shrugged. "I would fight for myself and what is mine. Nothing else matters."

"But what if you must fight with the Anglos?" Rubio pressed him.

"I do not trust the Anglos to fight by my side. They are a treacherous breed." Tomas nudged his gelding with his wide spur. "We will do best not to get into their fights."

Rubio shook the reins and his horse advanced beside Tomas's. "Stephen Austin is a good Anglo. He has done what he could to abide by the government's edicts, but the government cannot decide everything without listening to us. While Mexico ignores us, Texas suffers. We cannot stay out of the fight, if it comes. My heart says I must side with Mexico, but my mind says the Anglos are right in what they ask."

Tomas laughed. "You've got something more frightening than war to worry about."

"What's that?"

"Your marriage to Angelita." Tomas spurred his horse hard and darted for the ranch compound before Rubio could answer.

A quill in his hand and a frown on his face, Colonel Ugartechea glanced up from the stack of papers on his desk as Juan Paz entered his office. The colonel pursed his lips as he put down his pen and leaned back in his chair. Ugartechea did not trust Juan Paz, but the colonel knew he had to rely on the *arriero* for information and, if it came to war, for supplies for the Mexican Army in Texas. Because he traversed the province carrying supplies from Gulf ports and Rio Grande towns to Bexar, Goliad, and Victoria, Paz knew what was going on throughout Texas.

Ugartechea tolerated Paz because he could not alienate any of the Tejanos if it came to war, for all of them would be needed to defeat the numerous Anglos. Ugartechea had heard that Paz had squired Angelita Sanchez at Mexican Independence Day, instead of Rubio Portillo, her betrothed. What Angelita Sanchez might see in Paz confounded him.

Neither man spoke until the soldier who had escorted Paz exited and shut the office door. Paz smirked at the colonel and did not remove his hat. The colonel remained seated. They were men with values so disparate that neither felt at ease around the other.

As the door closed, a wicked grin appeared upon Paz's face. "*Buenas dias*, Colonel," Paz said. "You gave an excellent speech last night. Too bad few understood everything that you meant."

Nodding slowly, Ugartechea rubbed his hands together, pondering what Paz could want — save possibly war, to improve his business.

Though he was a soldier, Ugartechea did not prefer to fight — just yet at least. And until that day came, he knew he had to rely on men like Juan Paz, no matter their deviousness, to get a feel for the mood of the people. "Juan Paz, what brings you to see me after dancing all night with Angelita Sanchez?"

Paz grinned, proud that his activities with Angelita had been noticed. "The celebration, sir, was the best in memory."

Ugartechea knew Paz was lying. The celebration was subdued because of the uncertainty facing Texas.

"And your speech memorable, sir."

Ugartechea shook his head. "I did not know, Juan Paz, that you could be so moved by oration."

"I was moved because I understood it. It is time that the Mexican Army move against Gonzales to reclaim its cannon."

Ugartechea cleared his throat. "I said nothing about Gonzales, Juan Paz."

"No, sir, you didn't, but some of us knew."

"Some of us?"

"A few, sir, but I think you have but one man to worry about, possibly two."

Ugartechea smiled. "Would one of those men be Rubio Portillo?"

"Sir, how did you know?"

"I'm familiar with his reputation," Ugartechea answered, knowing that Paz would take any opportunity to besmirch the reputation of his victorious rival for Angelita's hand.

Juan Paz licked his lips. "Rubio can wait. Another man, an Anglo, is much more dangerous."

"And who would this be?"

"Donley Calder, the one that wears the lionskin hat like some Indian savage."

"And why is he any more a danger than any other Anglo?"

"Last night at the celebration he was drunk and his tongue said things others overheard."

"And what were those things?"

"That Gonzales must be warned."

Ugartechea leaned forward in his chair. "Did he say more?"

"Several heard him after your speech. He was so drunk he could not walk home, and another man, perhaps an ally, helped him to his jacal."

"Do you know this man's name?" Ugartechea picked up his quill.

Paz licked his lips and grinned like the devil's assistant. He appeared to enjoy his power. "I shall want favors for this, Colonel."

Ugartechea shook his head. "You shall get what you deserve."

Paz nodded. "What more can one ask for?"

"The name?" Ugartechea said impatiently.

"But of course." Juan Paz stepped to the desk, planted his hands atop it and leaned toward the colonel. "The second man was Rubio Portillo."

Ugartechea tossed the quill on the table. "Juan Paz, you are an evil man, defaming the name of a rival who has won the heart of a young lady you desire."

Paz leaned farther across the table, until the colonel could smell his acrid breath. "Others saw him with this man Calder and his half-breed daughter. Angelita tried to stop him from consorting with the Anglo and his vermin daughter, but he spurned his betrothed, Colonel. She came to me to console her wounded pride." Paz straightened. "I was glad to help."

"I'm certain you were." The colonel studied the distasteful arrogance in Paz's grin. "Do you have anything else?"

Shaking his head, Paz rubbed his callused hands together. "There is nothing more." He paused, then smiled. "Except that when you find out what I have said is true, you shall repay the debt."

"If the debt be worth repaying."

Paz turned around and stepped to the door. As he grabbed the handle, he looked over his shoulder. "Colonel, it will be."

Ugartechea stood up from his chair and marched to the door. The soldier standing outside straightened. The colonel watched Paz disappear down the hallway, then turned to the soldier. "Bring me Lieutenant Castenada, pronto."

"Yes, sir, at once." The soldier saluted, then scurried away.

Ugartechea retreated to his desk, angry at himself for not being more temperate in his remarks at the celebration, angry at Paz for being so deceitful, angry that the Anglos had ever been allowed to settle in Texas. If Texas was headed for war, he did not have soldiers enough to hold onto the province, the Anglos having poured into the state like bees from a disturbed hive. He must do everything to ensure that the Anglos did not take Texas, and first of all, he must detain Donley Calder. Then he must recover the cannon.

Shortly, Lieutenant Francisco Castenada appeared in the door and saluted smartly.

"Lieutenant, please enter and close the door."

The junior officer turned about, shut the door

and stepped toward the colonel, stopping three steps from his commander's desk.

Ugartechea paced back and forth behind the desk. "Lieutenant, do you know of a certain Anglo who wears a lionskin hat about these parts? His name is Donley Calder."

"I have seen such a man, though I do not know him."

The colonel nodded. "Find and detain him before he can leave Bexar. If you cannot find him, send out a patrol toward Gonzales. Use all the force necessary to keep him from reaching Gonzales."

"Yes, sir."

"When you have seen to that, Lieutenant, start preparations to take soldiers to Gonzales in five days. I want that Gonzales cannon returned to Bexar."

"As you wish, sir." The lieutenant saluted.

Mary Calder was crushing cornmeal for tortillas when the soldiers arrived that afternoon.

They burst through the door, their muskets crowned with bayonets pointing toward her.

"Donley Calder," the lieutenant said. "Where is he?"

Mary screamed, then scrambled to her feet and backed into a corner. "He is not here!"

"Where is he?"

"What has he done?"

The lieutenant advanced toward her, lifting his hand menacingly over her head. "Tell me," he yelled, then slapped her face.

Stunned, she fell back against the wall as the lieutenant stepped toward her again. Then, cat-like, she sprang for him and clawed at his face.

He lifted his arm to shield his cheek, successfully blocking her right hand, but her left slipped across his cheek and her nails left three long scratches.

The officer cried out and his men stepped toward her, threatening her with their bayonets. Mary trembled in fear. Her fingers were no match for the gleaming blades. What had her father done? Why had they come for him? She knew he'd gone to the river to bathe and wash away the pain in his head from too much drink.

"Tell me where he is," the lieutenant commanded, "or we will arrest you as well."

"For what? For what?" she cried.

"It is no matter of yours."

Mary's mind raced like swift waters. She had to get them out of here. The longer she refused to answer, the longer they would stay. If they lingered and her father returned, they would take him. Or worse, hurt him.

"Tell me where he is," the lieutenant shouted.

"Yes, yes," she said. "Just get your men out of here."

"Not until you tell us where he is."

"He left Bexar to go hunting."

Shaking his head, the lieutenant tapped his boot impatiently. "He has gone to warn Gonzales, hasn't he?"

Mary was confused. Who was Gonzales? "No, he's gone hunting."

The lieutenant laughed. "Your word is worthless. We may have to arrest you as well, until we find your treasonous father."

She had already told them he'd gone hunting, and she now declined to respond, remaining silent.

"Take her, men, and we'll put her in the jail."

The soldiers stepped toward Mary, their attention so focused on her that they did not realize her father had entered behind them.

She wanted to scream for him to run.

One of the soldiers reached for Mary, swatting at her wrist.

She dodged his hand and behind him saw her father's eyes widen in anger.

3

If the cool waters of the San Antonio River could have washed away Donley Calder's lingering hangover as well as they had removed the dirt from his body, he would've felt as good as a freshly minted coin. Liquor was the devil's potion, but a man was due an occasional lapse to drown himself in whiskey and forget his troubles.

Texas's troubles were just beginning. War was coming. Calder could feel it. He was unafraid for himself, but scared for his daughter. He had lived fifty-four years and had fought Apaches, Comanches, Kiowa, and Karankawa in Texas. He had ridden to Santa Fe, steered flatboats down the Mississippi to Natchez and New Orleans, paddled up the Missouri, stood at the foot of the Grand Tetons, and walked through fields of geysers and natural pots of boiling mud near the river named Yellowstone. But of all the places he had been, he loved Texas the most.

Now he had a jacal at the edge of town. It wasn't much of a legacy for his daughter, but its stick walls chinked with mud and its thatched roof provided more house than he'd lived in since he was a kid. When the war started and the

Texians whipped the Mexicans, Calder decided he'd throw out the Sanchez family and move his daughter into their fine stone house on the plaza. Then, when he crossed that final river into the unknown, he would at least leave his daughter a good home.

As he walked toward his jacal he adjusted the buckskin hunting coat that reached his knees. His tomahawk rode on his right hip, his skinning knife with a buckhorn handle angled from his left hip across his flat belly. His percussion pistol, converted from an 1826 smoothbore Navy-issue flintlock, was tucked in his belt just to the right of his belt buckle. He had left his long rifle, bullet pouch, powder horn, and loading block on the table in the jacal.

Come nightfall, Calder would fetch his horse, which he'd left staked by the river south of Bexar, and ride east to Gonzales, spreading word of Colonel Ugartechea's plan. He had told Mary he would be leaving, but not where he was going. Calder was a hunter, and Mary had long grown accustomed to his absences. As he turned down the path that led to his humble dwelling, he adjusted the lionskin cap and tightened the leather thong that secured it under his jaw.

As he approached his jacal, he realized something was wrong. A soldier stood in the doorway, looking inside and laughing. Though he wanted to challenge the soldier's presence, he'd learned that surprise was the best ally. Calder moved toward the preoccupied soldier until he was within reach.

Looking over the Mexican's shoulder, he saw Mary cornered by another five Mexicans. Swiftly, he freed his tomahawk and swung the blunt end at the soldier, hitting him solidly on the head. As the soldier crumpled to the ground, Calder snatched his rifle from his hands. In the close quarters, he knew the rifle and bayonet would be harder to handle than the tomahawk, so he tossed the weapon onto the thatched roof, beyond anyone's reach.

Then Calder softly slipped up on the five soldiers threatening his daughter. By the slight nod of her head, he knew Mary had seen him, but she was cagey and gave no other sign of his approach. At the lieutenant's command, the soldiers waved their bayonets at Mary.

Calder struck. He lifted the blunt end of his hatchet and swung for the nearest man. Steel cracked against skull. The soldier groaned and fell to the ground, dropping his gun and clutching the side of his head.

The three remaining soldiers and the lieutenant spun around, surprise widening their eyes. "It is him!" the lieutenant yelled. He jerked his sword from his scabbard. "Take him!"

Calder swung the tomahawk at the nearest soldier, delivering a glancing blow that dropped the stunned man to his knees. Out of the corner of his eye Calder saw another soldier jab at him with his bayonet. He jumped aside, the bayonet slicing the air not two inches from his gut.

The soldier, expecting to hit his target, stumbled and tripped over the downed man at his feet. The gun hit the ground hard and discharged.

Mary screamed.

Fearing she had been hurt, Calder glanced at her, but turned back in time to dodge the sword of the lunging lieutenant. He swatted the gleaming steel aside with his hatchet, then swatted at the officer's head, knocking off his hat.

"Watch out!" Mary shouted.

Calder twisted about to see the two remaining soldiers taking aim with their rifles. He flung his tomahawk at the closest one.

The solider gasped as the tomahawk stuck in his shoulder.

Calder lunged for a rifle at his feet, but realized he could not defend himself before the final soldier fired. He gritted his teeth, fearing he was about to die. But Mary was diving for the soldier's rifle, and he saw her shove it skyward just as it discharged, sending the bullet and a hundred sparks into the thatched roof.

"Run!" Mary cried.

Calder spun about and saw the lieutenant rise, sword in his hand. Mary still clung to the rifle of the other upright soldier. The Mexican shook the rifle viciously, trying to wrest it from her grasp, but she refused to let go.

Calder leaped toward the man clawing at the hatchet in his shoulder and wrestled it free. As the soldier collapsed in agony, Calder turned back to the lieutenant, who charged again with outstretched sword. The frontiersman fell to the ground to dodge the blade, and the lieutenant tripped over him, falling hard upon the soldier with the ruined shoulder.

Scrambling to his feet, Calder drew a deep breath, inhaling the pungent odor of smoke. Glancing over his shoulder, he saw a tongue of flame high to his left. He ducked instinctively, then saw the lieutenant desperately reaching for the sword in front of him. Calder kicked the sword beyond his reach, then plowed his foot into the officer's stomach. The lieutenant fell gasping for breath.

"Watch out!" Mary shouted.

Calder twisted around and saw that the one soldier still on his feet had wrenched his rifle from Mary's hands. The soldier thrust the bayonet at him. For a moment, Calder froze, then swung wildly with his tomahawk and managed to knock the blade aside.

Mary lowered her shoulder and dove into the attacker. The soldier's bayonet impaled the jacal's chinked wall. As the soldier tried to extract the bayonet, Calder clubbed him with the back of his tomahawk. The man fell like a rock to the floor.

Hot and sweating from the exertion, Calder danced around to face the next danger. He took a deep breath of acrid smoke and felt the heat of a growing flame. The thatched roof was ablaze. His pulse raced. Jumping over a groaning soldier, he grabbed Mary's arm and pulled her to her feet.

"Get out. Fire."

Mary stumbled toward the door. A soldier thrashing on the ground reached for her leg, but Calder kicked his arm and the man fell back, groaning.

The room was filling with smoke, but Calder saw that Mary had made it safely out the door. "Fire," he yelled at the Mexican soldiers, hoping they would worry more about escaping than capturing him.

The flames racing through the dry grass overhead began to lap at the walls. Calder darted into the next room, grabbed his rifle, powder horn, bullet pouch, and bullet block, then dove out the window. He felt the hot breath of fire upon his neck. Calder saw people scurrying toward the jacal, carrying buckets of water to fight the flames. He circled to the front of the burning hut and saw men dragging a soldier from the door. Frantically, Calder looked for Mary. Through the commotion he spotted her standing across the street beneath a mesquite tree.

As he ran toward her, he saw two soldiers stumble out the door.

"Are you okay?" he hollered.

She nodded and gasped for air.

"Let's get out of here!" He shoved his tomahawk in his belt, then draped the straps of his powder horn and his bullet pouch over his shoulder. He patted his belt to make sure he hadn't lost his knife or pistol in the fight. Both were still there.

Glancing over his shoulder, he saw the lieutenant and another soldier stumble out the door. The crowd was still preoccupied with the burning house, but shortly they were bound to come searching for him. Calder grabbed Mary's hand and jerked her away from the tree.

They ran down the street, turned down another, then another, heading toward the San Antonio River, where Calder had staked his mount. Finally, when they could no longer be seen, Calder allowed Mary to catch her breath. He looked behind him and saw the plume of rising black smoke that marked the destruction of his jacal. He cursed, then turned to Mary. "Are you okay?" She was bent over, her hands on her knees, heaving for air and coughing up smudges of smoke from her lungs.

She nodded. "You must leave. They know you plan to warn Gonzales."

"But how? I told no one."

Mary held up her hand, signaling for a moment to catch her breath. After a moment she straightened up. "You were drunk. You said things that people overheard."

"Everyone was celebrating. No one knew any difference." Calder stared at his daughter. "It was that Mexican that betrayed me. He's the one that did it." Calder felt anger rising as hot as lava.

"What Mexican? What are you talking about?"

"The Mexican that helped me home."

"He was a decent man. It was not him."

"How do you know?"

44

Though she said nothing, Mary admitted to herself that she couldn't know for certain what was in a man's heart or his mind, but this one had seemed a decent and honorable man.

"The Mexicans are treacherous," Calder said. "They cannot be trusted."

"Neither can you after a few drinks," Mary chided.

Calder grimaced, then took her hand and steered her down the street toward the river and the spot where he'd staked his horse. They moved cautiously along the riverbank, passing women washing clothes and men clearing the debris from the irrigation ditches. Behind them the smoke from what had been their house gradually disappeared. As Calder neared his horse, a pinto broken by Apaches, he left Mary hidden among the trees. The pinto looked up from grazing to see Calder, then dipped his head back into a clump of yellow grass.

Keeping his rifle at the ready, Calder casually squatted and unhobbled the gelding, then pulled up the stake rope. He put both the hobbles and the rope in the pouch tied to the back of his saddle. He grabbed the saddle's pommel, slid his foot into the stirrup, and lifted himself atop the animal.

Looking carefully around, his eyes still sharp despite his age, Calder nudged the horse with his knee, and the pinto turned toward his daughter. Calder gave Mary his hand and helped her climb up behind him, where she settled on the pinto's rump. Easily, Calder turned the horse toward Mission Road and Goliad. He watched for signs of danger as they followed the river past Mission Concepcion and then the deteriorating ruins of Mission San Jose. Occasionally, he felt Mary's hand patting him through the lionskin pelt that fell over his shoulders. At times he thought he felt her hand tremble.

The people they passed beyond Bexar gathered corn from the fields and paid little attention to anything but their harvest. Behind him, Calder saw no sign of soldiers, but as they rode, he spotted a string of pack mules approaching Bexar up ahead. As Calder passed the three mule drivers, one of them stared at him and Mary, but did not greet or acknowledge them in any other way.

When the mule drivers passed out of hearing range, Mary tapped her father on the shoulder. "Why are we taking the road to Goliad if it is Gonzales that we must warn?"

"The soldiers will be watching the Gonzales road. I will go south, then swing east to Gonzales."

"I can carry the message with you."

"I'm the one who must carry the message, and I must carry it alone. You must stay out of danger. If the soldiers pick up our trail, we cannot escape them, not two to a horse. I must find a place for you until that day you have the fine stone house on the plaza in Bexar. When the Texians take Texas from the Mexicans, I will make that house yours."

"That is not right."

"Neither was destroying our jacal."

"Is everything going to be all right, Father?"

"Once Texas is free of Mexico, everything will be fine."

Angelita Sanchez arose from her bed just before noon. As the daughter of a wealthy Bexar merchant, she could take her time. She dressed slowly, then found her brush and ran it a hundred times through her hair, a daily ritual. When she was dressed, she left her room and found her mother standing in the door overlooking the plaza.

"*Buenas dias, Madre,*" Angelita said.

Her mother shook her head. "Is it true you danced the night with Juan Paz and spurned Rubio?"

Angelita smiled, certain Rubio had already called to offer his apology and seek her forgiveness. "It is true. What did he say?"

Her mother shrugged. "Others told me. He has not been by."

"He should have. He insulted me at the celebration."

"My daughter, your pride and your beauty will be your downfall. Others speak of how rudely you left Rubio. It blemishes the family name when you act so childish."

"Are these others your women friends who sit around all day and cackle like fat hens? How can you listen to them and love me?"

"My love is not deaf, my daughter. Your father's is both deaf and blind for you."

Angelita turned up her nose. "Papa cares deeply for me."

"Indeed, for he has spoiled you beyond repair."

Angelita huffed. Turning away from her mother, she crossed her arms over her bosom. "That is not so."

"Can you cook a meal?"

"We have servants."

"Can you make a blanket or mend clothes?"

"I can get new ones."

"Not when you live on the rancho with your betrothed."

Angelita tapped her foot impatiently. "We shall live in Bexar once we marry. Tomas can work the ranch."

Her mother laughed. "Most women find it hard enough to control one man without having to dictate what his brother shall do as well."

Angelita shook her head angrily. Her mother had listened too much to the cackling hens who gossiped all the time. They were jealous of her beauty and her comfortable life. "I am grown and full of life, not like the old hens who are fat and ugly, with no young men courting their favors."

"Yes, my daughter, you are grown, but you are not mature."

Angelita stomped her foot. "That is not true."

"If not, then why would you dance the night with Juan Paz? You know Rubio does not care for him."

"Rubio doesn't control my life."

"And you don't control his. Juan Paz is an evil man, one who cannot be trusted."

"He is a good dancer."

Rosa stepped from the door and lifted her hands to the ceiling. "You think only of fun."

"And you think only of work! And gossip!"

"Your father is not a good dancer, but he's a good man. It was his goodness that spoiled you."

Angelita wanted to scream at her mother, but that would only give the old hens more to cackle about. Instead, she hoisted her skirt and prepared to storm back into her room, but stopped at the sound of her father's voice.

"Are my two women arguing again? I do not understand."

Both turned to the door. His wife nodded with embarrassment, but Angelita smiled broadly and darted across the room to hug her father. He was white-haired and stooped. He carried a cane to help him walk along the patchwork streets of Bexar.

"I am glad you are home, Father."

He smiled. "But I am hungry and worried."

Angelita stepped back and lifted her hand to her throat. She feared most that he would mention his disappointment that she had danced the night with Juan Paz.

"Rumors are about that Colonel Ugartechea plans to retrieve the cannon from the settlers in Gonzales," he said.

Angelita smiled, relieved that she hadn't caused

her father undue worry. She slipped her hand in his, smirked at her mother, and escorted her father to the table where the servants had prepared a meal of frijoles, tortillas, and boiled goat meat.

Indeed, her father did seem worried, for he said very little once he sat down. Angelita and her mother exchanged cold glances as they ate. When the meal was done, her father retired to take a siesta, and Angelita retreated to her room, to wait for Rubio Portillo to call and apologize. The longer it took for him to arrive, the more difficult she planned to make it for him. She spent her time combing her hair and tying it in various ribbons until she was pleased with the reflection in her tortoiseshell mirror.

When she tired of that, she sang soft songs, wishing Rubio would hurry to apologize so they could go for a walk. After her father's siesta, she heard him leave to return to the store. Then she waited some more, the time dragging by like a church mass.

Finally, just before dusk, she heard a loud rap on the door. She jumped up from her seat, ran her brush through her hair a final time, then looked at herself in the mirror. She smiled. Her beauty would make him sorry he had offended her. She heard her mother answer the door. "Angelita," she called, "you have a visitor."

Angelita smiled. Now Rubio would pay for offending her. She stepped gracefully from her room, ignoring her mother as she paraded to the front door, where her caller waited. She let her smile fall flat. She wanted Rubio to have to work for her forgiveness; only then would she accept his apology.

Her mother, though, grabbed her arm. "Do not invite him inside," she whispered before releasing her grip.

Angelita was surprised at her mother's change of heart. Perhaps her father had chided his wife to treat their daughter with greater respect. It was about time. As she neared the door, she saw the figure of a man outlined against the darkening sky.

When she approached, he failed to doff his hat, so unlike Rubio. Perhaps he was as mad at her as she was at him. His reasons, of course, were not as legitimate as hers, she thought.

"Buenas dias," she said, and still he did not doff his hat. Then he turned toward her and Angelita understood why. This wasn't Rubio at all, but Juan Paz. It was Juan Paz her mother had refused to invite inside. Angelita felt betrayed by her mother. And by Rubio! Why hadn't he come to apologize?

Paz offered but a slender smile. "Angelita, I have come to give you the rumors so you wouldn't learn from someone else."

"What is it, Juan?"

"Trouble. A house burned down today when soldiers went to detain an Anglo dog for treason."

"Why should I be concerned? That is a matter for the soldiers."

"Indeed, except that an acquaintance of yours

51

spent the night there with the Anglo dog's daughter, a certain half-breed."

Angelita shrugged. "Why are you telling me this?"

"Because you are betrothed to the one who slept with her."

Angelita gasped and her hand flew to her mouth. "It cannot be so."

"I'm only repeating what I've heard. I know for certain the soldiers fought this half-breed's father this afternoon because he planned to warn Gonzales that soldiers were coming to retake the cannon that rightfully belongs to the central government. Some say Rubio is conspiring with the Anglos against the government."

Angelita's mind whirled. Had Rubio spent the night with another woman? Hadn't her dispute with Rubio come over politics? Didn't he hint at siding with the Anglos? She couldn't sort it out, and it didn't help when her mother spoke.

"Do not believe gossip about Rubio, Angelita," her mother said.

"*Senora,*" Paz said, "it is true, I am sorry to say. Some of my men saw the Anglo and his squaw daughter escaping town today."

Angelita began to cry. "No, no, no," she screamed, uncertain whether to be angry at Rubio's betrayal of her or of his government.

Paz smiled. "Do not be troubled, Angelita. I have done what I could to save your betrothed from danger. I notified Colonel Ugartechea, and he is sending a dozen mounted soldiers after the

Anglo and his squaw daughter. Perhaps they can stop them before they can reach Rubio. Then no one might know."

"No, no!" Angelita cried. "Please leave, Juan Paz. I cannot take any more."

Juan Paz smiled. "I just wanted you to know before others said things about your betrothed behind your back."

"Say no more, Juan Paz," Angelita's mother demanded. "You have said quite too much as it is."

Paz laughed. "I was helping your daughter see what kind of man she would be marrying if she went through with the wedding."

"I know what kind of man Rubio is, and the kind of man you are. There is a great difference. The difference between night and day."

4

To the west a giant thunderhead turned amber from the light of a dying sun. The great cloud boiled over the horizon, and the sound of its distant thunder occasionally reached Mary and Donley Calder as their mount tramped farther from Bexar. Mary grew confident their escape had been successful. But even as she relaxed, her father seemed to tighten like wet leather in the hot sun. He glanced often over his shoulder, then looked at the roiling storm clouds and shook his head as he followed the road paralleling the meandering San Antonio River.

As the day darkened, frogs began to croak on the bank and fish to splash in the waters. In the trees, birds gave their evening calls. Mary saw a pair of deer watering. The sight of meat reminded her of her hunger.

They had left Bexar far enough behind that she wanted to stop for the night. Her legs and hips were sore from her awkward seat on the pinto, and her stomach murmured with hunger. She was relieved when her father finally drew up the reins and quickly dismounted. He went to his knees then, and placed his ear to the earth. Mary prepared to dismount, but her father motioned for her to stay where she was. He cursed as he bounced up.

"Riders, coming fast. It has to be soldiers. Quick, Mary," he said, gesturing, "ride on ahead."

"What about you? I won't leave you."

Donley untied his rifle from the saddle and gripped it in his left hand. Then he slipped his right hand through the leather loop that had just held the rifle and secured himself to the horse. "You ride the pinto. I'll run beside him Apache style."

Mary shook the reins and the horse pranced forward. Calder whistled and the horse danced into a trot. Mary looked to her side and saw her father, half running, half pulled by the pinto. She grimaced at the pain in her father's eyes, then turned her head to focus on the road ahead. How long could he run? How could they escape the soldiers again? The pinto misstepped. Her father groaned at the sudden jolt to his shoulder. He gasped for breath.

"Hurry, think of something." She glimpsed her father, his face pained. She looked ahead to where the road curved away from the river and started up a slight hill.

"At the top —" Calder gasped, "— of the rise — stop."

Mary eased back on the reins, then jerked them when the pinto topped the incline. The horse halted suddenly. Calder yanked his hand from the leather loop and doubled over, heaving for breath. Mary looked from him toward Bexar and gasped. Even in the dwindling light she could see a dozen mounted soldiers racing toward them.

Calder jumped behind Mary on the pinto's rump. "I'll run off — and leave you."

"What?" Mary cried.

"They'll follow — the horse. When — the road hits — the river again — I'll drop you off."

"Then what?"

"You hide . . . behind a tree — or under the . . . embankment," he heaved, slowly getting his breath back. "I'll lead them away." He took a deep breath. "It's our only chance. The horse can never carry us both." He pointed up ahead in the trail. "By the clump of trees . . . you must hide. There's a rancho to the east. . . . You can go there for shelter."

Reaching the copse of trees, Mary jerked the pinto to a halt and scrambled out of the saddle. Calder quickly slid into her place and slipped his feet in the stirrups. He jerked the tomahawk from his belt and handed it to Mary. "Take it and hide, but hurry," he gasped. "They're just a few minutes behind us."

He kicked the pinto's flank and raced off down the road.

Mary clambered into the trees, then skated down the embankment and hid behind the trunk of an uprooted tree. She waited, her heart pounding. As the hoofbeats of the pinto faded, she began to hear the approaching thunder of the soldiers' horses. Her throat tightened.

She peered over the embankment to watch the horses flash by, three, five, eight, a dozen in all. They galloped past, lunging, snorting, kicking up dirt and clods. Mary barely breathed, fearing even the slightest movement might give her away. She wondered if she would see ever see her father again.

When all was silence, she lifted her head farther, scanning for unseen danger. She trembled at the distant rumble of thunder. Daylight was seeping away quickly. She must get her bearings quickly if she was to find the rancho.

Cautiously, Mary climbed over the log and ascended the embankment, clutching the tomahawk. She looked warily down the road as she made it up the slope. Seeing nothing, she edged away from the trees and into the clear. Suddenly she heard something barging through the brush nearby. Mary lifted the tomahawk, then frowned at her own fright as an armadillo scurried across the road. She lowered the weapon. To the west she saw lightning illuminate the giant cloud, which glowed silver, then turned black. Moments later the sound of thunder rolled over her. The storm would surely hit her before she found the rancho.

She knew she must leave quickly. Afoot, she could not outrace the soldiers if they returned. As she stepped across the road, she heard another noise from the brush. Another armadillo, she thought as she turned to look. But instead she saw movement among the trees fifty yards farther down the road. It was a horse! With a saddle on it! Distant lightning cast a soft glow over the land. She gasped. In the sudden light, she spotted a Mexican soldier on foot not fifteen feet away.

He waved his steel-tipped lance at her. His face was slashed by an evil smile and his teeth shone bright against his dark skin. The white leather of his carbine strap and his cartridge box strap intersected in an X across his dark blue coat.

Mary's fingers tightened around the handle of the tomahawk. She had thrown a tomahawk before, but never when her life depended upon it.

"Alto!" the soldier shouted. "Do not move."

Mary hid the tomahawk beside her dress, hoping he wouldn't see it. She studied the spot on his chest where the two white straps crossed. She would throw at the center of the X.

Leaning forward in the saddle, Donley Calder slapped the pinto on the neck. His shoulder burned with pain as the horse lunged ahead, momentarily invigorated by the lighter load. Calder knew the horse's stamina was draining. He hoped he could lead the soldiers far enough away from Mary so she would not be captured. As for himself, he vowed they would never take him. He still had his rifle, his pistol, and his knife, weapons sufficient for a young frontiersman to hold off an army of Mexican soldiers. From the pain in his shoulder, though, Calder knew he was no longer a young frontiersman.

A veil of soft light seemed to overtake him, then the distant rattle of thunder rumbled toward him. As the horse raced down the road, the fur of Calder's lionskin cap flapped against his leather coat. It felt to Calder as if he was flying, and for those few moments he believed he might escape the Mexicans as darkness enveloped him. Then a terrible thought hit him: What if he did outdistance them and they retreated to Bexar? They might stumble upon Mary.

He eased up on the reins. The pinto slowed and finally stopped, shaking its head and blowing. Darkness was closing in on the land and Calder could barely see. He knew he could easily escape in the night, but Mary might not be so lucky. He would improve her odds. "Come on you bastards," Calder shouted. "Here I am. Come and get me."

Only silence answered him. He caught the aroma of distant rain. Finally, he heard the low rumble of galloping horses down the road. "You heard me, you bastards, come on," he screamed insanely. "I'll show you how a Kentuckian can fight." They charged ahead. Though he could barely see them, he wanted to make sure they didn't miss him. Lifting his rifle to his tender shoulder, he cocked the hammer, set the percussion cap, and snapped the trigger. The gun exploded, and so did the pain in his shoulder.

He grimaced and cursed as his jittery pinto danced beneath him. Calder steadied the horse, then whirled it around and retreated. He hoped the Mexicans weren't halfhearted soldiers who would be cowed by a single shot. He slapped the gelding, but it had little more to give. Calder knew the soldiers were gaining. Once they got close, he would be a dead man, especially if they carried lances.

It was time to make a stand rather than run. Through the darkness he strained to see cover. A glow of lightning helped him find a place as good as any to die in Texas. He tugged the reins on his pinto and aimed him toward a downed tree. The pinto jumped the log. Calder yanked on the reins, then slid from the saddle. He slapped the gelding on the rump and sent it jogging away.

Quickly, Calder pulled from his bullet block a charge of powder, wadding, and ball he had wrapped in paper for quick reloads. He shoved the wad into the barrel of his rifle. He jerked the ramrod from his rifle and tamped the load into his barrel. Removing the ramrod, he shoved it back in its nest, then fumbled for a percussion cap in his bullet pouch. Setting the cap in place, he swung the long rifle toward the road.

He heard soldiers approaching, though he could barely make them out in the dark. Kneeling by the tree trunk, he steadied his rifle barrel in the vee of a pair of displaced roots. He eased the butt of the rifle against his sore shoulder and gritted his teeth at the pain. He waited.

In a flash of lightning he spotted half the riders directing their mounts into the trees lining the bank. The others charged ahead on thundering hooves. One rode into the sight of Calder's long rifle. Calder led him a fraction, then squeezed the trigger. His rifle spit flame and kicked like a mule.

Calder cursed at the throbbing pain in his shoulder. His target screamed, but rode past without falling, the others following before Calder had time to reload. He watched them ride into the trees beyond him, realizing they planned to squeeze him from both sides, then kill him. If Mary survived, his stand would have bought all he wanted. He scrambled to reload his rifle and change positions so when the soldiers shot at where they'd seen his flame, he wouldn't be there.

From the Bexar side one of the soldiers issued orders in Spanish. Two men answered simultaneously from the Goliad side. Calder understood Spanish, so he knew they planned to slip up on him and charge from both sides, as he'd expected. "Come on you bastards," he said under his breath. "I'm waiting."

Calder listened to the noise of men working their way through the brush toward him. He inched back to a thick-trunked tree. He might be able to last the night, he thought, because darkness was his ally. He could hide and ambush one or two soldiers with his knife during the night, but come morning, the advantage would turn to the Mexicans.

His breath slowed as his trembling fingers loosened the leather thong that held his lionskin cap in place. The rustle of movement kept drawing nearer. He breathed lightly so they might not hear him. Meanwhile his fingers tightened around the rifle he could not reload without revealing his position. He pondered what weapons they would use. Lances would be impractical among the trees. Swords and muskets with bayonets were more likely. If he answered their fire with rifle or pistol, the flash would give his position away. Once he fired, they would charge. He could get at most two of them.

The brush rattled on both sides of him as the Mexican soldiers closed in. Calder knew if he remained motionless, their advance would leave him in a cross fire between the two lines. If he waited, he died. He opted to attack one wing of the soldiers.

He crawled toward the river, struggling to manage his rifle as quietly as he could. The soldiers seemed all around him. Easing down on his belly, he squirmed forward. After a while, his movements were so agonizingly slow he had no idea how long he'd been on the ground. His muscles were taut, like tightly wound springs, ready to burst loose on whatever approached. He turned toward the Goliad line of soldiers. They had to be close because their noises were more subtle now, not the crashing sound as they had plunged into the brush to spring the trap upon him. He heard the hiss of whispered words, spoken not to be overheard. By the river the frogs had stopped croaking. It was eerily quiet, the distant rumble of thunder only heightening the tension.

Before him, he heard the snap of a twig and

then the sound of a limb brushing against cloth. A Mexican soldier was close. Calder lay flat on his stomach and slid his hand under his belly. His fingers wrapped around the buckhorn handle of his skinning knife. He pulled it out of its sheath and slid it out from under him, shielding the shiny blade with the sleeve of his buckskin coat so lightning would not expose the knife to its intended victim.

Just ahead he thought he saw a dark form crouching low among the grass and undergrowth. The form came closer, and closer still, until not a body length separated them. Calder held his breath, preparing to spring against his enemy. Slowly, he gathered his legs beneath his hips, ready to lunge at the faceless soldier and slice his windpipe so the man could not yell a warning to the others.

But before he could leap, Calder caught movement out of the corner of his eye and realized another soldier was even closer. Had the second soldier seen him? The first would step on him if he didn't move. Calder took a slow breath, then clenched his jaw. He would attack the first soldier, then try to stop the second. Once he sprang the attack, the surprise would be over and he would have to move fast if he were to get away. With suddenness and fury, Calder leaped from the ground, leaving his rifle where it lay.

The Mexican before him screamed and discharged his rifle harmlessly into the night air, the flash illuminating both men and the steel of Calder's knife for an instant. The soldier retreated, then stumbled and collapsed on the ground, Calder falling upon him and plunging the blade into his chest. The soldier screamed, then groaned. To his left, Calder heard the shout of a second soldier and rolled off his victim just as the Mexican fired. The bullet thudded into the chest of the downed soldier, silencing his groans forever.

Calder bounded to his feet and charged the second soldier, who grabbed his musket by the barrel and swing it savagely toward him. A ring of soldiers cursed at Calder. He ducked, but took a glancing blow, the stock of the rifle catching the lionskin cap, which flew off and skidded along the ground. The attacking soldier hoisted his musket again and swung once more as others charged through the brush.

Calder tossed his knife from his right hand to his left, then jerked the pistol from his belt and fumbled to cock it, hoping the percussion cap didn't fall off. The metal snapped in place. He pulled the trigger. The gun exploded in flame and burnt powder.

The attacker cursed and stumbled forward, losing his grip on his musket, which flew into Calder's chest.

Calder caught his breath, then clambered away. He glimpsed the forms of two more soldiers within twenty feet and heard the shouts of other soldiers surrounding him. He had taken two down, but he could not take them all. After shoving his empty pistol in his belt, he dove for his rifle, his right hand slapping the ground where he thought he'd left it. Someone fired a shot that whizzed overhead, and the flash provided enough light for him to see the rifle and lunge for it.

Grabbing it with his right hand and steadying it, despite the knife still in his left hand, he rolled over on his back to meet the next soldier to reach him. The soldier kicked him, then drew back his rifle to stab Calder with his bayonet. Before he could, Calder lifted his rifle and fired at point-blank range at the man's stomach. It was Calder who cried out in pain, from the gun's recoil to his right shoulder, as the soldier's shirt caught fire from the burning powder. The man's momentum had sent him forward, toppling toward Calder as he stabbed at him with the bayonet. Calder jerked his head aside, but the blade sliced his face from cheek to ear. Screaming, Calder rolled away as the soldier collapsed.

The soldiers were approaching from all directions.

Calder knew he was a dead man unless he made it to the river. He jumped up and swung his rifle at the first soldier appearing out of the dark. He missed, but the momentum of the rifle carried it into another soldier Calder hadn't even seen. He released the rifle and charged toward the river. Somehow holding onto his knife in his left hand, he jerked his pistol out, to use as a club, and bolted for the water.

Behind him the soldiers cursed and chased. Several shots pierced the night, but missed him.

Calder ran with deerlike agility to the river. He tripped and fell on his face, but managed to hold onto his knife and pistol as he rolled toward the water. The yelling Mexicans poured after him like mad ants from their hole.

Calder lunged into the water, felt a cold shock from the frigid river. His feet hit bottom and he lurched away from the bank, paddling as furiously as he could with the pistol and knife in his hands. He clung to the weapons.

A soldier flew from the bank toward Calder, who planted his feet to meet his attacker and stood in chest-high water. The Mexican splashed just outside of his reach, the water blinding Calder. Drawing his sleeve across his eyes, Calder felt the soldier grab his neck to strangle him. He gasped as the soldier's hands tightened. As he drew back the knife, another soldier thrashed through the water, grabbed Calder's wrist and wrenched the knife from his grasp. With only the pistol for a club, Calder swung viciously at his two attackers.

He feared he would be smothered, that they would strangle him. Desperate, he flung the pistol, which thwacked against one of his attackers, who fell away. Instantly, Calder leaned back in the water and shoved his feet against the bottom, trying to get away from the soldier who gripped his neck. As he thrashed toward deeper water, the soldier attempting to strangle him laughed until he realized where Calder was dragging him. The soldier was suddenly overcome with terror.

Calder took advantage of the man's momentary uncertainty by grabbing him around the chest and squeezing as hard as he could. The frontiersman's right shoulder simmered like a bed of hot coals, and his neck was raw from the grip of the man's callused hands. Worst of all, his lungs were aflame for want of air. Still, he dragged his attacker underwater. The soldier released his vicelike grip on Calder's neck and flailed desperately to break free for air. When Calder felt his lungs were about to burst, he released the man and both of them shot to the surface, gasping for air.

Calder managed two giant breaths before his attacker reached for him again. He grabbed the soldier's hair, pulling him under. Seeing the flames of guns on the bank shooting at him, Calder jerked the gasping soldier back up and used him for a shield as bullets plopped into the water all around him. The soldier screamed, and Calder shoved him away, twisted around in the water and launched himself farther from the bank.

Filling his aching lungs with air, Calder dove under the surface and took giant strokes, swimming with the current, which pulled him downstream. He stayed underwater until he needed air, then broke the surface gently to reduce noise. Along the river behind him he heard soldiers shouting and running along the shoreline. Then he heard the sound of hoofbeats as they found their horses. He let the current take him to the far side of the river, then drifted along, easing to the opposite shore, where he found a clump of driftwood. He pushed it into the water and let it carry him away.

The surly sky became angry. The lighting became brighter, the thunder louder. Calder hoped the bright flashes of lightening did not expose him to the searching eyes of the Mexicans. Then the clouds opened up and a great downpour splattered against land and river. Calder laughed. He couldn't get any wetter, but the Mexicans on the bank could until they gave up the search.

He floated in the water until he lost track of time, then hid along the bank and waited for the soldiers to search for him. He never saw any. By noon Donley Calder was soaked, hungry, and weaponless, but at least he was alive, and he knew as long as he was alive, he had a better than average chance to survive.

Mary fingered the tomahawk as the soldier neared her, waving the lance at her bosom. She focused on his chest where the two white straps crossed. The soldier announced in awkward Spanish that she was his prisoner. Mary shook her head. *"No comprende."*

The soldier repeated himself.

Mary shook her head. *"Adios."*

"No, no," he answered. Angered, he waved the lance at her.

Mary screamed.

Uncertain what to do, the soldier lowered the lance.

Mary lifted her arm and drew it back over her shoulder.

"Alto, alto," he cried.

Mary's arm swung forward and she released the tomahawk.

The weapon swished through the air and struck the man, higher than Mary had aimed. The soldier had stepped toward her, and now staggered and fell to his knees, dropping his lance in front of her.

Mary heard his wheezing breath, then a bubbling sound as his hands grabbed for the blade stuck in his neck. He struggled with it before pulling it loose. The wheezing and bubbling sound grew louder while he remained upright on his knees. Then he simply tumbled over, the tomahawk falling at his side.

Mary had never killed a man, until now.

She grabbed the tomahawk and ran toward the soldier's horse. Untying the reins, she mounted hurriedly and urged the horse to the east, hoping to find the rancho her father had mentioned.

She was thankful that the lightning gave her occasional glimpses at the countryside, and a better chance to find the rancho, but the storm caught up with her. Lighting came in great streaks,which slashed the sky, and thunder exploded all around as the sky dumped rain upon her.

The water washed the blood from the tomahawk and would help cover her trail, but that would not matter if she didn't find the rancho . . . and if her father hadn't survived the soldiers.

5

From the western bastion, Rubio Portillo studied the storm clouds. In the flashes of lightning they looked like great entrails splashed across the sky. The air was sticky with the moisture of approaching rain. Rubio welcomed the rain. It watered the grass and slaked the thirst of his cattle. He watched many of his herd stamp their feet and toss their heads, nervous at the storm's approach.

Rubio felt as edgy as his cattle. War was approaching as sure as the distant thunderheads. Texas deserved more than remaining a district of Coahuila. And so did Mexico! But could President Santa Anna see that? By his ever-changing politics and policies, the president had shown himself to be an opportunist with the grand ambitions of ruling a country which would serve him. That was not right.

Despite that wrong, Rubio knew he must weigh his allegiance carefully for he would have to take up arms against his own flesh, his own people. Perhaps he would even have to fight against his own brother. He feared the thought. He wanted only to run his ranch and extend his father's legacy without the Mexican government taxing it into poverty.

Tomas thought they should ranch and let others fight. He believed they could avoid sides in any turmoil. Rubio knew better. A man who chose no ally was doomed to have two enemies rather than just one.

As the darkness engulfed the land, Rubio watched the bolts of lightning, then felt the thunder rumble over him. As one streak of lightning slashed through the sky, he saw his cattle turn and stampede across the prairie land, disappearing behind a rise. In a second flash of lightning, Rubio saw something that made him gasp.

There on the rise pawed a great — and ghostly — bull. It stood briefly visible during the lightning flash. Rubio rubbed his eyes and looked again. His imagination had tricked him. His eyes strained to see through the darkness. Then another bolt of lightning forked out of the sky, illuminating everything. In that brief instant he saw the huge, ghostly bull tossing its head, its nostrils flared, its eyes burning like glowing embers, its horns like bronze lances. The bull disappeared again in the darkness.

"Tomas, Tomas," Rubio cried, "come quick." Lightning branched across the sky, then Rubio saw the bull head over the rise after the stampeding cattle. "Tomas, hurry."

His brother came running. "What is it?" Tomas raced up the ladder and jumped beside Rubio.

Lightning lit the sky again, but the bull had disappeared.

"Was it Apaches?"

"No, the ghostly bull."

Tomas laughed. "You are crazy, Rubio."

"No, I saw it, just like father said. Big, gray, and furious."

"Have you been drinking?"

"No, no, no." Rubio shook his head vigorously. "He stampeded our cattle. I swear it is true, Tomas."

Tomas patted his brother on the shoulder. "The thunder scared the cattle. I didn't believe father and I don't believe you."

Rubio turned away, angered that Tomas wouldn't believe him. The wind picked up, bringing with it the aroma of rain. "You remember what father said about the appearances of the great bull?"

Tomas started down the ladder. "Rubio, I never believed it."

"The first visit brought war and bad luck. The second preceded peace and the return of good times. We are headed for war."

"Only if we join the war, Rubio. I do not plan to fight. You may be headed to war, but not me." Tomas disappeared from the bastion.

Rubio stood staring, his only company the occasional raindrops that fell upon him. He stared, but saw nothing in the lightning, except for the approaching shower. Where the bull had run, a wall of rain pummeled the earth with a roar. Rubio raced from the bastion, down the ladder and to his dwelling. As he reached the door and pushed it open, the rains hit. While he waited in the doorway, he wondered if he had actually seen the bull or if Tomas was right. He offered a prayer of thanksgiving for the rain, closed the door and waited inside until the cloud had passed. He then retreated into the compound to check on his horses and the dwelling of the old woman who cooked for him and Tomas.

The senora was fine, but Rubio could see the horses milling about nervously in the corral. He zigzagged between puddles as he walked in that direction, his boots making squishing noises with each step. Rubio took deep breaths of the fresh air cleansed by the rain. At the corral, he stood and rested his hands on the posts. The horses trotted back and forth, frightened by more than the receding storm. Then Rubio, too, heard a distant noise. It was an odd cry. Not like the scream of the mountain lions which occasionally roamed the area, but weaker, more plaintive, almost human.

Rubio wondered if he was going crazy. First he had seen the ghostly bull, and now he heard this strange noise. But if he was crazy, so were the horses, for they remained skittish. Then he realized the cry was human. He ran from the corral to the bastion and scrambled up the ladder to the wall. He looked around, but the darkness was thick and the lightning had abated. The noise came again like a cry for help. He strained to listen.

"*Hola.*" It sounded like a female voice.

A glow of lightning lit up the prairie once again, and Rubio saw a horse and rider fifty yards distant. By the rider's dress, Rubio confirmed she must be female.

"Hola," he answered. "Are you lost?"

"I don't know. I'm wet and looking for shelter."

"I can give you shelter and, come morning, direction."

"Gracias," the rider called.

The voice seemed vaguely familiar, but Rubio could not place it nor understand why any woman was out on such a night. He climbed down the ladder and sloshed across the rain-drenched ground to the gate. He lifted the heavy wooden bar and parted the gate for the rider to slip inside.

"Gracias," the woman said as she entered.

Rubio studied the horse as it passed. He was able to make out enough of the animal's rig to realize it was a soldier's horse. The woman had many questions to answer.

When the horse cleared the stone walls, Rubio closed the gate and quickly barred it. He trotted over to catch the horse and lead it to the corral. The woman tossed him the reins just as Tomas emerged from his quarters and ambled to check on the visitor.

"All is well," Rubio said. "Our guest is lost and seeks shelter." Rubio tied the reins to a corral post and offered his hand to the woman.

She dropped agilely to the ground. *"Gracias,"* she said again.

Rubio reached for her hand, then saw a toma-

74

hawk. "You are soaked and scared."

She nodded.

"I will have our cook take your clothes, to dry them by the fire. She can give you something to wear. Then we shall talk."

Rubio pointed to a door where the senora stood waiting. He reached for her hand again. "Please, give me the hand ax. It will scare the senora."

Reluctantly, she lifted the tomahawk and gave it to him.

Turning to his brother, Rubio pointed to the horse. "Tomas, would you unsaddle him and put him in with the other horses."

Tomas nodded.

The woman said nothing as they walked, and Rubio did not pry. As he reached the open door, he spoke to the old woman. "*Senora,* our night visitor is wet. Would you help her dry her clothes?"

"*Si,*" the senora answered.

As the unexpected visitor stepped into the soft light cast by the candles, Rubio saw her face clearly and recognized the woman whose father he had helped home at the celebration in Bexar.

"Mary? Mary Calder? It is you."

She nodded.

"We have much to talk about when you are dry," he said as the senora closed the door.

Rubio hurried back to the corral, where Tomas had loosed Mary's mount with the others. Tomas was carrying the saddle to shelter when Rubio reached him.

"Rubio," Tomas said, his voice excited, "the horse is a soldier's horse and the saddle is a soldier's saddle. What is this woman doing out here? It can lead to no good."

"She said little, but when she is dry, we shall find out."

"And I shall listen too."

Rubio nodded. He left the tomahawk with the saddle and started back for his dwelling, thinking what a strange night it had been — seeing the ghostly bull, then finding Mary Calder at his gate.

Surely God portended something good of this.

The senora led Mary Calder across the compound to Rubio's dwelling. Mary wore a borrowed skirt, tied around the waist with a leather thong, and a simple blouse the senora had given her. The clothes smelled of wood smoke, which reminded Mary that her house had been burned on this long day, that she'd killed a soldier and that her father was gone. She did not understand why the soldiers had come for her father. She wondered if she would ever know or ever find him.

By the time she reached Rubio Portillo's door, the storm clouds had passed and a sliver of the moon and a thousand stars sparkled in the sky. The senora rapped on the wooden door. When it swung open, Rubio was standing there. He dismissed the senora.

"Muy gracias, senora," Mary said, patting the woman's shoulder.

The old woman smiled as she shuffled back to her quarters.

As she stepped inside, Mary looked enviously about a receiving room lit by a dozen candles on an *arana* — a chandelier that could be lowered by pulley for easy lighting. She had stepped upon a coarse woolen rug and was embarrassed to be tracking mud across so fine a covering. In the corner a small fire crackled in a stone fireplace, casting faint shadows that danced behind a nearby chair. Mary wondered what treasures the carved wooden chest across the room held. As she walked past one of three wooden benches lining the walls, she realized she was not alone with Rubio. She reached for her throat in surprise as another man arose from a high-backed chair in the far corner. "Forgive me, *senor*, I have had many frights tonight."

Rubio stepped to her side. "Please, meet my brother, Tomas."

She bobbed her head and smiled. "I am Mary Calder."

"Welcome," Tomas said, a wide grin upon his face. "We do not receive many visitors on any night, much less a night like this, and especially not such a pretty visitor."

Her cheeks warmed with embarrassment.

"My brother is clever with flattery," Rubio said, pointing to a chair by the fireplace. "You will be warmer there."

As she stepped toward the chair, she did not know if she could trust Rubio, much less Tomas, but she had no choice. If she hoped to find her father alive or bury his body, she had to depend on these two men. There was a brotherly resemblance in their dark eyes, narrow mustaches, high cheekbones, slender hips, and broad chests. Rubio was slightly taller and more serious. Tomas, with a rakish turn of his lips, was more given to smiling and, Mary thought, to mischief.

She settled into the chair, her back stiffening as she began to tell them of events. "Soldiers came to arrest my father. I know not why. They burned our jacal — it was nothing grand like this — and we escaped riding his horse. The soldiers came and found us by the river not far from here. My father dropped me off and rode ahead. I heard shooting. I hope he is alive, but I do not know."

Rubio nodded. "How did you come by the soldier's horse?"

Mary swallowed hard. "I found it."

Rubio crossed his arms over his chest. "How did you happen to find it if they gave chase to your father?"

Mary felt her lips go dry. Should she tell him? If she could trust him, could she trust Tomas? "One soldier must've seen me. He slipped up on me and I . . ."

"Attacked him with the hand ax?" Rubio asked.

"Yes, the tomahawk. I killed him." She looked for a sign of emotion from them. Their silence made her nervous. "Come morning, I shall leave to look for my father's body."

Rubio paced the floor, rubbing his hands together, glancing occasionally at his brother. "Do you know why the soldiers came to arrest your father?"

"He planned to warn Gonzales."

"About the cannon?"

She shrugged meekly. "I am not certain."

"We can help," Rubio offered.

"No!" Tomas shouted. He strode across the room to his brother. "It is trouble if we get between the Anglos and the government, Rubio. We take no sides. We have chores, remember?"

"*Silencio,* Tomas. We are helping a woman find her father, not choosing an ally."

"It is the same to the soldiers, and the soldiers will return."

Mary stood up. "*Gracias* for your help, but I'll leave now."

"No," Rubio said. "You will share our food and roof tonight, and tomorrow I will help you find your father."

"It is a mistake." Tomas crossed his arms and shook his head.

"I am sorry," Mary said.

"Come morning I shall help you find your father. Tomas can return the soldier's horse to Bexar."

Tomas threw up his arms. "And tell them what?"

"Tell them that you found the horse and knew it was a soldier's."

"And if they ask more, my brother?"

79

Rubio grinned. "You, who can charm all the women of Bexar with your words, are asking me what to say?"

Tomas cocked his head, his flash of anger melting under a devious grin. "Forgive us, *senorita*. We get along most of the time."

Mary nodded. She could no longer hide her exhaustion. "Might I have a bite to eat and a place to sleep?"

"We shall ask the *senora* to bring food to fill your stomach. And we will ask her to bring bedding so you can rest here in our house, where it is warmest."

"Gracias."

Rubio smiled gently. "You have thanked us more than enough."

Mary was embarrassed and fumbled for her words a moment. *"Gracias,"* slipped off her tongue again. She laughed.

Rubio laughed too.

Mary liked the gentle sound of his laughter.

By sunrise Rubio was up, with both his stallion for himself and a gelding saddled for Mary. He hung a goatskin of water from each saddle, then filled a parfleche with jerked beef and tortillas. He wished he had some candy from Bexar to offer Mary. He took his musket and tied it to the saddle, then returned to the big house to grab his two pistols, his powder horn and bullets. He checked Tomas's room and found his brother still asleep.

"Tomas, Tomas, don't you want to get an early start for Bexar?"

Tomas groaned, lifted his arm and waved his older brother away. "I'll leave at noon. The ladies like me best in the dark. I'll be back tomorrow by noon."

"If you find liquor, you'll not even be over your headache by noon."

Rubio left his brother squirming deeper into his blankets and went to the kitchen, where the *senora* was preparing food. "Is the senorita up yet?"

"No, she sleeps soundly. Even now, her breath is tired."

Rubio sniffed the aroma of menudo boiling in a clay pot in the corner fireplace. The senora stirred the mixture, a stew of tripe, with a cotton-wood spoon, then touched it to her lips. Pleased with the taste, she nodded. "The food is ready."

"When I return, wake her so we can ride." Rubio left the kitchen and returned to the corral. He slid his pistols into scabbards mounted over the pommel, then snugged the saddles down and started back for the house. As he was leaving the corral, he realized they would need a third horse for Mary's father, whether they found him alive or not. Figuring her father was dead, Rubio put a harness but not a saddle on the third horse and returned to the house.

The senora had disappeared from the kitchen. As Rubio seated himself on the bench by the table, he could hear her waking Mary. The senora returned shortly and dished out two clay bowls

81

of menudo. She sat one of the steaming servings in front of Rubio, the other across the table from him, and put a cottonwood spoon by each.

Mary Calder entered the kitchen running her fingers through her hair. "I have no brush," she apologized.

"The horses will not care," Rubio said. "Please, eat."

After she seated herself, she attacked the food greedily, taking a second bowl when she was done, and seldom looking at Rubio.

Once he'd finished, Rubio stood up and stretched. "When you are done, meet me at the corral," he said. "Then we'll find your father."

He hurried to the corral, led the horses out and tied the two saddled animals to the fence posts. The third he tied behind his own saddle.

Shortly, Mary emerged from the kitchen, wearing her own clothes, from the previous night. When she arrived at the corral, Rubio helped her into the saddle, then untied the lines and handed her the reins. Loosening his horse, he mounted and they headed for the gate, where he bent over, lifted the bar and pushed the gate open. Tomas could bar the gate later, he thought.

They said little as they rode away from the compound. Rubio concentrated on finding Mary's trail, and in an hour they were beside the river. Rubio found a discarded lance and a blood-stain where Mary had killed the soldier. Dismounting, he took the lance and studied the blood-soaked ground where the soldier had fallen. He looked up to Mary. "How far was the fight from here?"

"Down the road. Toward Goliad."

Rubio remounted and led Mary in that direction, scanning the ground between the road and the river for signs of battle. They had gone a league and a half when they saw droppings where several horses had been tied. They dismounted, led their horses into the trees by the river and started following the trails where men had crawled on hands and knees.

Finally, they came to a downed tree and a small patch of flat ground where the grass was bent and torn, the ground chewed up in a scuffle. Rubio spotted a long rifle and picked it up.

"It's father's," Mary said.

Rubio found many splotches of blood. He followed the trail of blood toward the river, then heard Mary gasp. As he turned, she lifted her father's lionskin cap. It was stained with more blood.

Mary cried as she clutched the skin to her breast.

Rubio followed the path of the fight down the bank to the river. "If your father fell into the water," he said. "we may never find his body."

Mary sobbed. "We should keep looking."

Though Rubio knew the search would be fruitless, he acquiesced.

6

"He got away?" Colonel Ugartechea slammed his fist against his desk. "The man who would warn Gonzales of our plans got away?" The colonel stood up and marched around his desk to the window, where the morning light slanted in. He stared out across Bexar, his anger white-hot like the morning sun.

Lieutenant Francisco Castenada stood stiffly in front of the colonel's desk. He did not know what he could have done differently to capture the human wildcat. "We could not see well."

"Nor could he, Lieutenant. Isn't that right? Are his eyes better than those of a Mexican soldier?"

Castenada clenched his jaw, then took a deep breath. "No, sir."

"How many soldiers did you have with you?" The colonel strode back and forth in front of the window, pounding his fist in his hand.

"Twelve in all."

"Two were killed and four wounded by one man?"

Castenada nodded. "It was dark. One of our men fell behind and was killed away from the fight with Calder. Perhaps he had allies."

84

"Surely, there were more. Twelve soldiers scared away by one?"

"He was a fighter."

"I don't care if his mother was an alligator and his father a bear! My soldiers should capture an old man and his daughter. Lieutenant, I expected better from you and my men."

"And I expected more of myself, Colonel."

"Very well. I shall give you a chance to redeem yourself."

"Thank you, Colonel."

"You shall have one week to find the traitor and any who assisted him. They shall be brought to Bexar and put in jail. If they are not in jail at the end of the week, then you shall be relieved of your services. You would not want that, would you?"

"No, Colonel. I am a soldier."

Castenada felt the sting of Ugartechea's tongue. He had failed at his duty, and he vowed not to fail again, no matter what. He returned to his men's quarters. They were slowly rising after the long night.

"Get up, and be quick," he commanded. "We must leave to find the man Calder."

"He's drowned," the sergeant said.

"Then we should find his body and detain any who assisted him."

"There were more?" the sergeant asked, scratching his head.

The lieutenant nodded. "Without allies, how else could the Anglo have gotten away?"

The men laughed.

"He couldn't," the sergeant suggested, "unless he was the devil incarnate."

At dawn, Donley Calder left the water and denned up in a clump of trees to get some sleep. Rest did not come easily. His shoulder hurt so badly, he could barely lift his right hand. And his face throbbed where the bayonet had gashed his cheek. He ached all over from the fight and knew he was lucky to survive.

He wondered how his daughter had fared. She was a tough young woman wise in the ways of the frontier. He knew she could survive on her own in the wild, what with her Apache mother's natural instincts and his own wiles bred in her. Calder remembered the first time he saw Mary's mother. He'd never seen a more beautiful woman. She'd been bathing with other Apache women, and she was the most striking. No man had ever risked more for the right to marry an Apache woman than Donley Calder, and no man had ever lost more when the Comanches killed her in a raid upon their small dwelling north of San Antonio. Calder's eyes watered at the recollection of his dead wife. He knew he was getting old, because old men got sentimental. Young men got revenge. He'd had his revenge upon her murderers, but it hadn't brought her back.

Calder weighed whether to seek Mary or to make his way to Gonzales to warn the citizens. He opted for Gonzales. Mary could take care of herself better than the settlers at Gonzales could defend themselves. Too, he didn't want her to see him beat up and limping.

By his estimate, he was at least forty miles from Gonzales, maybe fifty. Were he not hurt and hunted, he could make that afoot in fourteen hours of sunlight. But he knew he must travel some at night and cling to cover if he was to make it undetected. Even so, he had to start his journey soon. He listened for riders, then stood. His buckskin coat and the checkered linsey-woolsey shirt beneath it were still damp and cool from his night in the river. He eased to the water, knelt down, and with cupped hand sated his thirst. When he left the river and cut toward Gonzales across the broken prairie, he knew he'd be able to find water in the hollowed-out cores of tree stumps, in small depressions upon the prairie, and perhaps even in springs that the strong rains might have sent to flowing.

At high sun Calder started walking downriver. A half mile distant the road came within thirty feet of the river. Calder crossed there into a ribbon of trees that wove along a shallow draw about a hundred yards from the river before flattening out onto the prairie. He limped along, then paused to pick up a tree limb for a staff to help him manage. He wondered if he had the stamina to reach Gonzales.

Hearing a horse nicker behind him, Calder fell to his knees, then crawled behind a tree. Cautiously, he eased his head out from behind the tree and peered up the road. Squinting against the sunlight, he saw two riders weaving through the trees by the river, the one in front holding a lance upright.

They had to be soldiers looking for his trail, since they were skirting the river instead of following the road. Calder weighed his chances and grinned. At least they weren't Comanche, bear, or puma. If they continued to ride one behind the other, he could knock the first rider from his horse and spear him with his lance. If the horse didn't bolt, perhaps he could pull a pistol from one of the saddle scabbards and shoot the second rider. Then he would have two horses he could alternate in a hard ride to Gonzales.

Calder slipped back across the road to a mesquite tree with a low hanging branch. He slipped his staff under his arm, planning to use it as a spear, boosted himself onto the thick, gnarled limb and climbed to a higher branch, under which the riders would surely pass. He stretched out, turning his face away from the approaching riders so the white of his skin might not be seen from afar. Waiting for the approaching soldiers, he hoped he had enough in him to kill them.

Rubio Portillo had seen no sign of hope for Mary Calder's father, not after inspecting the site of the desperate struggle. If Calder had even survived the fight, which Rubio thought unlikely, he had probably drowned or been shot in the river. If so, the body might drift to Goliad or beyond.

On Mary's slim hope that she might find her father, he had ridden three leagues beyond the southern border of his property. It was near high sun and he was about to suggest they return to the rancho when he saw a patch of flattened grass where someone might have slept. Then he saw the ghost of a moccasin track by the water's edge. Was it Donley Calder or deadly Comanche? He looked over his shoulder at Mary, but she failed to pick up the sign. He looked at the butts of the pistols on either side of his pommel and considered discarding the lance and pulling a pistol. He hesitated, fearing he might alarm Mary or tip off whoever might be lurking nearby.

Rubio guided his stallion, followed by the trailing horse, toward a mesquite tree with a thick limb overhanging the trail. He heard the sound of his mount and the river, but nothing else, not even no birds.

While under the mesquite tree, he heard a shriek like a wounded mountain lion and twisted in the saddle. A man dropped from the branch above before he could spur his stallion. Rubio jerked the reins, desperate to stay in the saddle, but the weight of the attacker was too much. He tumbled to the ground, entwined with his assailant. The stallion and the trailing horse bolted forward.

Before Rubio could collect his senses, he found himself on his back, beneath a man in buckskin who raised a sharp stick with both hands to plunge it into his neck. Rubio squirmed helplessly as the man brought the stake toward him.

"Stop, Papa!" Mary yelled. "He's a friend."

Then Rubio recognized his attacker as Donley Calder. The frontiersman looked stunned, even more so when Mary Calder dropped from her mount beside him. She grabbed him, crying and then hugging him, even while her father straddled Rubio.

"You're alive, you're alive," she repeated.

He stood up awkwardly and embraced Mary. "And you too."

Mary pushed him back and looked at him, gasping at his face. "You've been hurt." She touched the tender gash.

He flinched. "Just a scratch."

Mary shook her head. "Many more scratches like that and we'll have to sew you together."

Rubio got up and dusted himself off, picked up the lance and walked to a patch of grass where the three horses grazed. He gathered their reins and returned.

Calder eyed him coldly, then turned to Mary. "What are you riding with a Mexican after what they did to our jacal?"

"He helped me find you." She went to her gelding and pulled the lionskin cap from its rump. Holding it up, she pointed at the bloodstains. "I feared you were dead."

"That's Mexican blood. It's bad blood."

Mary pointed at Rubio. "Not all of it's bad."

Calder grabbed his cap and fitted it on his head. "He won't turn against his own kind. They're a treacherous breed."

"He gave me food and shelter in his fine house last night."

"One day, Mary, when we take Texas from his kind, you'll have the finest house in Bexar. I know the house I'll claim for you."

"I've told you before, Father, it won't be right."

Calder grinned. "Maybe not, but it'd be yours."

Rubio picked up his hat and dusted it off. He moved to his stallion and dug into the leather parfleche, retrieving a handful of jerky. He offered it to Mary and she gratefully accepted a couple of strips. Rubio then offered Calder some of the dried meat. He took it grudgingly, but ate it greedily.

Mary pointed to her mount. "I found your musket."

"And your hatchet is in my parfleche," Rubio announced around a mouthful of jerky.

"I'm obliged," Calder finally said.

Rubio nodded.

"You wouldn't have any dry powder? Mine's ruint after my swim. I lost my pistol and knife."

"I've a little powder to spare and I can give you one of my two pistols. You may need them to reach Gonzales."

Calder froze. "How'd you know I was going to Gonzales?"

"You talk too loud when you drink."

"You ought not to be listening to what others are saying."

Mary stamped her foot. "Don't treat Rubio that way. He has been good to me."

"So have other men, white men."

Mary slapped her hands together, then pointed her index finger at her father's nose. "How can you insult a man who helped me find you? He even brought a horse for you. You be cordial with him."

Calder grimaced.

Rubio turned and untied the extra horse, handing Mary the reins. He got one of the pistols from his saddle scabbards and offered it to Calder, who accepted it without comment.

"Thank him, Papa."

Calder sighed. *"Gracias."*

Rubio lifted the strap of his powder horn over his head and shoulder. "I can get more at the rancho."

Calder eyed the powder horn. "Is it Mexican powder?"

Rubio nodded.

"Mexican powder ain't worth a damn. You can get a bigger bang with charcoal dust."

"My powder's dry. How good is yours when it's wet?"

Calder studied Rubio a moment, then grinned. "You've got a point there, Mexican." He offered his hand to Rubio.

Rubio shook Calder's hand warily.

Calder removed his powder horn and exchanged it for Rubio's. Rubio hung the strap over the pommel, untied the parfleche and tossed it to Calder. The frontiersman grimaced as he caught it.

"There's beef jerky and tortillas inside, enough to get you to Gonzales. You won't have to build fires, in case the soldiers are looking for you." He offered Calder a goatskin of water as well. "That'll quench your thirst."

Mary stepped past Calder and hugged Rubio. *"Muchas gracias."*

Rubio patted her on the shoulder, then led her to the gelding and helped her climb astride the animal. When Rubio turned around, he saw Calder adjusting the strap of his powder horn over his shoulder. Calder gave the goatskin of water to his daughter, positioned the lionskin cap on his head, and tied the leather thong beneath his chin. He then stepped to the saddleless horse and pulled himself atop it. *"Adios,* Mexican."

"His name is Rubio Portillo," Mary corrected.

"Adios, Rubio. Thanks for taking care of my Mary."

Rubio nodded as Mary and her father rode by. He watched them cross into the line of trees that followed the draw away from the road. When they disappeared, he picked up the lance, mounted his black stallion, and rode for his rancho.

He ran the stallion until he got back on his property, then slowed the horse down. As he cut through the heart of his land, he looked at his cattle, which numbered three thousand or more. He would have a better count when he and Tomas finished the fall branding.

It thrilled his heart to ride his land and watch his herds. One day, he thought, he would be rich enough to have Angelita Sanchez for a wife. But he couldn't help but wonder if he might not be richer still with Mary Calder for a spouse.

Tomas Portillo left the rancho an hour before high sun. He rode his favorite horse, a gray stallion with a spirit as wild as his own. The stallion, though, was hampered by the poor-spirited, poorly fed army horse tied to it and trailing along behind. Tomas had saddled the government horse with the awkward saddle the government provided for its mounted soldiers. He was ashamed to be seen leading such a miserable-looking nag. He knew it would not impress the women when he rode into Bexar and delivered the horse to the soldiers.

After high sun, he smiled at his luck when he saw a troop of mounted soldiers approaching on the Goliad road. The soldiers could take the horse. He saw the officer leading the approaching patrol twist in his saddle and say something. Shortly, the soldiers, who had been riding two abreast, fanned out.

"Buenas dias," Tomas called when the soldiers were within hearing distance.

The lieutenant neither smiled nor acknowledged him. When the officer was within twenty feet of Tomas, he halted, but the riders on either side of the road swung on past until Tomas was surrounded.

"I am Lieutenant Francisco Castenada of the Mexican Army," he announced. "Where did you get that horse?"

"I found him running loose."

"Are you sure you didn't kill the soldier who rode him?" The lieutenant's voice brimmed with venom.

"No," Tomas said as the soldiers leveled their muskets at him.

"Did you help an Anglo dog escape from us?"

"No, no," Tomas repeated. "I was returning the horse to Bexar."

"To hide your part in the fight?"

"What fight?" Tomas demanded.

"The fight that killed two of my men and helped an Anglo dog escape."

The officer was crazy, he thought. "I would help no Anglo against the soldiers of Mexico."

"Detain him," the lieutenant ordered.

Four soldiers nudged their mounts closer to his.

Tomas grimaced. "I have done nothing against Mexico."

"Disarm him," the lieutenant commanded.

The soldiers rode within reach.

Tomas rattled his reins and drove his spurs into the flank of his stallion, but the horse reared rather than run into one of the soldier's mounts. After Tomas slapped the horse on the neck, the stallion bolted into a soldier's horse. The stallion stumbled, and one soldier grabbed the reins and jerked the horse to a halt. A second lifted his

95

musket and clubbed Tomas with the butt.

Screaming, Tomas swatted at the soldier holding his reins, then tried to duck the blow of the rifle butt. The hard wood of the rifle caught him up beside the head. He saw a flash of light and felt an explosion of pain. He wobbled in the saddle and grabbed the pommel to keep his balance.

"Take him," the lieutenant ordered harshly, "and put him in irons."

Tomas felt strong arms close around him and pull him from the saddle. Next, cold metal was clamped onto his wrists. The weight of the irons tugged on his arms and shoulders as he stood unsteadily on his feet. He clenched his eyelids to fight the pounding headache.

He heard the sound of other soldiers dismounting, then felt someone grab his jaw. Tomas parted his eyelids enough to catch a glare of sunlight and the sneer of the lieutenant.

"You tried to escape," he growled. "That alone convicts you."

In spite of the pain, Tomas jerked his head from the lieutenant's grasp. The sudden motion left him momentarily dizzy. He gasped, then staggered toward the lieutenant. "You are wrong," he managed.

The lieutenant slapped him.

Tomas wobbled, then fell to his knees. His cheek burned and his mouth tasted of blood.

"You are Tomas Portillo, are you not?" the lieutenant asked.

Tomas nodded.

"And the brand on the gray stallion, is it not the brand of the Rancho de Espiritu Toro?" The lieutenant answered his own question. "*Si!* Now, three of you men take the prisoner back to Bexar. The rest of you, accompany me to the rancho to arrest your brother as well."

"No, no," Tomas cried, his mind muddled. "I was the only one involved."

The lieutenant shouted, "First you denied it and now you say you were the only one involved. You lied before. You are a traitor."

Two soldiers grabbed his arms and jerked him to his feet. "I'm no traitor. I've always been loyal to the government of Mexico."

"Don't lie again." Castenada slapped Tomas once more.

"I have always — been loyal to Mexico," he gasped.

The lieutenant struck him again.

"Until now," Tomas said defiantly.

Rubio Portillo took his time returning to his ranch fortress. He circled his property looking for unbranded cattle. He saw many, and guessed his herd could even top thirty-five hundred cattle. Though the season was gradually changing to fall, the recent rains had revived the grass, promising good grazing for the winter. With the clouds building on the horizon, there was the promise of even more rain. With so much rain, 1836 couldn't help but be a good year. But he worried if Angelita could ever be happy with him on the ranch. She was accustomed to Bexar's festivities, and the rancho provided no match for that.

Rubio smiled at the remembrance of Mary Calder's reaction to his modest dwelling. He had seen her eyes widen with envy when she entered his home. Not so Angelita on her single trip to the rancho. She had stared with disbelief, then inspected Rubio's quarters, shaking her head all the time. No doubt Angelita had a feisty spirit, and he liked spirited horses. And yet, Tomas liked spirited horses and women even more than he, but his disdain for Angelita knew no bounds. Rubio could only hope that with time Tomas would come to appreciate Angelita as much as she would surely come to love the Rancho de Espiritu Toro.

As he turned his mount toward the rancho compound in the distance, Rubio had a sense that something was wrong. Maybe, he thought, he was just jittery after seeing the ghost bull. His father had said the first appearance of the bull brought bad luck. Only upon the bull's second appearance had good luck been redeemed. A sudden panic overtook Rubio, though he could not explain why. He slapped his stallion with his reins and galloped for the compound.

As he approached, he knew his instincts had been right. Both gates were open and the corrals empty. The senora should be cooking the evening meal by now, but he saw no smoke rising. He dashed through the open gate into the middle of the compound and jerked on the reins of his stallion; the animal wheeled around.

"Is anyone about?" he cried. No one answered. He whistled loudly. Only silence answered. He pulled his pistol from its saddle scabbard and cocked it, uncertain what he should fear.

Rubio tensed at a sound behind him, then jerked his horse about to face the dwelling of his cook.

The senora stood in her doorway, her eyes wide. She shook her head.

Lowering his pistol and releasing the hammer, Rubio nudged his stallion forward. "*Senora,* what has happened?"

"The soldiers came. They have arrested Tomas and they are looking for you. They took our horses too."

"But why?"

"Though it is untrue, they say you and Tomas killed two soldiers when Mary's father escaped."

"And Tomas?"

The old woman shrugged. "He was taken to the prison in Bexar, I was told."

"I must ride to Bexar to free Tomas."

"But patrón," the senora continued, "they said they were looking for you as well, that you were seen plotting with the Anglo Calder during the celebration of independence."

Rubio bit his lip. It hadn't been the bull that had brought back luck, but Donley Calder and his daughter, Mary.

7

The next night, Rubio Portillo slipped into Bexar, leaving his stallion tied to a tree along the banks of the San Antonio River. With his hat low over his brow and a serape draped over his shoulders, he ambled toward the square and Angelita's house. He met a soldier and nodded, wondering if the man had had a part in Tomas's arrest. Rubio clenched his fist at the thought, then glanced over his shoulder to make sure the soldier went his own way. He did. Rubio's fist melted.

In the square, Rubio looked for a sign that someone might be watching Angelita's place. When he was satisfied no one stood guard, he angled across the plaza and stopped outside her door. He lifted his hand to knock, then hesitated at the sound of her laugh. With his ear against the door, he heard muffled voices, one Angelita's, the second that of a man. The voice was too strong to be her father's.

Rubio backed away from the house and retreated across the plaza. He sat down with his back to a stone wall, his knees bent. As he sat watching her door, his hand slipped to his belt and he fingered the handle of his knife.

Who was talking with Angelita? he wondered. How could he get Tomas from the prison? Had Mary Calder reached Gonzales safely? These and other questions floated through his mind, each untethered to an answer, as time crawled by. An hour or more passed before Rubio saw Angelita's door open and a lean man emerge. In the brief instant the man was illuminated in the soft candlelight, Rubio recognized Juan Paz. He cursed, then waited until Paz disappeared from the plaza. Looking around, he slowly arose and ambled across the plaza.

Outside Angelita's, he gazed warily up and down the street, then rapped softly on the wooden door. He saw the handle twist and the door open slightly.

"Juan . . ." Angelita said.

Rubio shoved the door open wide enough to slip in, then shut it quickly behind him.

Angelita gasped and her hand flew to her throat. "What are you doing here?"

Rubio glanced at the vacant room. "Why was Juan Paz here?"

She lifted her nose in the air. "I can have any visitor I want."

"I am your betrothed, am I not?"

The question hung unanswered.

Angelita moved away, but Rubio grabbed her arm with his hand and pulled her to him. "Am I or not, Angelita?"

"Once you were."

"But no longer?"

She shrugged weakly.

"Tomas was right. You wouldn't make a good wife."

Angelita slapped his cheek. "Tomas is in prison and they are hunting for you," she spat. "Were I to scream, they would find you. That I don't is my parting gift to you, Rubio."

"Were you to scream," he said, "you would never scream again."

She hissed at him: "You've turned against your people."

"No, the government has turned against its people."

Angelita scoffed. "You're a traitor to Mexico and your people. Juan Paz has not turned against his people."

"He's on nobody's side save his own."

"The Anglos cannot win," Angelita said, "and you are throwing away your future by allying with them. The army will defeat all who side with them. Just today Colonel Ugartechea has learned that 550 troops under General Cos have landed on the coast. They will strengthen the presidio in Goliad, then come here. They will crush the Anglos and all who side with them. And then you will lose your fortune and your place."

Rubio shook his head. "You were always more interested in my wealth than in me."

She smiled. "You are nothing without your wealth."

"And you, Angelita, are nothing with yours. Or, should I say, with your father's."

"Leave before I scream."

Rubio shook his head. "You deserve Juan Paz."

"He will stay rich."

"In money, perhaps, but never in spirit."

"At least he is not being pursued by the soldiers."

"Tomas saw your heart of stone long before I did."

Angelita raised her finger and pointed to the door. "Leave, Rubio, and never come to see me again."

Rubio backed to the door, eased it open and slipped back outside. He left the door cracked. Finding his stallion, Rubio untied the animal, mounted and rode away from Bexar.

He had a long time to think on the journey back to the ranch compound. After he gathered his powder and supplies at the compound, he knew he had but one place to go — Gonzales.

Donley Calder looked at the high waters and shook his head. "The Guadalupe's on the rise. The rains must've been stout upriver."

Mary peered through the early morning gloom as sunlight squeezed between the trees. "It's bad, isn't it?"

"No, it's good. It'll keep the Mexican Army from crossing."

"But how will we cross?"

Calder pointed. "There's a ferry upstream. The Texians should still hold the ferry. Let's move."

They reached the ferry in a half hour. The

ferryman asked for a fare, but Donley Calder talked him out of it. "I've messages for the alcalde, unless you want the Mexican Army taking over your ferry."

The ferryman relented and began to pull Calder, his daughter, and the horses across.

"If you want to be safe," Calder instructed him, "keep to the east bank. The Mexicans will be coming shortly."

"Why for?"

"The cannon," Calder replied.

On the other side, Donley Calder and his daughter mounted and rode the short distance to Gonzales. Calder headed directly for the town square. Mary was surprised by the smoldering anger in his eyes. She had never seen her father this way. But then, he had never been beaten by soldiers before.

Calder stopped beside a small cannon mounted on a primitive cart frame with two iron bands. Two solid wooden wheels gave the cannon more a comical than a dangerous appearance. Only a handful of men were out as he stood in his stirrups and loosed a wild yell. "Somebody fetch the alcalde! Pronto!"

The men shrugged and moved on, apparently thinking he was a drunk or a lunatic. Calder lifted his lionskin cap and waved it in the air. "The Mexicans are marching on Gonzales, and not a man will listen to me or fetch the alcalde," he cried out.

A short man on horseback reined up opposite

Calder. "I'll get the alcalde," he said, and galloped away. As he rode off, the other men gathered around Calder or called for others. In five minutes a crowd of thirty men, nearly all of them carrying arms, circled Calder, imploring him to tell more.

Calder shook his head. "Only when the alcalde arrives."

"Who whipped you?" one man asked him.

"Soldiers who tried to keep me from delivering this warning."

Shortly, the murmuring crowd parted to make way for a lean man with leathery skin and serious eyes. "I'm Andrew Ponton, alcalde for Gonzales," he announced. "What kind of rumors are you spreading?"

Calder eyed Ponton, then ran his trigger finger down the scabbed slash across his cheek. "A Mexican bayonet did this to stop me from delivering this message: The Mexicans are marching upon Gonzales."

"We've been loyal to Mexico," Ponton said, puzzled, "and most sentiment in Gonzales favored the government . . . well, at least until two weeks ago," he admitted, "when Adam Zumwalt caught a Mexican deserter stealing from his storeroom. Adam tried to stop him, but the soldier beat him with his musket. Folks are still plenty riled about that."

"Soldiers could be marching on Gonzales right now," Calder said, "and these aren't deserters."

"But why Gonzales?" Ponton asked.

Calder pointed to the artillery. "Colonel Ugartechea wants the cannon back."

"That little thing?" Ponton said incredulously. "Why, it's just a noisemaker to scare off the Comanches. It doesn't have any value other than that."

"It does to Colonel Ugartechea."

Ponton turned to the other men. "As your alcalde, I'm not prepared to give up the cannon. We saw what happened to Adam Zumwalt. We can't chance that happening to another of us."

The men cheered. Someone yelled, "The cannon stays."

Ponton turned to a man near Calder. "I'm appointing Albert Martin our captain in the face of hostilities. No one'll take our cannon."

The men cheered again.

"I'll stand with you," Calder announced. "I've a score to settle with the Mexicans. As long as the river's high and the ferry's on on this side, the Mexicans can't reach us or the cannon."

The new captain stepped forward. "He's right, men. I want two of you to go upstream and two down and order folks to keep their boats on the east side of the river. We'll keep outriders across the river, looking for the enemy. Once they're spotted, we'll send out an alarm and converge here to meet them. Everyone understand?"

The men nodded.

"Then keep your powder dry," Martin cried, "and be ready to fight on a minute's notice. We're the grandsons of the men who whipped the British, and we'll do the same with the Mexicans."

The men rushed away, leaving Martin and Ponton alone with the Calders. "We are grateful for the warning, and that you're standing with us," Ponton said.

"There's a fight brewing," Calder replied, "and I intend to be a part of it."

Juan Paz slapped Angelita Sanchez and she fell to the floor, tears spilling out of her eyes. Paz drew back his foot to kick her. Angelita shook like a leaf until he lowered his foot.

"Rubio was here last night after I left?"

Angelita nodded nervously.

"And you didn't send for me?"

Angelita nodded. "I feared that he might hurt you."

Paz scowled. "Had you come to me, we might have caught the traitor and reunited him with his brother."

Angelita began crying. "I'm sorry, Juan, believe me."

Juan turned away. "If he ever returns and you do not tell me, I will kill the both of you. You are my woman now, and I want all of Bexar to know about it."

Angelita nodded feebly.

Juan spun for the door and stormed away in disgust. He could hear Angelita sobbing behind him as he stepped onto the plaza. Rubio Portillo could have been captured had only she alerted him. She had much to learn if she intended to be his wife.

Paz marched across the plaza, past the church and onto the Military Plaza where Colonel Ugartechea had his office. Paz barged inside to the colonel's room and found Ugartechea talking with Lieutenant Castenada. Both men were startled by his sudden entrance. He enjoyed the surprise on their faces.

"I have information for you, Colonel."

Ugartechea nodded and looked at the lieutenant. "Please wait outside for a few minutes, Francisco."

The lieutenant nodded, tossing Paz a hard stare. Paz smirked, pleased that he had clout enough to interrupt a meeting among soldiers. The lieutenant marched briskly past him.

"Don't forget to shut the door," Paz said.

When the door closed, Ugartechea stood up, shaking his head. "Why do you gall people so, Juan Paz?"

"It gets results, like whipping a mule."

Ugartechea nodded. "I'm not one of your mules."

"Rubio Portillo slipped past your guards last night."

"It does me no good to learn that now, Juan Paz."

"He visited Angelita Sanchez." Paz folded his arms over his chest. "She didn't tell me until today, but if he slips into Bexar again, she knows to come to me immediately."

"Why would she? Aren't they betrothed?"

"They were, but no longer. She has fallen for me." Paz laughed.

"I'm certain, Juan Paz, that you didn't come here to announce a wedding date."

Paz stroked his chin. "Odd, isn't it, that she's broken her betrothal with a wealthy rancher for a man who drives mules and carries freight. Of course, Colonel, with Rubio Portillo wanted by the government, I should like to own Rancho de Espiritu Toro before I marry Angelita Sanchez."

"From what I have heard about the temperamental Angelita," the colonel said, "you deserve each other."

"Are you sending soldiers to his ranch to capture him?"

"More pressing matters have come up, Juan Paz."

"The cannon in Gonzales."

Ugartechea shrugged. "In ten days my soldiers will march on Gonzales."

"Why wait?"

"General Cos and his five hundred and fifty men will be moving to secure the presidio at Goliad and marching to Bexar. I will wait until his men are closer. The Anglos will see we mean to take the cannon and that we have the soldiers necessary to enforce the wishes of President Santa Anna. You know, of course, General Cos is the president's brother-in-law?"

"What difference does that make?"

"Santa Anna sends his brother-in-law where

the trouble is greatest."

Paz nodded. "Never should we have let the Anglos settle in Texas. It can only mean war."

Ugartechea laughed. "And war can only make you rich, Juan Paz. Your men will freight supplies from the coast to our army and make a tidy profit, and when it is over, you'll be able to claim Rubio Portillo's ranch and his woman for your own."

"Don't expect me to thank the Anglos."

The colonel stroked his chin. "Juan Paz, I don't expect you to thank anyone."

Rubio Portillo saw the rider disappear into the trees. Leaning forward in his saddle, he lifted his pistol from its scabbard on the pommel. Slowly, he lowered the pistol until he held it behind his leg. The rider was the first person he'd seen since abandoning his vacant rancho. It had taken him three days since he had left his place and ridden for Gonzales, and he knew he now must be within a league of the Guadalupe River itself. Rains and caution had slowed his trip.

He felt guilty for abandoning Tomas in Bexar, but he also knew he could do nothing alone to change that. His only hope was to ally himself with Anglos chafing under Mexican rule. He planned to throw in with them at Gonzales. Seeing the ears of his black stallion flick forward, Rubio surveyed the path that meandered between trees and thickets of brush toward the river. He moved forward slowly, and when he was within fifty paces of the river, saw the stallion's ears flicked again.

Before he could lift his arm and pistol, a man appeared from behind a tree, another to his right from a thicket of bushes, and a third to his left. All had their guns pointed at him.

"What's your business, Mexican?" the one before him asked.

"I'm here to fight against Mexico."

"Who are you?"

Before Rubio could answer, the man to his right announced, "The Mexican's holding his pistol behind his leg."

"If he lifts it," said the man blocking his path, "kill him."

Rubio flinched.

The man at his side rushed over and took the pistol

"Now, who are you?" the man in front demanded.

"Rubio Portillo from Rancho de Espiritu Toro. And who are you?"

"Albert Martin. I'm captain of the Gonzales volunteers. What are you doing here?"

"You sure he ain't spying for the soldiers?" the man holding Rubio's gun wanted to know.

"I'm looking for Donley Calder."

Martin cocked his head. "You a friend of his?"

"I don't know if Calder has any friends, much less any Mexican friends."

"That's Calder all right, but just in case you ain't on the square, Rubio, we'll take your weapons until we check it out with Calder."

The two men on either side took his musket and his knife, then stepped back.

"Since we're afoot, you follow me to the river," Martin instructed. "Now, if you were to make a run for it, or even if your stallion was to bolt, Rubio, we'd be obliged to shoot you."

Rubio shook his head. "I've got more troubles behind me than ahead of me."

"We can't say the same thing about Texas." Martin turned toward the river, and Rubio followed at a slow pace, the two volunteers on either side eyeing him warily.

By the flooded river, Martin disappeared behind a thicket of bushes and reemerged with three horses. The trio then mounted and pointed him north.

"There's a ferry a mile away. We'll cross the river there."

They didn't say much the rest of the way, though Rubio saw them signal to other sentries stationed periodically along the river to be especially watchful for approaching soldiers.

At the ferry, Rubio guided his horse through the muddy approach and onto the wooden craft, which was adequate to carry a wagon or a half dozen horses. The ferryman glanced at Rubio, then at Martin as the captain rode on board.

"Catch you a spy?"

Martin shrugged. "Don't think so, but I've got to check."

"He's a Mexican, ain't he?"

Martin glanced down at the ferryman. "You

112

gonna jaw all day or pull us across?"

The ferryman grumbled, took hold of the rope and began to yank the ferry through the fast-moving waters an arm length at a time. Rubio thought it was customary to help the ferryman pull the craft, but Martin made no effort to assist. When the ferry reached the opposite bank, Martin followed Rubio off and pointed him toward town. Rubio's other two captors followed.

Gonzales was a small town built around an abundant square where some fifty armed men stood guard. Several stepped out to meet Martin. Rubio was uncomfortable with their hard stares.

"Where's Calder?" Martin asked.

"Here I am," Calder answered from behind.

Rubio turned to face Calder.

Squinting at Rubio, the frontiersman adjusted his lionskin cap.

"You know this man?" Martin pointed at Rubio.

"He gave me a horse after the fight with the soldiers."

"Can you vouch for him?"

Calder scratched his head. "I don't vouch for nobody except myself."

Rubio was stunned.

"I can vouch for him," Mary Calder shouted, elbowing her way through the men. "He saved me and found my father."

"But he's Mexican," a young soldier challenged.

"I can vouch for him," Mary repeated, "and if

113

you don't accept my word, I'll quit cooking for some of you. You can starve for all I care."

"She makes a point," Martin said. "Give him his weapons."

His two other captors offered Rubio his pistol, musket, and knife. As he took them, Martin spoke.

"You don't be riding out of Gonzales."

Nodding, Rubio slid his pistol in his saddle scabbard, then slipped the leather cover over his musket and inserted his knife in his belt. As he dismounted, the others returned to their duties.

Mary, though, stood waiting. As soon as his feet touched the ground, she walked over and hugged him.

Calder growled. "Don't be clinging to him like bark to a tree."

"I'll do what I please," she answered back, "or you'll be cooking for yourself."

Calder grumbled and walked away.

Mary smiled at Rubio. "I didn't get to thank you enough for saving my father."

Rubio grinned. "You saved me, remember? If you hadn't been there to pull him off of me, I'd be a dead Mexican."

"Did you come to join the volunteers or to see me?" she asked.

Rubio was uncomfortable yet pleased with the question. "They put my brother in prison."

"Did it have anything to do with Papa's fight?"

Rubio nodded. "That's what the senora told me. The soldiers want to arrest me too."

"I'm sorry," she said. "Maybe I could cook for you too. I owe it to you. You'd be welcomed to throw your bed near ours."

"You sure your father wouldn't mind?"

"I'll tell him you're betrothed? You are, aren't you?"

"I was, but I'm not sure anymore."

"I'm sorry," Mary said, but it seemed to Rubio that her response lacked sincerity.

The afternoon shower came suddenly and washed through Bexar. The rain was borne on a cool breeze that seeped through the narrow slit of a window that provided all the light in Tomas Portillo's prison cell. His wrists were raw from the irons around them, and the cell had been stifling hot. He was kept alone in his cell, except for the two or three rats he'd seen, and the brazen cockroaches. The guards beat him, ate his food, and taunted him for killing one of their comrades. He received water but once a day, and only a single meal, a bean soup that was more water than bean, if his guards didn't eat it.

As the rain pummeled the ground outside, Tomas leaned against the wall slit, letting the hint of a breeze cool his face. The opening was not even large enough for him to stick his hand through so he could cup his palm and catch some of the aromatic rainwater. He pushed his nose into the slit and opened up his mouth, hoping some drops might strike his tongue, but the wall was too thick and his dry tongue felt like a rasp over his cracked lips.

The rain came in sheets, occasionally whipped by the wind, until Tomas could almost swallow its flavor, but not its moisture. He tried to push his nose and mouth deeper into the opening, as if a hair's width might bring his tongue within reach of the water. He cursed his thirst. He cursed Mexico. And he cursed its soldiers. He hoped that Rubio had escaped them, but he had no way of knowing.

The rain came down even faster, tantalizing Tomas even more. So much water was falling from the sky, and all he wanted was a dozen mouthfuls, a chance to fill his belly until it was heavy. As the roar of the rain began to recede, he heard another tantalizing sound — dripping water. He jerked himself away from the wall and spun around. Water was trickling from the ceiling. A dozen rivulets poured through. Like a madman, he raced from one leak to another, tilting his head, opening his mouth and letting the water pour in. The water tasted gritty and sour, but it was wet and it cut the thirsty crust on his tongue, his lips, and in his mouth. He danced from leak to leak, taking all the water he could swallow. And when his thirst had been sated, he stood under the leaks and let them soak his hair. He shouted with pleasure and wondered if he was crazy.

Tomas knew Rubio had always thought him crazy because he liked the young ladies and spent so much time preening for them. He must have been with every pretty young lady in Bexar at one time or another, yet not a one had come to visit. Tomas knew the soldiers would not let them visit him, but he also knew they could pass by and just call his name through the slit in the wall. That would be enough. All his play had gotten him nowhere when he needed friends. Rubio, who had always been interested in work and in politics, had done no better. His politics had caught him up in the same whirlwind.

Two brothers so different, yet caught in the same storm. Maybe the Anglos were right, Tomas thought. Maybe a man should have a say in his government. It had never occurred to him that it would matter, but then he'd never been held in prison before, nor had he been so desperate for water that he drank ceiling leaks.

Tomas did not know if he would ever drink clear water or eat a roasted beefsteak or sleep with a young maiden again. He did not even know if he would leave this dungeon alive. But if he ever did get out of prison, he vowed he would kill many soldiers in retribution.

8

In the week since Rubio Portillo had arrived in Gonzales, the makeshift army recruited to protect the cannon was gradually evaporating. With each passing day, more men returned home to protect their families or gather their crops. Each day, too, brought more and more resentment against Donley Calder. Many called him a crazy old man behind his back. Some even suggested that both Calder and Rubio were spies for the Mexicans. Each morning during breakfast Captain Albert Martin would appear, as if checking to see that Rubio had not escaped during the night.

On this morning, Martin was standing with arms crossed when Rubio emerged from the bushes. He shook his head. "We're down to eighteen men this morning. Why haven't you left?"

"There's nothing to do, nowhere to go, Captain. All the guard posts are accounted for."

Martin rubbed his hands together. "Why haven't the Mexican forces come?"

Rubio shrugged. "I heard more soldiers had landed on the coast and were headed for Bexar." He pointed to the cannon. "Such a small cannon for such a big fuss."

Martin scratched his chin. "A small ember can start a big fire."

"If they come, what will you do with eighteen men, Captain?"

"Stall. The river will protect us."

"But one day the river will fall. Then what?"

"My men will fight because Texas is their home. It will be easy for us. It's men like you I pity. Your heart may be with us, but your skin sides with the enemy. Some men can't overlook that."

Rubio heard his name and turned to see Mary waving to him.

Martin smiled. "Breakfast must be ready."

Rubio nodded. "What watch do you want me to take?"

"Finish your breakfast, then stay out until noon, when I'll have somebody spell you." Martin looked around. "Come tomorrow morning, I wonder how many men will be left besides you and me."

"And Donley Calder."

Martin laughed. "He could be enough to whip half an army."

Rubio retreated to breakfast. Calder squatted Indian style by the fire, eating his sliced salt pork and biscuits. He greeted Rubio with his customary morning grunt.

Mary offered Rubio a tin of coffee and a plate of bacon and biscuits. He downed the coffee quickly, then Mary lifted the pot from the fire with a rag and filled his cup again. Rubio sat on the ground beside Calder.

The old man scowled. "What watch were you assigned?"

"Morning watch." Rubio bit a chunk from a biscuit.

"I always get guard duty right before dawn, when a man's at his sleepiest." Calder looked around. "If men keep leaving, it may be just you and me keeping guard."

Rubio gobbled down his breakfast, then handed his plate and empty cup to Mary. Retreating to his bedroll, he picked up his musket and pistol, powder horn and bullet pouch. He strolled to the corral, saddled his black stallion, then rode to the ferryman, who transported him across the river.

Rubio found the guard he was to replace beneath an oak tree. "I ain't seen nothing," the sentry said. "I think I just as well head back home and do what I can with my crop."

Rubio nodded. "It's been a long wait for nothing."

The man mounted his horse and galloped back to the ferry as Rubio guided his horse through the trees to a spot where he could see more than half a league down the road.

Sentry duty was boring, monotonous work, lulling a man into lethargy. The morning passed at a snail's pace. When his stomach began to growl with hunger, Rubio knew his watch was almost done. Glancing over his shoulder, he saw his replacement riding toward him. Rubio smiled, then turned to take a final glance down the Bexar road. His throat tightened when he saw a single rider in uniform looking over the countryside with a spy glass.

Before his replacement could reach him, Rubio watched two more mounted soldiers join the first. They were dressed like Ugartechea's dragoons. Rubio wondered how many more there were.

Rubio's replacement drew up beside him and spotted the soldiers. "Mother of God," he exclaimed, "they've come." The volunteer reached to pull his pistol from his belt. "We've got to sound the alarm."

Rubio grabbed his hand. "Don't fire. We must be careful."

The volunteer reluctantly released the butt of his pistol. "What will we do?"

"Retreat to the ferry and cross the river."

The two men spurred their horses toward the Guadalupe.

"They've come," the volunteer yelled to the ferryman.

Rubio followed the volunteer's mount onto the ferry, then both men jumped from their saddles and helped the ferryman pull the craft across the river. As the ferry glided to the eastern bank, both men jumped on their horses and raced off and toward town.

"They're here!" the volunteer yelled. "Get your weapons!"

Men at the camp scurried to load their muskets and saddle their horses. Shortly, Captain Martin and the remaining fifteen men joined Rubio and the volunteer.

"How many?" Martin asked.

"We saw only three," Rubio answered, "but there will be more."

Martin guided his horse out in front of the others and lifted his hand. "No one is to fire unless I command. Once we see their numbers, I'll dispatch some of you to spread the alarm."

The men nodded, then mounted their horses. They followed Martin to the river and spread out across its bank. Rubio sat near the captain to serve as a translator. He watched a line of about a hundred Mexican dragoons approach. Eighteen men could not hold out long against such a large force. For several minutes the volunteers returned the hard stares of the Mexican soldiers, then a single rider broke from the dragoons carrying a flag of truce.

Martin turned to Rubio. "Accompany me to the water's edge." Twisting about in his saddle, Martin gave additional instructions. "Do not fire unless I give the command or unless I'm shot down myself. I plan to buy enough time so others can join us." The captain nudged his horse forward and Rubio followed. They waited at the water's edge for the Mexican officer to reach the opposite bank.

"*Buenas dias.* I am Lieutenant Francisco Castenada. I carry a message for the alcalde," Castenada shouted.

Rubio translated for Martin.

"Tell him the alcalde is out of town."

Rubio obliged.

Castenada seemed confused for a moment. He dug into his pocket and pulled out papers he waved over his head. "I must cross the river to deliver the message."

Rubio translated Castenada's words. Martin instructed Rubio to tell the lieutenant no man would be allowed to cross the river. "Tie the message to a rock and throw it over," Rubio called. "We will carry the message to the alcalde."

The lieutenant dismounted, stabbed the shaft of the flag into the ground and found a rock. He folded the message, then tied it to the rock with a pair of leather thongs. He heaved it across the river.

One of the volunteers picked up the rock and delivered it to Martin. He passed it to Rubio, who separated the paper from the rock and read aloud the demand that the cannon be returned. When Rubio finished, Martin told him what to say.

"We will deliver your message once the alcalde returns," Rubio shouted scross the river in Spanish, "but you must keep your troops on the west side of the river."

"When will the alcalde return?" Castenada asked.

"Two, maybe three days," Rubio answered, according to Martin's instructions.

"We shall wait three days, no longer, then we

shall be forced to take other action," Castenada called back.

Martin nodded that he understood. When Castenada retreated to his troops, Martin backtracked to his own. Rubio followed.

The men huddled around Martin. "We are outnumbered," the captain said. "Until more men can join us, we must hide the cannon." Martin called out three names, then told them to bury the cannon.

Quickly, the three men retreated to the cannon. Martin turned to two more. "Spread the word and get as many men to return as you can."

"When do we get to the killing, Captain?" Calder asked.

"The shooting starts when I give the word, not before," Martin told him.

"I came to fight," Calder said.

"So did they," Rubio replied.

Reinforcements began arriving at Gonzales that afternoon. For two days a steady stream of men swelled the ranks of the Texians to almost two hundred men. They were a surly lot, spoiling for a fight.

By the end of the third day, the Texians held the numerical advantage. Martin ordered that the cannon be recovered from its grave and that the Texians prepare to cross the river after dark. Rubio hungered for the fight, hoping to rout the enemy and follow them to Bexar, where he could free his brother.

Just before dusk, several men pulled the cannon on its awkward carriage out of the woods. The men cheered at its sight and at the flag one man waved behind it. A cannon had been painted on the white cloth. Below the cannon someone had painted *Come and Take It.*

Toward seven o'clock word was passed for the men to slip quietly to the ferry. Mary hugged her father as he led his horse toward the river, then she turned to Rubio. "Take care of yourself," she said, and kissed him on the cheek.

Rubio smiled. "I'll be fine."

He followed Calder to the river and led his horse onto the ferry. A dozen men and horses crowded on before it started across. The men whispered among themselves, wondering if a dozen of them could hold off a hundred dragoons until others were ferried across.

They slid over the waters, disembarked cautiously and made their way up from the river. With every step, Rubio feared that a musket shot might crack through the night. But their luck held and no sentry raised an alarm.

Word was passed that once the infantry were in position, the Texians would attack. Rubio was ready. This would be the first step on his return to Bexar to free Tomas. Finally the infantry were ferried over and they fanned out in uneven ranks behind the mounted soldiers. Men cocked their weapons and pointed them at the enemy position on high ground some three hundred paces from the river.

Rubio licked his lips nervously as they advanced toward the hill. When he realized Calder rode beside him, he felt safer. "They haven't seen us yet," Rubio said.

"I think they knew we were coming and high-tailed it."

"They scared to fight?"

"No, but they may have gone upstream to find a crossing where they can circle Gonzales," Calder suggested.

Rubio grimaced. Mary was in Gonzales. "We've got to find them."

"We will. They can't be far."

When they reached the high ground, the soldiers confirmed Calder's suspicions. The Mexicans had abandoned their camp.

Captain Martin rode to the front. "They've retreated," he said. "We'll wait until light to follow."

"No," Calder said. "If we don't stay on their tail, they can circle around behind us and take Gonzales, even surprise us."

Martin pondered Calder's words. "The Mexicans can't see in the dark any better than we can. We'll advance, but I'm ordering Donley Calder to lead."

"That suits me, Captain."

"I'll ride with him," Rubio said.

"That's fine by me too," Calder said. "I want you fellows to remember one thing," he added, looking at the men. "Rubio is a Mexican, but when the shooting starts, I don't want any of you firing at him."

"Our aim's not that bad," a soldier countered.

"It's not your aim I'm worried about as much as your brain."

Several laughed.

Calder held up his hand. "We'll stay twenty or thirty paces ahead of you. Don't any of you fellows get nervous and fire off your guns in our back." With that, he shook his reins and his horse moved forward. Rubio following.

The night was dark as ink and the atmosphere heavy as they advanced stealthily, weaving among the trees. Occasionally, Rubio heard sounds that made him fear they'd stumbled upon the Mexican camp, but Calder always identified the noise.

"Deer," he whispered once. "Armadillo," he said another time. Behind them they heard the soft sounds of their own men advancing and the occasional curses of the men maneuvering the cannon in the dark. After midnight fog set in, making it almost impossible to see. Still the Texians inched forward.

By three o'clock Rubio was drowsy in his saddle and ready to rest, but the yelping of a dog not thirty paces ahead cleared his brain quickly. He straightened in his saddle, lifting his musket toward the sound.

"Stay here and don't make any sudden movements," Calder whispered. "We've found their camp. I'll go take a look for myself."

"You won't see much, not with the fog."

Calder disappeared into the haze, then a shot cracked through the stillness. Rubio ducked instinctively, heard Calder's horse nicker and squeal, then a thud, followed by the sound of hooves approaching. He cocked his rifle and just made out the silhouette of a riderless horse trotting by.

It was Calder's horse! Rubio nudged his stallion forward, intent on finding Calder, to see how badly he was hurt, if he was alive at all. As his horse advanced he heard Calder's loud whisper. "That you, Rubio?"

"Yes. Are you okay?"

"The gunshot spooked my horse and threw me. I bloodied my nose in the fall, but nothing else. The Mexicans are just up ahead."

Suddenly, Calder loomed out of the darkness and fog. Rubio extended his hand and helped pull him onto the back of his stallion. Several other gunshots erupted from the trees ahead of them. Rubio ducked, turned his horse about and retreated.

"Don't shoot," Rubio called. "It's me and Calder."

"Is Calder okay? Someone caught his horse."

"I'm fine, dammit, just got a bloody nose."

A couple men laughed. "What'd you try to do, Calder, stop the bullet with your teeth and miss?"

Calder growled. "We'll see who's laughing after the fighting."

Once Rubio passed the line of Texians, several answered the Mexican gunshots with their own weapons. As the sound of shots rang through the trees, Rubio helped Calder down and dismounted himself. He staked and hobbled his horse. Like the other men, he dug in behind a log and waited in case the Mexicans attacked.

After the initial flurry of gunfire, things went silent and the men stared through the fog toward an enemy they could not see. Dawn arrived shrouded in mist. Up and down the line, Texians checked their weapons for the battle that was coming.

Gradually, the sun began to burn away the fog. Rubio could see the Mexicans upon a rise two hundred paces away. Occasionally, one of the Texians took a shot with a long rifle at a careless soldier. Emboldened by the Mexicans timid response, forty or more Texians left their hiding places and advanced into a clearing between the two camps. They shot again at the Mexicans, then laughed at them and taunted them with words the enemy likely didn't understand.

Rubio heard a commotion behind him and turned to see men pulling the tiny cannon into position. They wheeled it to the middle of the line and placed powder and buckets of nails beside the wooden wheels. One soldier waved the banner with the "Come and Take It" challenge. As he watched the Texians load the petite cannon, Rubio heard galloping hooves from the Mexican camp. Twisting around, he saw fifty dragoons pour over the rise and out of the camp. They charged toward the Texians in the clearing.

Calder shouted, "Make your aim count!"

The dragoons raced toward the outer Texian line. The men in the clearing fired their muskets, then retreated to the trees. Once they were under cover, the second line of volunteers fired. Donley Calder stood up beside Rubio, jerked his musket to his shoulder and took steady aim. He squeezed off a shot, then cursed. "Missed." Calmly, he reloaded his musket without stepping behind a tree or dropping behind a log for cover. The smell of gun smoke engulfed the woods as Rubio fired his gun. It felt good to spend powder and lead on his brother's captors.

The volley, though doing little physical damage to the attackers, broke the Mexican troops' resolve. They wheeled their horses about and retreated to their camp.

"Cowards," Calder yelled, shaking his fist. Other Texians stood and cheered, waving their hats and caps over their heads.

"Any men hurt?" Captain Martin shouted as he ran along the line.

"Not a scratch," someone yelled.

"Hurrah," Martin called. "Calder's nose is our only wound yet."

Calder spat and cursed. The men around him laughed.

Shortly, a flag of truce appeared in the Mexican camp.

Martin called for Rubio. "Ask what they want."

Rubio yelled in Spanish to the enemy camp. Lieutenant Castenada answered. "He wants to parley, Colonel." Rubio said.

"Tell him we will meet on open ground in fifteen minutes. Him and an interpreter will meet you and me. Tell him no weapons."

Rubio relayed the message, and the lieutenant accepted the terms. Martin turned to his men. "If they try to take us prisoner, I'll throw my hat in the air. That'll be the signal for you to fire."

Rubio gave Calder his musket, powder horn, pistol, and cartridge box for safekeeping. Calder propped the rifle against the nearest tree, then hung the powder horn and cartridge box over a broken limb. He tucked the pistol in his belt and grinned at Rubio. "Don't let the lieutenant out-talk you."

Captain Martin stepped up to Rubio and handed him a short limb with a murky kerchief tied to one end. "Our flag of truce."

Rubio took the stick and nodded. "I am ready."

Together the two men walked side by side and emerged from the trees into the clearing. From the rise where the Mexicans hid, the lieutenant and a second officer appeared. They walked with stern faces and serious intent, meeting Rubio and Martin in the middle of the clearing. Neither side offered pleasantries or showed respect for the other's rank.

Rubio stared at Lieutenant Castenada, hating him for imprisoning his brother. He fought the urge to attack him with his fists. The lieutenant spoke first, and Rubio translated. "He says he has been ordered to request the cannon be returned to Bexar."

Martin glanced back over his shoulder and pointed at the piece. "There it is. Our flag says 'Come and Take It.' "

Rubio translated, and Castenada's interpreter nodded that he agreed with the interpretation.

Castenada's lips tightened and he answered in a menacing tone. Rubio nodded as he translated. "The lieutenant says he has no orders to fire on the colonists, and he desires to know why the colonists have taken up arms against Mexico."

"Tell him," Martin said, "that by acting on behalf of Santa Anna, he and his troops are defying the constitution of 1824. We do not want to fight. We only want to see that the constitution is restored so that we can be represented in the government."

Rubio translated the message, then listened to Castenada's response. "He says he is a federalist too, but he is a soldier first and will not become a traitor to his country."

"Tell him he already has," Martin replied.

Instead Rubio told him the Texians would not return the cannon.

Castenada's interpreter, though, translated Martin's harsh words for the lieutenant. Castenada shook his head and gritted his teeth, then spoke heated words, which Rubio translated.

"He says to delay returning the cannon can only bring war and misery to our people. Even as we speak, the great General Cos is marching on Bexar. He has more than five hundred men with him. If rebellion breaks out, many more will come and crush you like ants."

Martin nodded. "Tell him we have nothing more to discuss. The cannon stays with us unless they take it."

Rubio hesitated, then asked a question of the lieutenant. "Do you have Tomas Portillo in the Bexar prison?"

"For killing a soldier, *si*. And for killing a soldier and siding with traitors, you too will one day be there." The lieutenant shook his head. "You should be fighting with your people, not against them."

"You are not my people."

Castenada pointed a finger at Martin. "But neither is he."

Rubio shook his head. "My captain says we have nothing more to discuss because the cannon stays."

"Much blood will be spilled because of this," Castenada said, then turned around and started toward his camp.

Rubio and Martin returned to their men, who yelled questions. Martin did not answer, but marched straight to the cannon.

"Gentlemen," he ordered, "load the cannon and fire it upon the Mexican Army when you are ready."

The artillerymen cheered. Yells were heard up and down the line as men were told the command.

"When the cannon sounds," Martin cried, "arise and charge. It is better to die free men than to live as prisoners to a government in which we have no voice."

Up and down the line men checked their powder and cocked the hammers on their muskets. Rubio ran for his weapons, grabbing them from Calder, then started for his horse.

"No," Martin cried when he saw men untying their horses. "We will attack by foot."

The artillerymen announced the cannon was loaded.

"Fire when ready!" Martin shouted.

The men lit the cannon, and it discharged loudly.

As one the men rose and charged the heights, screaming with exhilaration. They shot, reloaded, and shot again.

The Mexican soldiers, though, held their fire. And when the Texians reached the top of the rise, they saw why. The cavalrymen were mounting and racing toward Bexar.

The Texians cheered and danced with one another. Martin raised his hat in the air, shouting, "We routed the enemy without a casualty — save Calder's nose."

9

Juan Paz marched into Colonel Domingo Ugartechea's office unannounced. "My muleteers could have put up a greater fight than your soldiers at Gonzales."

The colonel slammed his fist against his desk. "Leave, Juan Paz. I am busy."

"How will you explain your men's failings to General Cos?"

"Leave, Juan Paz. I have important matters to consider."

"Don't insult me, Colonel. It is my muleteers your army must rely on if war comes. If you do not accommodate my wishes, I may have difficulty managing yours if war comes."

"You are quite the patriot, Juan Paz." Ugartechea arose from his desk, shaking his head.

The freighter smiled. "All I ask is your power upon occasion."

Ugartechea nodded. "And this is one of those occasions?"

Juan Paz smiled. "Indeed. I want permission for me and a guest to see the prisoner, Tomas Portillo."

The colonel stepped around the desk.

"And why is that?"

"To acquire his rancho."

Ugartechea laughed. "You are greedy, Juan Paz."

Paz shook is head. "The rancho is not for me, but for my wife-to-be. Rubio has dishonored her name by turning traitor. I should like the ranch to give her as a wedding present. We shall be married on Christmas Day, when she had planned to marry Rubio."

"You are devious as well, Juan Paz."

"Perhaps, but I am loyal to Mexico."

Ugartechea shook his head. "You are loyal only to yourself." The colonel bent over his desk, took up his quill and dipped it in ink. He quickly wrote out an order allowing the bearer and his guest to visit Tomas in his prison cell. The colonel handed the paper to Paz. "Take it and be gone."

Paz pinched the corner of the order between his thumb and forefinger, then marched out onto the Military Plaza. He held the document up toward the sun so the ink might dry quicker, then strode to Angelita's house.

Reaching the entrance, he lifted the handle and let himself in without knocking. "Angelita," he called, "join me." He saw her scurry out of the kitchen toward him.

"Yes, Juan," she answered with a tremor.

Paz enjoyed the fear in her eyes. "Come with me."

She patted her hair, then her cheeks. "I am not presentable."

"No matter, Angelita, we have a friend to visit."

"I must change, Juan, please."

Paz grabbed her arm and squeezed until she grimaced. He smiled. Angelita had been a free-spirited mare, but he planned to break her spirit to make a better wife. Angelita protested weakly as he steered her out the door, not bothering to shut it. With every step Angelita tried to straighten her hair or pat her cheeks to add color.

"Why are you humiliating me, Juan?"

"Why were you not ready for me when I came?"

"You did not tell me you were coming, Juan."

"You are always to be ready for me."

"Where are we going, Juan? Please tell me just that."

"To prison."

"They have captured Rubio?"

Paz tightened his grip. "You no longer care for him, do you?"

"No, no," she gasped. "It is you I fear — I mean love."

He jerked his hand from her arm as they reached the prison. "It had *better* be me that you love."

The guard at the outer door stepped in front of Paz. "Your business?"

"I'm here to see a prisoner."

"No one can visit without the written command of the colonel."

Paz offered him the colonel's orders.

The soldier took the paper, studied it, and returned it to Paz. The guard nodded. "Follow me." The soldier unbarred the door, then led them down a dingy hallway lit with two candles and lined with thick plank doors. At a middle cell the soldier unbarred the door and swung it open.

Paz took a candle from the closest holder and walked inside, grabbing Angelita's arm when she hesitated and dragging her with him.

In the back corner of the small cell, Paz saw an emaciated figure shielding his eyes from the light of the candle.

Angelita gasped. "Tomas?"

Tomas nodded weakly, the chains on his wrists rattling as he tried to rise. "Angelita," he wheezed. "Is Rubio okay?"

Angelita shook her head. "I do not know."

Tomas sank back against the wall.

Paz laughed. "This is what becomes of traitors."

"Juan Paz? You've no reason to visit me except for evil."

Paz stepped to Tomas, bent over, then slapped his cheek.

"No, no," Angelita cried.

"I came to help you, Tomas," Paz chided, "and yet you mock me."

Silently, Tomas licked the blood from his lips.

"I can see that you are released. For a price, of course."

"I'd rather die in prison than seek a favor from you."

Paz laughed. "That may happen unless you do what I say."

Tomas stared blankly ahead.

"Sign away your rancho to me and I will see that you get out."

"It is Rubio's and mine. I'll die before I would sign it away." Tomas spat blood at Paz's feet.

Paz struck Tomas savagely across the cheek.

"No, no," Angelita cried, rushing to help Tomas.

Paz grabbed her arm and flung her aside. He pulled a roll of papers from beneath his serape. He waved them in front of Tomas's nose, then dropped them in his lap. "I will return tomorrow."

Tomas flung the papers aside.

"Need a quill to write with?" Paz bent for his boot and jerked out a stiletto. He grabbed Tomas's weak hand and jabbed the knife in the tip of his forefinger. "Sign it in blood."

Paz shoved the stiletto back in his boot, then straightened. "You are a prideful man, but you face the fate of a traitor. Only I can help you."

Angelita whimpered. "I'm sorry, Tomas."

Paz grabbed Angelita's arm and pulled her to him. "Angelita and I are marrying on your brother's wedding day."

"Why did you bring me to see this?" she screamed.

"So you would know what would happen to you if you spurned me, Angelita." He shoved the colonel's orders in her hand. "Keep this in case you want to visit Tomas someday and see his fate." He pulled her out the door. The guard barred it behind them as Paz replaced the candle in its holder. Then the three moved back down the dingy hall.

As they stepped out the door and into the sunlight, Paz pushed Angelita away. "Remember what you saw, and don't ever cross me."

Angelita sobbed and stumbled across the plaza, but hardly a pedestrian noticed because of the commotion at the other end of the street. A line of mounted officers had just turned onto the plaza, and behind them came a column of infantry four abreast.

Paz and the others stopped to watch General Cos enter Bexar.

—Rubio Portillo estimated four-hundred-plus Anglo colonists, leatherstockings, and adventurers had arrived in Gonzales as word of the Mexican defeat was carried across Texas. Some sixty Tejanos like himself had joined to fight Mexico as well. The Anglos argued among themselves whether the fight was to restore the constitution of 1824 or to seek total independence. After he freed his brother, Rubio thought, he would decide what he was fighting for. Until then, nothing else mattered.

"Every time more volunteers arrive," Donley Calder groused over a cold biscuit one night, "we've got to elect new officers. We'll spend more time electing than fighting if we don't find a leader."

Rubio agreed. He was anxious to march on

Bexar and end this dispute so he could return with his brother to his rancho.

The next day, though, when a tall, thin man rode into the noisy camp, whispered word preceded him and the men fell silent, several removing their caps and staring with reverence at the emaciated stranger. Rubio had never seen the man before, but he had heard the name: Stephen F. Austin. Many of the colonists called him the "Father of Texas." Even from a distance Rubio could see that he was pale and weak. Several spoke of him having been imprisoned for some two years in Mexico. Though he had been jailed before, he had never been deterred from his mission of seeing Texas survive and survive peacefully. Some said that was because Stephen F. Austin was a weak man without the constitution to fight.

Many men reached out to touch him, but he rode past them into the center of the crowd. When he halted his horse, he surveyed the ragtag army. The men carried muskets and fowling pieces and pistols galore, but Rubio could see no weapon upon Stephen F. Austin.

Finally, Austin shook his head to acknowledge the army's reverent silence. "From the day I first set foot on precious Texas soil," he called in a surprisingly strong voice, "I have been a disciple of peace. I had hoped and prayed that we could colonize Texas not only in harmony with the land, but also with the people of Mexico. I believe with all my heart that peace is still the preferred

141

course for Texas. But we cannot have peace if we cannot have freedom. The government of Mexico refuses us the freedom even to represent ourselves through legally called elections."

The men stood silently, transfixed by his words. The only sound was of a Tejano translating the remarks for those who could not understand English.

"I have been a disciple of peace for years, and what has it gotten us? An army under General Cos is advancing upon Texas with orders to dispel troublemakers and to take the arms from all colonists so we cannot shoot food for our families or protect ourselves from marauding Indians. I have had doubts, I must admit, over which course to take, but no more," he called out, his voice rising. "No doubts, no longer. No submission to Mexico. I cast my voice for freedom. I am but a humble voice one day to be stilled, but I hope to live to see Texas forever free from Mexico."

Austin lowered his head and closed his eyes as if he were praying. For an instant the men were silent, then they broke into spontaneous cheers. Those surrounding his horse reached out to touch him, and he seemed invigorated by their response. Rubio found himself cheering and turned to see Calder yelling and whistling. Calder ripped his lionskin cap off and placed it atop his gun barrel, then thrust it in the air like a war trophy.

When Rubio glanced back at Austin, the statesman was moving his horse through the crowd, aiming for the tent of the latest man voted commander. By dusk the soldiers had called for a new election and overwhelmingly voted Austin their new commander.

The volunteer army lingered for two days at Gonzales while Austin and his officers plotted their move. Good news arrived the second day when a contingent of colonists came from Goliad. They brought news that once General Cos departed for Bexar, Texians had recaptured the presidio at Goliad and taken its store of supplies, arms, powder, and lead. A cheer went up through the army that Goliad was in friendly hands again. By controlling Goliad, the Texians blocked General Cos's shortest supply route from Bexar to Copano Bay.

On the morning the army was to depart, Rubio awoke before dawn and gathered his gear. The morning was cool and peaceful, with doves cooing from the trees. Mary stirred in her blanket on the ground, then stretched and yawned. Out of the corner of his eye Rubio saw her climb out of her blanket, but instead of moving to her pit to start a fire for breakfast, she ambled to him.

"Be careful on the march."

Rubio realized for the first time that she would not be going with the army. He had been around her so much during the past weeks, he'd taken it for granted that she would go where her father went. "I'll watch out for your father," he offered.

She smiled bashfully. "Look after yourself too. I would hate for something to happen to you."

"Once I get my brother, everything will be fine."

Mary grimaced. "It's my fault your brother is in prison. It should be me. I killed the soldier." She began to cry.

Rubio put his arms around her. She nuzzled against his chest and draped her arms around him. He liked the feel of her and the aroma of wood smoke in her hair. They stood silently until they heard her father stirring, then broke their grasp.

She turned away and moved toward her pit to begin building a fire for a final breakfast. Rubio resumed packing his belongings. Donley Calder stood up and stretched, then ambled off to relieve himself. When he returned, Rubio was rolling up his bedding. The aroma of coffee, salt pork, and biscuits hung in the air.

Calder ambled by and swatted Rubio on the back. "You ready to free your brother?" Calder wriggled his lionskin cap over his head and tied it beneath his chin. "I always figured Mary needed a man to look after her once I was gone, but she never took much interest in any man until now."

"I thought you didn't like Mexicans," Rubio said.

"I don't, save one or two."

"You puzzle me, Calder."

"I'm getting old, Rubio. Before I cross that final river, I'd like to know that someone'll be around to look after Mary. She's a half-breed, and that's a bad mark upon her among many white men."

Rubio shook his head. "I'm not saying I'll take care of her or marry her, anything like that."

"And I'm not asking you to, Rubio. Just that if you decide you could take a liking to her, I won't stand in your way. Even if you are a Mexican, you're an honest one who can stand and fight with the best of them."

Rubio grinned. "And can fight without getting my nose bloodied."

"You're to blame for it all." Calder glanced over his shoulder at his daughter. "She's a fine woman, Mary is," Calder said. "She'd make a fine wife."

"Why are you telling me this?"

"Rubio, I got a feeling I won't leave Bexar alive. You wouldn't hold it against a man for being superstitious, would you?"

Slowly, Rubio shook his head, thinking of the ghostly bull he had seen the night all the trouble began. "A man can see sign. I've seen sign before, but I haven't always understood it."

"It's easy to understand dying, Rubio. It's living that's hard to understand, why one man's rich and another's poor, why one woman's pretty and another's ugly, why one horse is fast and another's slow, why one Mexican's treacherous and another's as decent a sort as ever walked the earth." Calder grinned. "I've pegged you as a decent sort. Maybe I'm getting old. Old folks do tend to ramble on."

"How old are you, Calder?"

"Can't rightly say. I was about thirty-three when I fought with Andy Jackson at New Orleans. That was eighteen and fourteen. It's eighteen and thirty-five, so that puts me about fifty-four. That's a long life for a man of my tendencies, drinking, fighting, those types of things."

When Mary called, they ambled to the fire. She forked them out biscuits and bacon, then poured coffee. She didn't say much, and Rubio feared she might have overheard her father.

"Good food," he managed, but nothing more.

Mary remained silent. She went about her chores until word was passed for the men to form up and start the march for Bexar.

Calder grabbed his daughter and gave her a bear hug. "You'll be safe here, Mary. I'll send for you when the fighting's over."

Mary began to cry, then turned to Rubio. "Be careful. I hope you find your brother alive and well."

Rubio nodded his thanks, then picked up his gear to go saddle his black stallion. After he secured his belongings on his mount, he pulled himself atop the animal and joined the other mounted men. About half the volunteers had horses and half were afoot.

As he rode away he glanced back over his shoulder and saw Mary wave.

Though Rubio left Gonzales in high spirits that soon he would be in Bexar fighting to free his brother, his elation soon flagged. It took a week

146

for them to march the forty odd miles to the outskirts of Bexar. Along the way the carriage to the cannon that had started it all broke an axle, so they buried the artillery piece.

Though Stephen F. Austin made a good speech, Rubio thought, he did not make a good general. Austin had called himself a man of peace, and it showed when he came to make war. He was timid and afraid, fearing to risk anything for fear of losing even more. But there were among his officers men of known fighting mettle. Jim Bowie, a man so fearsome with a blade that a knife had been named for him, was one. Colonel James W. Fannin was another, a man who had training at the American military college called West Point.

When the Texian Army set up camp five miles east of Bexar, the officers could see with their spy glasses the Mexicans building fortifications around town and around an abandoned mission across the San Antonio River. The vacant mission had since come to be called the Alamo for a nearby grove of cottonwood trees.

The army moved the next day to Mission Espada, south of San Antonio, and camped the night. The officers clustered in the chapel and argued what course to take as the impatient soldiers waited. As Rubio Portillo marched around the camp, he heard the men complaining about their leaders and wishing for a quick battle to whip the Mexicans and send them packing to Mexico. The mission grounds were familiar to him, as he had walked them many times as a boy. He strode past the granary, its walls crumbling and pilfered for stones to be used in houses or fences along the river. He stopped in the door of the old workshops, the tools and workbenches long since removed. A few families had claimed dwellings within the mission grounds as homes. The mission had once thrived with great ranches, including what was now his own. Then the Spanish government had claimed unbranded church cattle as its own, and the wealth that had accrued to God's church had been stolen by the king of Spain.

As Rubio walked, he heard someone running toward him, calling his name. He turned to see Calder, who grabbed him.

"Come with me," Calder said. "Someone wants to see you."

"Who?"

"I can't say." Calder led him toward the chapel.

For a moment Rubio smiled, thinking Mary had come to join her father, but as he neared the chapel he realized this was an army matter. At the chapel, Calder pushed opened the door and entered. Several of the two dozen men standing around a table where the altar would have been looked up from the maps they were inspecting.

Rubio swallowed hard. Stephen F. Austin and Jim Bowie, among others, stared at him.

"This is Rubio Portillo," Calder announced. "He knows these parts and every tree and every crook in the river between here and San Antonio.

He's a good man, a trustworthy man too, one who could marry my daughter without objection from me."

Austin motioned for Rubio to join them at the table.

Rubio stepped forward, but Calder hesitated. "You too, Donley," Jim Bowie called. "I'll want you to accompany us. You're worth three alligators, a dozen wildcats, or a hundred Mexicans in a fight."

Calder laughed. "Glad you remember, Bowie."

Together Rubio and Calder joined the others. Rubio removed his hat, uncomfortable plotting war in what had once been the house of God.

Stephen F. Austin extended his hand. Rubio grabbed it, but Austin's hand was weak and it wilted within his grasp. Rubio shook the hands of several men, but Bowie's was the strongest of all. He had an iron-clad grip and stare.

"We must move close to San Antonio," Austin said, "and take up a defensible position. We need you to scout for Jim Bowie and help him find that place."

Rubio nodded. "I will."

"The other missions," Bowie asked, "are they defensible?"

Rubio scratched his head. "Mission Concepcion is the closest to Bexar. It is this side of a bend in the river, sheltered by high banks and a good stand of trees. It is defensible, especially since the bell towers can be used to watch the approaches."

Bowie nodded. "Can you guide us so I can see for myself?"

"I can."

"Good," Austin said, turning to Bowie. "Take no more than a hundred mounted men come morning and inspect the mission, Jim. When you've done that, return to camp here and we'll decide our next move. But be careful and be quick. It is unwise to split our forces, but we have no choice in this matter if we're to succeed for Texas."

All the men around the table nodded, except Jim Bowie. "We will do what's best for the men," he answered.

As the meeting broke up, Bowie strode over to Calder and threw his arm over his shoulder. "You're riding with us tomorrow."

"I'm here to do a little fighting," Calder admitted.

Bowie grinned. "It'll be like the old days."

10

By the time a sliver of light cracked the eastern horizon, a column of horsemen was lined up outside the walls of Mission Espada. Stephen F. Austin stood on a pile of rubble by a section of collapsed wall. Jim Bowie reined his horse toward Austin and called for Rubio to join him. Both men approached the commander.

"Colonel Bowie," Austin called, "go only as far as you can comfortably return by dark. It is risky to split our force."

Bowie nodded. "I will do what is best for Texas."

"Then Godspeed."

Bowie jerked the reins on his horse and turned about. Rubio followed him. With a wave of his arm, Bowie started the column toward Bexar. Rubio's heart pounded with excitement. Perhaps this day he might free Tomas, if he were still alive. He could not accept that possibility nor easily dismiss it. Rubio pointed Bowie toward the tree-lined banks of the San Antonio River. "We should cling close to the bank. The journey is longer, but we can approach Bexar unseen."

Rubio rode into the lead and saw Donley Calder direct his horse beside Bowie. The men grinned and began an animated conversation that lasted much of the morning. It was noon or later when the column neared Mission Concepcion. Rubio had seen occasional Mexican scouts, but they seemed to have missed the column of Texians. Rubio halted the column before he came in sight of the mission and reported to Bowie.

"We must stick to the river's edge from here on. If they have sentries in the bell towers, we can be spotted."

Bowie instructed his men to ride in the water where it was shallow and cling to its bank where it was deep. He ordered the men to remain silent the rest of the way. Concepcion was but a league from Bexar, and the town could be easily seen from the mission's twin bell towers. The column advanced until Bowie ordered it to halt in the middle of a U-shaped curve in the river. He dismounted and slipped up the riverbank. Rubio knew Bowie could see Bexar to the north across the river and the mission five hundred yards at his back.

Bowie studied the timber-lined riverbank which rose six to ten feet above the water to the level of the surrounding plain. Then he retreated down the slope to Rubio and Calder. "This spot can be defended," he announced. "With our long rifles we can make a stand here. With a sentry in the bell tower, we can see for miles."

Rubio pointed to the sun. "We can make faster time going back and reaching the others before dark like Austin wanted."

"We're not leaving, Rubio. The position is strong. We can make a strong stand here."

Calder nodded. "That's why we're here, to fight."

Rubio grinned. Perhaps by nightfall he would be in Bexar.

With the approach of the rebel army, Colonel Domingo Ugartechea had sent Juan Paz and two dozen of his muleteers to Concepcion to appropriate the mission's supplies for his troops. Paz relished the task because the padres had always requested a tithe of him. Now he would appropriate their grain and foodstuffs. Already his men had taken one load to Bexar, and he expected them back shortly for the next. Paz enjoyed his power when the priest visited him once again, imploring him not to take any more supplies.

"The winter will be long and our food too little," he begged.

"Colonel's orders," Paz replied. "Leave me alone, dammit."

"You should ask forgiveness for your unholy language in this sacred place." The priest chanted something in Latin.

Paz shoved him aside and scurried up the stairs to the bell tower. He looked toward Bexar to see if his men were returning. They weren't. He cursed again, then took a step toward the stairs, but stopped dead when movement along the river caught his eye.

He saw three men standing on the bank in the middle of the wide river bend opposite the church. The men had to be Texians. Paz bolted down the stairs, ran past the padre, flew down the center aisle and out the door behind the baptistry. He raced for his horse.

He had to stop his muleteers from returning, and to warn Colonel Ugartechea that the Texian army was within sight of Bexar. He jerked the reins loose, jumped into his saddle and used the mission to screen his escape. When he was far enough away that the Texians could never catch him, he turned his mount for Bexar. At the edge of town he found his muleteers forming to return to the mission. He reined his horse up savagely. "The rebels are at Concepcion."

Paz slapped his horse into a gallop, racing down the street toward the Military Plaza. Seeing the colonel inspecting troops beneath the flagpole in the center of the square, he charged for the troops, then reined up hard. "Colonel!" he cried.

Ugartechea dismissed Paz with a wave of his hand.

"The rebels are at Mission Concepcion. There are many."

"I shall notify General Cos," Ugartechea answered.

Paz grinned. The Texians would be crushed, but one especially he wanted to die: Rubio Portillo. He suspected that Portillo was with the Texian army. Paz knew of one more person he should warn in case Rubio accompanied the rebels: Angelita Sanchez.

As Ugartechea rushed to inform General Cos, Paz left the square and rode to Angelita's house. He slid out of the saddle and shoved the door open. "Angelita," he cried, and enjoyed the look of fear in her eyes as she shot up from her chair in the front room.

"What is it?" she asked meekly.

"The rebels are at Concepcion."

She grimaced.

Paz stepped to her and grabbed her cheeks between his thumb and forefinger. "If Rubio Portillo slips into Bexar to find you, you are to come and tell me."

"And if I don't?"

Paz laughed. "I will kill you."

Toward dusk Jim Bowie ordered Rubio to return to Mission Espada to inform Stephen F. Austin that their contingent would not be returning after all and that Austin should bring the rest of the army up to join them. Rubio had requested to stay and fight, or even slip into Bexar to determine the enemy's strength, but Bowie insisted that he carry the message, since he knew the terrain best.

Rubio mounted his stallion and left the others behind. He reached Mission Espada around nine o'clock and was taken to the chapel. Bursting inside, he found Austin pacing the floor in front of his subordinates.

"Thank God," he cried, "Bowie and his men have returned."

Rubio grimaced. "No, sir, only I have returned."

Austin exploded. "I gave specific orders, and now our army is split. I command the Texian army," Austin shouted, then turned to his officers. "We must prepare to advance at sunrise. If we delay, the war could end with our deaths."

Rising from their chairs, the men moved quickly out of the chapel to issue Austin's orders. Rubio turned to leave, but Austin called to him. "I'll want you to lead us by the quickest route in the morning, before the Mexicans discover we're a divided army."

Rubio nodded, then left Austin alone. He retreated to his horse, made his bed, and caught what sleep he could until the army stirred in the morning. Rubio cursed when he rose. The ground was shrouded in fog, a thick fog. He could see twenty paces at best. He felt a great weight upon his shoulders. The fate of both parts of the army rested on him. He could follow the old mission road, but it meandered along the river and it would take longer to reach Concepcion. The quickest route would be over the rolling prairie, provided he did not get turned around in the fog. Rubio lowered his head, made the sign of a cross over his chest and said a quick prayer. Then he untied his stallion and led it through the ranks of the makeshift army.

He found Austin by the chapel, preparing to

mount his horse. Austin seemed weak and barely able to pull himself into the saddle. When he mounted, he tugged nervously at his hat. "Are the men ready?" he asked, fidgeting in the saddle, looking from one side to the other. "We must hurry. Where's Colonel Travis?"

"Here," William Barrett Travis answered.

Rubio turned to see a lean man with dark hair leading a white gelding by the reins.

"The cavalry is assembled. Shall I lead them to Bowie's rescue?"

Austin hit his thigh with his fist. "No, no, no," he said. "We cannot split our forces any more. Colonel Bowie is to be reprimanded for his failure to obey my orders."

"He should be," Travis answered, climbing atop his gelding, "but he is a fighting man who knows favorable terrain."

Austin frowned. "And I know enough not to split my forces."

Travis responded with an exaggerated salute and a curt, "Yes, sir." He circled his horse and rode away, shouting orders.

Austin looked about and spotted Rubio. "Can you direct us to Concepcion quickly?"

"I can advance no faster than our slowest foot soldier, but I am ready to lead as you command," Rubio answered.

Austin issued orders to his subordinates to form up the troops. When his officers reported back to him, he nodded to Rubio. "We will follow you."

Rubio shook his reins and rode to the head of

the forming column. It was hard to tell because of the fog, but he estimated an hour at least remained until dawn when he turned his stallion out onto the mission road. By sunset he hoped to be in Bexar, freeing his brother from prison.

The going was slow at first, even along the road, because of the darkness and fog. Though it was a bit farther along the road, he followed it until the darkness was eroded by the dim gray light of dawn creeping over the fog. He forded the river at the shallows. Though the infantry grumbled about getting their feet and leggings wet, Rubio knew he would not have to cross the river again to reach Mission Concepcion.

He rode across the prairie, skirting the eastern bank of the river on occasion. As the morning lengthened, the fog began to thin. Rubio hoped they reached Bowie before Mexican troops did.

Then, from the distance, he heard slight pops that he knew must be gunfire. They were followed by explosions that could only be cannon.

General Austin rode up to him. "Is that the sound of battle?"

"Yes," Rubio replied.

Colonel Travis galloped to Austin, saluting as he yanked the reins. "Let me take my men to assist Colonel Bowie."

"No," Austin replied, his voice high-pitched and nervous. "We cannot split our forces further."

Travis cursed. "They may not be split if we do not assist Bowie. We may be all that are left."

"I said no. The infantry will advance at a trot, Colonel Travis, but you are not to advance any farther than them."

Rubio hoped his decision — and Austin's — were correct ones.

The damnable fog. Donley Calder cursed and spat. He knew the whole Mexican Army was out there, creeping toward him. He could feel it in his bones as surely as he was still breathing. Like the others in Bowie's command, he had slept on the slope of the riverbank, his long rifle at his side. When he awoke, he let his eyes focus overhead on the thick branches of the pecan trees and cottonwoods. Even in the fog he could see clusters of pecans ready to drop.

Calder rolled over on his belly and lifted his head to look toward the mission. He could not see it in the fog. At times he thought he heard noises that sounded like soldiers on the move, but fog could play tricks on a man's ears as well as his eyes. Even if Mexicans were approaching, Bowie had chosen ground that men with long rifles and good aim could defend, even against a superior force.

Bowie had positioned them below the banks of the horseshoe bend in the river, half the men on the left side of the U and the other half at the bottom. The river cut made a natural trench where men could secure their horses out of sight, fire their guns, then drop down behind the cover of the bank to reload. With the river at their back, they had all the water they would need, and a course of escape that could take them directly to Bexar or, in case of a retreat, closer to Austin's troops, who would surely be marching to their aid. Once the fog lifted, Calder didn't think all the soldiers in Texas could dislodge them.

Gradually, the fog thinned, but not enough for the mission to appear. Calder knew the sentries posted there by Bowie would have little time to escape if the Mexicans slipped up on them in the fog. All along the river Bowie's men began to stir, checking the loads in their guns or making sure their horses were securely tied.

Calder's stomach growled and he reached for a couple of pecans that had fallen upon the ground by his blanket. He squeezed them together in his palm and cracked the hard shells, then pried the meaty pecan halves from the shells. As he ate the nuts, his hand froze at the sound of what seemed like a low growl. Calder brushed his hand against his leather coat and grabbed his long rifle. It could only be the Mexicans. Austin would not arrive with the remainder of the army so soon after daybreak, not with fog as thick as it was. The low growl grew until there was no doubt it was the approach of dragoons on horseback. Occasionally, Calder thought he heard the sound of rattling metal or chains.

A gunshot erased all doubts about what might be approaching. From near the mission a sentry yelled out. "Boys, the scoundrels are here." A second shot answered the first, then a half dozen more replied. Calder knew both sides were shooting blindly.

Bowie yelled to his men, "Our sentries'll be dropping back. Don't fire until we're sure they're all back."

Shortly, the sentries, seven in all, materialized out of the fog. Calder watched them, figuring visibility was between fifty and seventy-five paces. He glanced toward the east. The sun was little more than a bright glow through the fog. He thought it might burn off quickly. For the present, he liked it just like it was because the Mexicans would have to find them.

Bowie ran behind the line, encouraging his men. "Seven sentries are in, that's all of them. Save your fire until you're certain of a hit. We've neither a man nor a bullet to spare."

Calder cocked his rifle and slipped a percussion cap in place. He stretched out on his blanket and rested his long rifle on the bank. Pulling his rifle to his shoulder, he took aim at the fog. On either side of him men had unsheathed their knives and were cutting brush to give them a better field of view, or were scratching out a swath of bank to give them more protection.

Then horsemen appeared out of the fog. They guided their mounts ahead tentatively, knowing they were approaching an unseen enemy. Along the riverbank the Texians whispered patience to one another. Calder sighted his rifle on a rider who appeared to be headed straight for him. As his finger slid over the trigger, a man crawled beside him. Calder glanced quickly and recognized Bowie, then focused his full attention on the enemy line.

"Dragoons," Bowie said.

The horsemen advanced, coming within fifty paces.

"Now," Bowie yelled.

Calder squeezed the trigger. His gun convulsed in a cloud of smoke. Several other rifles barked along the line. Calder slid down the bank, rolled over on his back and began to reload. He pulled a paper wad of powder and lead from his cartridge box, bit off the end and poured powder down the barrel. He shoved the wadding and lead in next and jerked the ramrod free, quickly shoving it in the barrel and setting the load. He moved in fluid motions as he extracted the ramrod, then slid it back in its holder. As he crawled back to the blanket, he pulled a percussion cap from his pouch. He set the cap, then wormed his way beside Bowie, who had yet to fire.

"That volley stung them," Bowie announced, "and they retreated."

"They'll be back for a second helping."

Bowie laughed. "And you'll enjoy dishing it out."

"Indeed I do."

"Well, I ain't worried about you, but I ought to walk the line and calm the younger fellows. It could be a long day, especially if Austin doesn't come in a hurry." Bowie slid back down the bank, then moved back and forth, telling his men what to expect.

Toward the mission, Calder heard the clinking sound of chains and metal. Though he could see nothing, he knew the Mexicans were bringing up cannons. He hoped Bowie's men held steady in the face of artillery, but if their cannon was no bigger than the piece that had started the ruckus in Gonzales, the Texians were safe.

Shortly, the men and cannon materialized out of the fog. Two cannons were dragged into place while three lines of infantry formed up behind them.

Bowie yelled, "Don't shoot until they've fired the first volley with their rifles. Our long rifles'll carry farther than their muskets, but I don't want them to know that."

The Mexican artillerymen scurried in front of their cannon, setting them in place and aiming them toward the river. Calder figured he'd let the other men shoot for the infantry. He'd spend his time picking off the cannoneers. As close as they were, Calder knew he could knock one off with every shot.

"Keep low until after the first volley," Bowie commanded.

Calder watched the cannoneers load powder and then ram canister down the barrel. He ducked and waited. A cannon exploded, then a second. Instantly, shot whistled through the trees overhead, cutting leaves and branches and rattling pecans from the limbs. The cannonade was followed by a volley of musket fire.

Calmly, Calder lifted his head and pulled his long rifle to his shoulder. He sighted in on the artilleryman ramming powder into the cannon barrel, then pulled the trigger. His Mexican target collapsed in front of the field piece. Calder slid back down the embankment and calmly reloaded his rifle. He worked quickly and efficiently, meanwhile listening to the sounds of battle. He liked what he heard. The men around him dispensed measured, unhurried shots, while the Mexicans were wasting their ammunition with ineffectual shots, shots that made an odd fluttering noise that confused Calder. He'd never heard bullets make such a sound. He wondered what it could be as he inched up the bank and downed another artilleryman. The other cannoneers danced nervously around the fallen man, uncertain whether to fire or retreat.

The Mexican infantry advanced in ragged lines, never building any momentum because the sharp aim of Bowie's men kept cutting holes in their ranks.

Once again Calder slid back, turned over on his back and reloaded. He saw that the fog was thinning overhead. When it cleared, all the Mexicans would be exposed on the prairie, while the Texians would have the cover of the riverbed. As he wormed back up the incline, Calder studied another artilleryman, aimed and pulled the trigger. The rifle smoke blinded him for a minute, but as the smoke cleared he saw his target slumped over the cannon wheel. This time others broke and abandoned the two field pieces.

Calder raised his fist to celebrate, then screamed as something slammed into his shoulder. He'd been hit. He cursed himself for allowing his pride in marksmanship to offset his battle wits. Dropping his long rifle, he rolled down the embankment and grabbed his shoulder. He winced at the pain, then looked at his hand. Where he expected to see blood, he saw fingers smudged only by powder and sweat. He looked at his shoulder, expecting to find a hole in his coat. There was nothing, except a greasy smudge where a ball had hit leather. He shook his head, then laughed. That explained the odd noise of the bullets. The Mexican powder was so poor that it didn't give the bullets the velocity to do much harm at long range.

Calder crawled back up the bank. Seeing a couple pecans that had fallen on his blanket, he grabbed them, cracked the shells, and ate the meat before picking up his rifle. A man tough enough to stop a bullet without it breaking the skin deserved a break in fighting, he told himself.

Calder was still chewing the pecans when he started reloading. After he finished, he looked over the bank at the prairie and smiled. The fog had cleared enough for him to see the mission's bell towers. A line of dragoons was held there in reserve.

It puzzled Calder why the Mexicans didn't send the cavalry with their lances. They could have quickly overpowered the Texians; unless, of course, their lances were no better than their powder. In the face of the steady Texian fire, the Mexican infantry wavered, then began to fall back, first in pairs, then in squads. On either side of Calder men stood and cheered.

Jim Bowie darted up the bank. "The cannons, boys, take the cannons."

Bowie dashed for the artillery pieces, a stream of Texians behind him screaming like demons and jumping over Mexican bodies. Calder climbed up the bank but did not charge for the cannons. That was for younger men. He calmly loaded his rifle and scanned the perimeter. All was clear as far as he could see in the fog.

He watched Bowie's men wheel the cannon about. The Texians fired one into the backs of the retreating infantry and shouted gleefully. Calder retreated down the bank and untied his horse. He jumped on the animal and galloped to the cannons.

When he got there, Bowie was ordering a dozen men to man the cannons and half the remainder to set up a perimeter around the field pieces in case the Mexicans charged again. Texian riflemen continued to down terrified Mexicans with their long rifles. Bowie ordered the remaining men to retreat to the river and protect the horses.

"On to Bexar!" several men shouted.

"Hell, no," Bowie cried. "The walls of Bexar are their riverbed. We can't take them there. Chase them a ways to make them think we'll follow them all the way to their graves, then pull back." Bowie pointed at Calder. "Calder'll lead. When he says fall back, fall back."

Calder turned toward the river, his command following on foot. "Be quick, Texians. Every Mexican we kill today is one less we must kill tomorrow."

At the top of the embankment Calder reined up his horse. The men ran down the bank, several stumbling and falling before they could reach their horses. Some cursed, but many laughed at the exhilaration of seeing the enemy flee. In seconds they were astride their horses and riding up the embankment. Calder wheeled his mount about and raced past the cannons and toward the Mexicans.

A few more Mexicans would die before this day was over, Calder thought as he led the charge.

The fog began to break up, and Rubio Portillo caught a glimpse of the twin bell towers of Mission Concepcion. They had heard the gunfire and now they could see the mission. Rubio stood in his stirrups to view the battleground, but the field was shrouded with smoke and it was hard to make out what had transpired. Then he spotted ragged Mexican troops running toward Bexar. He saw horsemen giving chase and firing at the Mexican dragoons. Behind him, he heard Colonel Travis yell to his cavalry.

Suddenly, the ground around him thundered and Travis's men charged by. He could no longer wait. He slapped his stallion into a gallop with them, pulling his pistol from the saddle scabbard and shouting gleefully. In the distance he could see Bexar. They could be in the town in minutes. By nightfall he would free Tomas from prison.

When Rubio spotted the man leading Bowie's contingent of cavalry, he laughed and screamed all at once. It was Donley Calder, his lionskin cap flapping in the breeze as he ran. Then the old man reined in his horses and stopped the charge. A thin line of Mexican dragoons had turned about to cover the infantry withdrawal.

Rubio could not believe that Calder had not charged all the way to Bexar. It was there for the taking.

He spurred his mount toward Calder, reining up hard when he reached him. "Why are you stopping short of Bexar?"

"Following orders," Calder replied. "We cannot take Bexar."

Rubio cursed.

"We held the river. They hold the town. What happened to them will happen to us if we charge," Calder said.

Angered, Rubio turned his horse away, just as Austin rode up.

"Attack men, attack!" Austin cried.

"No," Calder answered. "This battle has been won. We will take Bexar another day."

Rubio felt bitter tears run down his cheek. He wondered when that day would come.

"I came here to fight, not freeze," Donley Calder groused as he sharpened his knife blade on a whetstone. He leaned toward the crackling fire that fought lamely against the frigid air. "It's been a month since the mission fight, and I ain't done nothing but stand guard and freeze."

Rubio Portillo shivered. "We should've chased them into town, taken our chances when we had them on the run. We had an army then."

He studied the camp. So many soldiers had gone home that the Texians couldn't close the ring around Bexar. Colonel Ugartechea had managed to slip a hundred dragoons out of Bexar undetected, and they roamed somewhere to the south or sought reinforcements. Colonel Bowie had resigned in disgust. Colonel Travis had left on cavalry patrol and had yet to return. Many soldiers had deserted to tend their families or finish gathering their crops. A few soldiers had gone to San Felipe de Austin on the Brazos to frame a provisional government. Rubio sighed. While men met in San Felipe and the army sat on its haunches outside of Bexar, Tomas languished in jail.

"Will things improve when a government's formed?" he asked.

Calder held his knife to the fire, studying the sharp blade, then lowered it to his knee and continued sharpening. "Government's the problem now. Creating another one's not gonna get rid of the one we have. Spilling blood's the only way to do that. The only question is whether it'll be theirs or ours."

"It'll be our blood if we keep sitting," Rubio said.

Calder spat into the fire. "Stephen Austin's an impresario, not a soldier. He started colonies, but he can't finish a war. He can lead men in peace, but not men at war," Calder said without rancor.

Rubio wriggled his fingers at the fire, then knotted them into fists to trap the warmth. "Why won't he lead us into Bexar?"

"He's sick. Just yesterday I saw him try to mount his horse and he had to have men help him. And he's scared of the enemy and the unknown. Most men that ain't fought don't know the enemy's just as scared as him, and the less a man's fought, the more 'fraid he is of the unknown. Austin don't know how fortified Bexar is 'cause he ain't had anybody that could scout it."

Rubbing his hands together, Rubio looked around to make sure no one was listening. He leaned toward Calder. "I could scout Bexar."

Calder looked at Rubio with narrow eyes. "You sure you wouldn't be recognized? It might get this army off its tail."

"I'd risk it, if Austin would permit it."

Calder grabbed Rubio's arm. "I don't know that he'd be thinking straight, him being as sick as he's been. And he can't say no if you don't ask him. Say nothing of this to anyone. Tomorrow night, before the moon rises, I'll help you slip into Bexar."

Rubio licked his chapped lips. If he could get into Bexar, he could see where the Mexicans had placed cannons and strongholds. With that information, the Texians could take Bexar and he could free his brother.

Releasing Rubio's arm, Calder wagged his trigger finger. "You must do this for the army, Rubio, and take no unnecessary risk."

Rubio nodded.

Calder shook his head. "You don't understand me, Rubio. You mustn't try to free your brother."

Rubio bit his lip. "I cannot let him rot in prison."

"His is just one life. You must do what's best for the army, the many, rather than just one man. Otherwise, we could all rot in prison. Or worse, in graves."

Juan Paz was furious.

General Martin Perfecto de Cos smiled politely, his small, effeminate mouth and chin accentuated by a thick mustache and long nose. His thin eyebrows arched over dark eyes as he straightened his high uniform collar, which made his neck appear too long for his body.

"Colonel Ugartechea has spoken of you, Juan Paz," Cos said, studying him intently, "and he has not spoken well of you."

Paz glared at the general. "I have not been paid from the treasury for the supplies I have delivered. I have risked the lives of my men and animals to provide for you and your men."

"We are at war, Juan Paz. Even my men have not been paid. But when the hostilities end, they will be paid, as will you. I speak with the authority of his excellency the president, General Antonio Lopez de Santa Anna."

"I have not been paid, yet you order me to go with your soldiers to bring more supplies to Bexar." He crossed his arms over his chest.

"You are a smart, though greedy, man, Juan Paz. I can understand your greed, but not your impatience. The president will smile favorably upon you when this rebellion is drowned in the blood of the traitors. When that is done, you will be handsomely rewarded . . ." Cos paused, his lips curling into a sarcastic smile. ". . . for your patriotism."

Paz gritted his teeth and stared at the wall behind the general.

"You have a choice, Juan Paz." Cos offered him a feeble smile. "You can do as I command, or you can join the traitors if you think they have the money to pay you for your services."

"You leave me little choice, General."

"But Juan Paz, a third choice exists. I can imprison you."

Paz's lip quivered. He had seen Tomas Portillo in prison. The confinement had reduced him to an animal eating bugs and even the papers Paz had left him to sign. Paz did not care to share his fate. "You are right, General," Paz said. "I'm an impatient man, but I am not a traitor. I stand ready to serve you and your army."

"Once again, Juan Paz, I am overwhelmed by your patriotism."

Paz felt his shoulders sag.

"I understand," Cos said, "that there is a ranch you would like, owned by one of the traitors."

Paz looked up, eyed the general and nodded.

"It shall be yours as well, as your pay, when these troubles are behind us. You see, Juan Paz, if you help Mexico, Mexico will help you."

"What do you want me to do?"

"Tonight when it is darkest before the moon rises, be prepared to leave Bexar with my soldiers. Thirty shall be assigned to guard you and your men. You are to scour the countryside, taking food and supplies from the colonists. Take any guns and powder you may find, and any livestock as well, to help us through the winter. With spring, the president himself will lead an army into Texas."

"I look forward to that day," Paz replied.

"Of course," Cos grinned, "because that is the day you will be paid for your patriotism." The general turned his back on Paz. "I am done with you."

Paz spun about and marched from Cos's headquarters. Outside, he tugged his serape tight to block out the cold. His anger burned hot as a poker. He knew he should go tell his men that they must leave Bexar and the warmth of their homes after dark, but he made his way first to Angelita's. He knocked on her door, which was answered by her mother.

"*Bueno,*" she said, but Paz could tell she didn't mean it.

"I have come to see Angelita."

The old woman frowned. "She is not well and seeing no one."

"I am her betrothed."

The senora nodded. "And especially not her betrothed."

Paz pushed the old woman aside and stepped into the dwelling. Angelita's mother cried out and Paz lifted his arm to strike her.

"No!" Angelita cried.

His temper flared hotter when he saw Angelita charge across the room at him. He lifted his arm again, to strike the senora, but Angelita managed to grasp it. She tried to wrestle him away from her mother, but with his powerful arm, Paz flung her aside. She tumbled into a wooden bench.

Her mother defiantly lifted her chin, daring Paz to strike her.

Angelita screamed at Paz. "Don't hit her! You don't own me!"

Paz snatched Angelita's arm. "I do own you, because I alone can provide you the wealth you so greatly desire."

"You forget Rubio Portillo."

"He is a traitor to his country, his people, and to you."

"At least, *he* is decent."

Paz jerked her arm behind her back, then lifted it until she gasped. "But I shall be your husband, and don't you forget that." He released her arm.

Angelita backed away, rubbing her arm and shaking her head. She pointed to the door. "Leave."

Paz stepped to her, grabbed her behind the head and pulled her to him. He pressed his lips against hers and kissed her savagely, then pushed her away. "When I return, I'll want more than just a kiss."

He strode outside then, and heard her sobs as he walked away.

Rubio shivered behind a cottonwood tree clinging to the bank of the San Antonio River. He felt Calder's hand upon his shoulder.

"Hard as it is, Rubio, think of the many, not just the one."

Rubio nodded but said nothing. How could he forget his brother? He tugged his hat lower over his eyes. Beneath his serape he adjusted his pistol and knife as well as the pistol and tomahawk Donley had loaned him. He had left his rifle back at camp, since it could not be so easily hidden.

"I'll return before dawn with the horses, Rubio. If you cannot make it back by then, you should hide during the day and I'll return at dusk to this same spot."

Rubio nodded. He wanted to tell Calder to bring an extra horse for Tomas, but he didn't.

Calder clamped his hand on Rubio's arm. "Don't risk yourself or Texas for your brother."

Rubio clenched his lips, then pulled himself away from Calder and the cottonwood tree. He crouched and advanced, turning to look at Calder, but the frontiersman had evaporated in the darkness. Rubio moved stealthily from tree to bush to depression along the riverbank. He paused regularly to listen for the sounds of danger. Mostly, he heard his labored breath and the rustle of the chilly breeze through the trees. When the wind was right, he could hear the sound of sentries around Bexar, calling out that all was well.

Nearing Bexar, he paused longer, listened more closely, and stared harder, looking for sentries. When he was within a hundred paces of the outermost dwelling, he heard muffled noises and dropped to the ground. His eyes tried to cut through the murkiness of night.

He saw ghostly dragoons, two dozen or more, strung out along a trail that paralleled the river, and several more men afoot, leading possibly sixty mules. They were muleteers, likely Juan Paz's men. After the caravan passed beyond Rubio's hearing range, he rose and slipped closer to

Bexar. At the edge of town the river made a horseshoe bend east toward the Alamo. Rubio saw the dark walls of the abandoned mission. The fires behind those walls cast a soft glow on the facade of the crumbling chapel.

Rubio picked up the scent of wood smoke. It gave him an idea. If he picked up an armload of wood, he would have an explanation for being out. He crouched and began to pat the ground, groping for wood. He found a half-dozen pieces of dried wood, loaded them in his arms and advanced.

Taking a deep breath, he emerged from the cover of the trees and scurried to the nearest building. He leaned up against the cold stone wall, listening for any sounds of danger. He was about to move when he heard a sentry call out that all was well. The voice carried deceptively in the night air. Rubio thought the sentry was on the opposite side of the house, but he could not be certain. He eased to the end of the house and peeked around the corner. Seeing no one, he stepped out into the street.

"*Alto!*" a sentry cried.

Rubio heard the click of a musket being cocked.

"Do not shoot," he said in Spanish. "I was just gathering wood to warm my family, that is all."

"No one save soldiers is to be out after sunset."

"*Si,*" Rubio answered. "That is true, but the night is cold and our wood was low. Soldiers have taken many of our blankets and I must keep my family warm." Rubio hoped the soldier would advance near enough to be clubbed with one of the limbs in his arms.

The soldier edged closer, but not within reach.

"I will escort you home," the soldier said. "Where is it?"

Rubio caught his breath. He had no home in Bexar, but he had no choice. "It is on the Main Plaza." He wondered if Angelita would betray him.

The soldier waved the bayonet in front of him. "Lead the way."

Rubio weighed the chance of attacking the guard, but decided he could not subdue him before the sentry raised an alarm. Instead, Rubio walked toward the Main Plaza. The street was quiet and dark, and he noted sentries and strong points. It seemed his capture by the sentry had been fortuitous, because he was able to observe the enemy without raising any suspicions.

Until he reached the Main Plaza, Rubio saw few signs of soldiers, hearing only an occasional call from one that everything was okay. At the plaza, he saw freshly dug ditches. Log-and-earthen barricades slashed across the corners of the square so that cannons could be aimed down either approach. Each corner was manned by three or four soldiers, while an additional soldier marched back and forth along each side of the plaza. One of the sentries glared at Rubio as he passed, then called to his captor, "Is he enemy?"

"He was gathering firewood."

"Maybe he's passing messages to the rebels.

Are you certain he is a Bexarano?"

The guard grumbled. "I am certain only that he is my captive."

Rubio continued to march forward.

"Where is your home?" the guard asked.

"It is there," he said, nodding toward the front door of the Sanchez house, then looking over at the bell tower of the San Fernando Church which loomed over the plaza. He saw the silhouettes of two guards.

Rubio stopped at the door and was about to knock when the sentry brushed his arm away with the side of his bayonet. The guard leaned past him and pounded on the door.

Rubio caught his breath. If his bluff didn't work, he might soon feel the blade of the bayonet slicing into his back. Impatient that nobody answered immediately, the soldier beat on the door again. Shortly, Rubio heard the sound of the wooden bar being lifted.

"Open or I will batter the door down," the soldier called.

The door widened and Rubio saw both Angelita and her father, a flintlock pistol in his hand

Angelita's face widened. "They've captured you, Rubio," she cried, lifting her hands to her cheeks.

"Sí," Rubio answered, trying to keep Angelita from revealing the truth. "You told me they would, but I had to bring us firewood."

"Yes, my son," Angelita's father said, "we were running low, and it is my fault for not sending you in the daylight."

The soldier finally spoke. "This man, you know him?"

"*Sí,*" Angelita said. "He is my husband."

The guard grumbled to Rubio, "Stay home after sunset or you will be thrown in prison."

"*Sí,*" Rubio replied, staring at Angelita. At least she still cared enough about him to lie for him. Even in the dim light of the single candle, she was as beautiful as he'd remembered. As her father closed the door, Rubio moved to the corner fireplace and dropped the wood.

The moment he did, Angelita wrapped her arms around him and nuzzled into his chest, crying softly.

"You should not have risked your life to see me," she sobbed.

He put his arms limply around her, but the gesture seemed inadequate because he no longer knew how he felt about her.

She shoved his arms off, then pushed herself away. "You didn't come to see me, did you?" she cried, hitting his chest.

Before he could answer, Angelita's mother stepped into the room and pointed her finger at Angelita. "Why should he see you after you broke the betrothal and promised to wed Juan Paz?"

Rubio felt his shoulders sag.

Angelita planted her fists on her hips. "Juan Paz has not betrayed his country."

Her mother shook her finger at Angelita. "I don't care for politics, only for decency. Rubio is

180

a decent man. He's never hit you like Juan Paz."

Angelita slapped her mother, staggering the old woman, who Rubio steadied with his hands. She shook her head and cried.

"You have learned this disrespect from Juan Paz," her father scolded. "It is not how I taught my daughter."

"No," Angelita screamed, "you do not care for me or my happiness. Juan Paz can provide for me. Rubio cannot, even if he survives. Do you not think of my future?"

"Every day," her mother answered, "especially if you marry Juan Paz." The old woman hugged Rubio. "You are welcome in this house any time. Forgive my daughter's foolishness. She is young and stubborn."

The old man stepped beside him as well and patted his shoulder. "You are welcome, yes, but you are not safe here. Certainly not when Juan Paz returns."

Angelita scowled. "Rubio has betrayed his country."

"The politics of Mexico change, foolish daughter, but the people do not."

Angelita held her nose arrogantly in the air. "The army of Mexico controls Bexar. It is foolish not to side with the army."

"It is more foolish, Angelita, to side with Juan Paz," her father answered.

"I cannot stay," Rubio interrupted. "I came only because the soldier caught me and I had nowhere else to turn."

Angelita pointed her finger at Rubio. "You came to spy, didn't you, Rubio?"

Rubio wondered if she had ever really cared for him, or if it had just been his land. "I came to learn of my brother."

Angelita looked away.

Rubio cursed to himself. She knew something. He grabbed her by the arms. "Is he dead? What do you know?"

She bit her lip.

"What do you know of him? Tell me, I beg of you, if you ever cared for me."

Angelita looked up, her gaze locking on his. She nodded as he stared into her dark eyes.

"Por favor," he pleaded. "Is he alive?"

"I have seen him but once," Angelita told him, "but that was weeks ago. I do not know since."

"Where is he, *por favor?*"

"In the guardhouse. He did not look well. They say he killed a Mexican soldier. They treat him accordingly."

Rubio's mind raced. What could he do? He could not leave him in Bexar, yet neither could he save Tomas against the entire Mexican Army. He grimaced, knowing the odds, yet also knowing he had to do something.

Angelita seemed to read his thoughts. "They will kill you, Rubio, if you try to free him. You must leave town before light. Too many people know you here. They will notify the army."

"What difference does it make to you, Angelita? You have chosen to side with the army."

"No, Rubio, I have chosen to side with Mexico."

"And to marry Juan Paz!"

Angelita Sanchez was confused. Deep within her stirred a longing for Rubio. As he held her arms, she could not deny the desire for him. If only he had chosen Mexico or had avoided politics, like most in Bexar, she would have chosen him over Juan Paz. But Juan Paz would be rich when Mexico squashed the revolt. And Rubio Portillo would be poor, if not dead.

So much bewilderment flooded Rubio's gaze that Angelita turned away. Even in the dim candlelight he seemed desperate and vulnerable. She'd seen anger and even jealousy in his eyes, especially when she would flirt with Juan Paz, but never had she seen him like this.

Rubio had not treated her as poorly as Juan Paz, she admitted, but Juan had scorned her in private. Rubio had scorned her in public by siding with the Anglos. She resented him for it, and always would.

"You betrayed me, Rubio."

He shook his head. "You left me for Juan Paz. No man is worse."

"I will not stand for you to talk about my betrothed that way," she said.

"Once, I was your betrothed."

"But you did not love me. You wanted me to live on your rancho. I wanted to live in Bexar."

Rubio nodded. "Your words do not ring true.

183

I would never have wanted someone I did not love to live with me on my rancho." Then he turned toward the door. "I must go."

Angelita watched her mother and father step forward to block his departure.

"No," her father said. "They will kill you."

"I have seen what I came to see," Rubio replied. "There is only my brother that I care for now in Bexar."

The words cut Angelita. She grabbed his arm.

"I must leave," Rubio told her.

"I will extend to you one last favor, Rubio."

"You have nothing to offer me, Angelita."

"You are wrong," Angelita replied.

"What can you give me that I cannot give myself?"

"I can get you inside the prison to see your brother."

12

Rubio Portillo was stunned. He did not know how to respond. Just when he thought he understood Angelita, just when he thought she was a mean woman to the core, she surprised him. He bit his lip. Was she trying to help him or to lure him outside where a soldier might kill him? He didn't know, and didn't care. It was worth the risk to see his brother. "Why are you doing this, Angelita?" he asked.

"My heart says it is right, even if my heart no longer says you are right." Angelita took the candle and started for her room.

Rubio stepped after her.

"Please wait," she said softly.

Rubio froze as she disappeared, bewildered about what she would do next. When she returned, she offered him a sheet of paper. As Rubio took it from her hand, she lifted the candle for him to see. He unfolded the paper and read the writing in an elaborate hand. It was an order from Colonel Ugartechea allowing the bearer and a visitor to see Tomas Portillo. "Where did you get this?"

"It doesn't matter. It will get you in to see

Tomas. Isn't that what you want?"

Rubio knew he must take the risk to see — and perhaps free — his brother. It was too chancy to try to reach the prison so soon after being escorted to Angelita's house, but in the hours before dawn, he might. *"Gracias,"* he said to Angelita.

She shook her head. "It will get you in to see Tomas only if you can get to the prison, but you may not even reach the prison because many in Bexar know you are a traitor." She turned away. "When you chose Texas over Mexico, you abandoned me. Do not return here or I will alert the soldiers myself, and you too will go to prison."

Rubio turned to Angelita's parents. "I am sorry I have troubled you, but if I may stay until the early hours of the morning, I will not return to bother you again."

The old woman wiped a tear from the corner of her eye. "How can we deny you? You have been like a son to us."

"Gracias," Rubio said.

Angelita turned and gave the candle to her father, then disappeared in the darkness of her room. "Viva Mexico!" she said.

Her parents stood in the flickering candlelight, then her father patted Rubio's shoulder. "Angelita has changed, but as long as this is our house, you shall always be welcome."

Rubio shook the man's hand, then hugged his wife. *"Gracias,* but I shall rest by the door and leave quietly before dawn."

The old man crossed himself. "May God bless

186

you and walk beside you." The couple turned and left the room.

In the darkness, Rubio refolded the paper, then eased to the wall by the door. He sat on the floor and leaned against the cold limestone wall. He wondered how different things might have been had he not sided with the Anglos. But they were right, he thought, and Mexico and Angelita were wrong. If he could no longer love Angelita, neither could he hate her, for she had given him the one gift no one else could provide — the chance to see his brother. It was the best present he'd ever received . . . unless it was a trap.

As Rubio pondered, he heard the occasional sounds of the soldiers outside, making their rounds, calling out to each other. He planned to leave the house a couple hours before dawn, hoping that the soldiers on guard would be tired and sleepy so he could slip past them and behind San Fernando Church to Military Plaza, where the prison fronted the governor's quarters.

Rubio dozed intermittently, never allowing himself to fall fully asleep for fear he would not awaken before dawn. When the hour finally came, he rose, stretched his arms and legs, then checked the weapons he carried under his serape. He pulled each pistol and replaced the percussion caps. Then, with Colonel Ugartechea's order, he slipped out the door. He saw soldiers posted at the cannons at each corner of the plaza, but they were circled around their small fires, trying to stay warm. Rubio waited, watching the square's perimeter for patrolling sentries. Seeing none, he closed the door softly behind him.

Clinging to the darkness and the wall, he eased to the end of the house and waited, eyeing the bell tower of San Fernando Church. He spotted a single sentry, who seemed to be looking in the other direction. Rubio glanced from the tower to the three soldiers gathered around a cannon not fifty feet away at the corner of the plaza. He wondered if he could pass them unseen. He had no other choice except to abandon his attempt. Pulling his hat down tighter over his forehead, he inched along the wall, reaching the corner of the plaza. The soldiers stood so close he could hear them complaining about their hunger, the cold, their homesickness, and their bad luck in being assigned to the early morning watch.

Rubio paused. From beneath his serape he pulled a pistol and hid it in the folds of his wrap. He eyed the movements of the men by the cannon. They were preoccupied with cursing General Cos. When the trio looked away, Rubio caught his breath and scampered across the road. To his ears, his footfalls seemed to echo across the plaza, but when he reached the opposite wall, all he heard was his hard breath.

He lingered a moment, to calm his pounding heart, then slipped along the wall toward the church. He froze when he thought one of the soldiers manning the cannon stared at him, but the soldier turned away. Rubio advanced to the corner of the building across from the church and paused, surveying the church and trying to see the tower guard without being seen. But the angle made it impossible.

Clutching his pistol in one hand and the signed order in the other, he walked softly around the corner of the building, then angled for the church wall, where the sentry in the tower could not see him. He moved quickly to the back of the church and surveyed Military Plaza. It was smaller than the Main Plaza and not quite so heavily guarded. Small fires across the square illuminated two more cannons, each manned by three soldiers. The cannons pointed away from the church. Once again Rubio looked carefully for signs of moving sentries. He saw none. The only other guards he saw, two of them, were standing on opposite sides of the square. Each stood beside a door dimly lit by a single candle in a covered holder. One door was the entrance to the Governor's Palace, and the other was the barred door of the prison.

Spotting no other guards, Rubio thought he had a chance to reach the prison, though the sentry in front of the Governor's Palace could not help but see him, if he was alert. He had come too far not to try to reach his brother, however. And at this point, Rubio realized, retreat was just as dangerous as advance. He tucked his pistol back in his belt and pulled his knife.

Moving quickly away from the church, he scurried to the walls of the neighboring building, then advanced to the corner of the plaza. He waited to catch his breath, then angled across the street and stepped toward the sentry. He tried to hide from the guard across the plaza, without making the prison guard unduly suspicious. He was within ten paces when the sentry called out.

"*Alto!* Who approaches?" The guard lowered his musket and pointed it at Rubio's chest.

Rubio gritted his teeth. The call had been too loud. The sentry across the way and the men at the cannons surely had heard his command. He realized no guard would allow a man inside the jail at this time of the night. He had been foolish to think otherwise. Perhaps he could bluff. "A friend of General Cos," Rubio announced, "with an important message."

The sentry waved the musket barrel at Rubio. "You shouldn't be out until daylight. The dawn is less than an hour away."

"But I must see him."

"What about?" the guard asked suspiciously.

Rubio advanced, careful not to step into the faint ball of light cast by the lamp. "It is a matter I cannot discuss with anyone but the general."

"I must call my superior."

Rubio could see doubt in the sentry's eyes. He shook his head. "Your superior might be angered to be awakened."

"I must seek his permission to send you to the general."

Nodding, Rubio detected uncertainty in the sentry's reply. "The future of Texas depends upon General Cos receiving this message. If you have doubts about me, lock me inside the prison, then at dawn seek out the general and deliver this message. He will free me and punish you." Rubio held up the paper for the sentry to see. "This is the message. General Cos will be angry if it is delayed, and outraged if it never reaches him."

The soldier squinted as he tried to make out Rubio's features. Finally, he nodded. "Unbar the door," he ordered as he slid from beneath the candle.

Rubio slipped his knife back in his belt as he eased to the prison entrance, careful to keep his face screened from the sentry. He knew his bluff had failed, and that as soon he stepped inside, the guard might close and bar the door behind him. He grabbed the wooden plank and lifted it. He stood it on end beside the door and dropped the paper on the ground. As he bent to pick it up, he eyed the guard, trying to gauge him.

The sentry motioned for him to step back, and Rubio obliged. The guard then twisted the iron handle and eased the door open. "Get inside."

Rubio stepped for the opening, intentionally brushing the wooden plank as he entered. The plank clunked onto the ground in the doorway so the door would not close.

The guard cursed Rubio and bent to pick up the plank. As he did, Rubio dropped the orders and lunged for him, grabbing the guard by the shoulders and jerking him inside. The guard's musket clattered at his feet and he yelped, but Rubio drove the man's head into the hard-packed dirt floor. The guard's hat flew off and he groaned. Stunned, he gasped for breath as Rubio grabbed him by the hair and pounded his head against the dirt.

The guard's nose splattered blood on the floor and then he went limp. Rubio pulled him all the way inside, then grasped the wooden plank and jerked it in as well. He poked his head outside to see if anyone had witnessed his attack. He saw nothing amiss. He looked across the plaza, where the inattentive guard remained in front of the Governor's Palace.

Rubio slipped back inside the thick walls. The narrow corridor was lit by candles on each side. He went from each barred door to the next calling softly, "Tomas, Tomas."

It seemed to Tomas Portillo that he'd been in prison forever, and he knew he teetered somewhere between sanity and lunacy. Food had been withheld much of the time, and he only received water once a day. He had caught a couple rats and eaten them, as well as the papers Juan Paz had brought for him to sign. His face was overgrown with a scraggly beard and itched incredibly from the vermin that had taken residence there. He was always cold, often shivering until his teeth chattered. He sat on the cold ground and leaned against the cold stone wall. He slept on the cold earth, went to sleep cold and awoke cold. When he received food, it was cold. In all his daily existence, he had but one source of warmth —

his hatred. It was an ember that burned deep within him, and he hoped to one day exact revenge on the Mexican Army for its injustice against him.

Sometimes Tomas's mind tricked him, his cravings for food and company becoming almost real. He spent his nights trying to sleep, but it was always an uncomfortable sleep, broken by nightmares of what the Mexicans would do to him. Sometimes he would see visions of senoritas he had courted in the past. Often he would see his brother and hear him talking of the great, ghostly bull.

And occasionally Tomas would wish he were back on the ranch, paying more attention to the chores Rubio always said needed doing. Some days he sobbed, wondering if Rubio was even alive anymore. Tomas knew his brother would not abandon him, for that was not Rubio's way, but he had overheard the guards talking of battles with the Texians, and occasionally he heard the sound of gunfire. It never seemed to last long enough to be anything more than a skirmish, but Rubio could have been in that or any other fight and could be dead.

If he were ever freed, Tomas vowed, he would join the Texians and fight the Mexican Army until it was driven from Texas forever. If only he lived that long. At times, he doubted he would. Many nights he sweated and shivered with a fever that left him delirious, until he had even more difficulty sorting out what had actually happened with what he'd imagined. He hated the night. He dreaded the day. And he feared the tricks his mind played on him, because they sapped his hope. Over the chatter of his teeth he heard a voice. The voice sounded like Rubio's. His mind played with him again.

"Tomas? Tomas? Answer me. Which room are you in?"

Tomas turned on the hard ground, waking enough that the voice went away, but only for an instant. Then, it returned!

"Tomas, wake up."

Tomas lifted his head and shook it vigorously, but the sound of Rubio's voice persisted. "Rubio, Rubio, is that you?"

"Tomas?" Rubio replied. "Have I found you?"

"*Si, si,*" Tomas cried, shocked at the grating of his own voice. Hearing the door being unbarred, Tomas squinted toward the hallway. He shuddered with anticipation as the door swung open. He saw Rubio silhouetted against the pale candlelight.

Rubio moved toward him. "It is me, Tomas, your brother."

Tomas began to cry. It was Rubio, not a trick. "You're alive."

"I'm here to take you away," he replied. "Hurry, arise."

Tomas struggled against himself, but he seemed anchored to the hard cold floor. "Go, Rubio. Leave me before they capture you."

"No."

Tomas felt Rubio's hands grab his shoulders. He felt limp as a doll as Rubio lifted him to a sitting position.

"You must try to walk, Tomas. I cannot carry you, but I cannot leave you."

Tomas wanted to escape, more than anything else, but he was weak. He sat for a moment, shivering so much that he didn't know if he could even stand.

"You're cold," Rubio said. "Do not move. I will be back."

Rubio scurried out of the cell and grabbed the unconscious guard by the hands. He pulled him beside Tomas and began to yank the sentry's clothes off, first the white cross belt from over his shoulders, then the blue blouse. He moved down the soldier's legs and jerked his shoes and splatterdashers off, then pulled his coarse sailcloth trousers off.

"What are you doing?" Tomas asked.

Rubio cringed at the sound of his brother's voice. Tomas seemed so helpless, he wondered if he could make it out of the dungeon, much less out of Bexar. Without answering, Rubio jerked off his serape and draped it over Tomas to warm him. Then Rubio began to yank on the uniform over his own clothes.

Tomas seemed bewildered. "I cannot make it, Rubio."

"You must, Tomas. I will wear the soldier's uniform so the others will think I'm a soldier. I'll tell them I caught you outside and I'm returning you to your house."

"It'll never work."

"I'll say you're drunk. It's our only chance." Rubio finished dressing, then tried to help his brother up. Tomas seemed little more than dead weight. "Please, Tomas, try."

Tomas nodded. Slowly, with Rubio's help, Tomas arose, standing as wobbly as a new foal for a few moments. "I'm dizzy."

Rubio nodded. He could not press Tomas too hard, yet they could not tarry or the Mexicans and daylight would slip up on them. Tomas took a tentative step forward, then a second. Rubio guided him out the door. Tomas stopped and leaned against the wall.

Rubio cursed to himself, wondering how his brother would ever make it out of town. As soon as he was out of the cell, Rubio closed the door, then barred it. Rubio removed his hat, placed it on Tomas's head, stepped across the corridor to pick up the infantryman's shako hat and put it on. Then he grabbed the guard's musket.

Rubio slipped to the front door, opened it and peeped outside. The sky was paling overhead. They were running out of time.

Retreating to Tomas, Rubio put an arm around his shoulder. "You think you can make it?"

Tomas shrugged.

"We'll make it, Tomas."

"If I can't, you save yourself," Tomas said.

Rubio pushed the door slowly open, then

stepped outside. Tomas followed him. Once outside, Rubio slipped behind Tomas and lowered the musket. He considered retreating along the same route he'd taken into Military Plaza, but decided against it. That route was longer. The most direct route, though, would take him closer to the soldiers manning the cannons. Deciding to chance it, he nudged Tomas with his musket barrel. "Go that way and be quiet."

Tomas mumbled something.

"Cling to the wall, Tomas," Rubio whispered.

They advanced along the wall, reached the end of the building, then turned north, down a side street. It seemed forever before they reached a cross street that would take them out of sight of Military Plaza, but they finally made it undetected. They would have to be careful, yes, but Rubio could almost taste freedom for his brother and himself.

As they neared Acequia Street, which ran on the west side of the Main Plaza and in front of the church, Tomas slowed. Rubio jumped beside him, steadying him, then looking down the street toward the cannon on the corner of the plaza. Rubio did not even see sentries. He grabbed Tomas's arm and helped him across the street. When they were close to the walls of a building across the road, Rubio sighed. "Just one more street, Tomas, and the worst is over."

With each step, though, Tomas seemed to wobble more. Rubio held his arm tighter and took in the eastern sky, where a pink glow was lighting the horizon beyond the Alamo. He could see sentries posted at the corners of the abandoned mission which the Mexicans had claimed for a fort.

Rubio cursed himself for not thinking of the danger from the Alamo. The sentries there would be able to observe his and Tomas's movements once they cleared town and headed toward the San Antonio River to meet Donley Calder. "Can you move faster?" Rubio asked.

Tomas shook his head. "I do not have the strength."

"We don't have far to go," Rubio assured him. They kept plodding toward Soledad Street. As they neared it, Rubio slipped in front of Tomas. "Make it across this street, then I can help you the rest of the way. Can you do it?"

"I'll try."

Rubio supported his brother with one hand and the musket with the other. He stepped out in the street, glancing toward the the barricade on the corner of the Main Plaza. He smiled. He didn't see any soldiers. Fifteen paces and he and Tomas would be out of their sight. "We're almost there," Rubio said.

Tomas suddenly leaned heavily into Rubio, then fell forward. Rubio tried to catch him, and dropped the musket in the street. The weapon clattered on the hard-packed ground. Rubio lunged to catch Tomas, but his brother slid to the ground.

The noise alerted the plaza sentries. *"Alto,*

alto!" they yelled.

Rubio grabbed Tomas by the shoulders and dragged him across the street. Soldiers fired their muskets. Rubio heard the whiz of the musket balls as he desperately tugged Tomas to cover.

As he pulled Tomas out of sight, he saw two of the soldiers charging down the street with their bayonets. Rubio cursed. He dropped Tomas and fumbled to lift a pistol from under his soldier's blouse. When he jerked the pistol free, he cocked the lock and extended his arm straight at the nearest of the two men. He fired and the soldier screamed, dropping his rifle and falling to his knees, clutching at his shoulder. The second soldier charged until Rubio pulled his second pistol, then the man lunged for a doorway and cover.

Rubio retreated around the corner with the loaded pistol in his hand, the empty pistol tucked into his belt. He bent and scooped Tomas from the ground. Surprised at how light his brother was, Rubio ran for the San Antonio River, praying that Donley Calder was there.

Behind him he heard shouts and an occasional shot. Musket balls sizzled through the air. Rubio ran as hard as he could. Looking over his shoulder once, to see if the soldiers were gaining, he almost tripped. Heaving and panting, he lumbered for the canopy of trees along the river to hide him from the pursuing men.

Then, from the Alamo, he saw a couple of soldiers emerge on horseback and ride toward the river to cut him off. His one loaded pistol would do little to fend them off, or to repel the soldiers chasing him on foot. He knew the men behind him were gaining. He stared at the river, looking for a place to make his stand.

Rubio doubted now that he could save himself and his brother, but neither could he leave his brother.

Then he saw a flash of light from the river, and heard the boom of a rifle. He feared he'd been surrounded by the Mexicans until he heard the scream of a soldier behind him.

There could be but one explanation: Donley Calder.

13

Donley Calder didn't know what to make of things. In the dim light he could see a Mexican soldier running toward him, carrying another man. Calder thought he recognized Rubio's serape, but why would a soldier be carrying him out of town? Something had gone wrong, but what?

Several other Mexican soldiers bolted from the streets of Bexar and shot at the fleeing soldier. If other soldiers were firing at the escaping soldier, Calder decided, then he must be an ally. Leveling and cocking his rifle, he aimed at the cross belt on the nearest pursuing soldier. He squeezed the trigger and watched his target tumble to the ground. The other soldiers dropped as well. Since the battle at Concepcion, they'd learned to take cover in the face of long rifles.

Rolling over on his back, Calder calmly reloaded his rifle, set the percussion cap, and glanced toward the Alamo, where two riders were angling for the escaping soldier. Calder sighted in on the closest horse and fired. The animal flinched but kept charging.

"Damn you," Calder spat, then glanced back

to Bexar and the escaping soldier with his captive. He replenished his rifle, ready to shoot at the horse again, when he saw the animal slow to walk, then stop and lay down despite the dragoon's flailing at him with a quirt. The second horseman, less courageous without his ally, reined up.

The escaping soldier, weighed down by the man he carried, kept plodding toward Calder. A pursuing soldier would occasionally pop out of the grass, but his aim was always as bad as his powder. "Stand up," Calder taunted, hoping for a clear shot, then looking over his back toward the Alamo. He saw the sun begin to peek over the horizon and smiled. With the sun at his back, the soldiers would have a more difficult time spotting him. He looked toward Bexar again and studied the escaping soldier. Recognizing Rubio in the uniform, Calder knew he was carrying his brother.

Rubio lumbered toward Calder, narrowing the distance from fifty paces to thirty and then to ten. Finally, he stumbled down the embankment and fell beside Calder, dumping his load on the ground. He gasped for breath, heaving and shuddering on his hands and knees.

"He's my — my brother," Rubio huffed.

"Hell, son, I didn't figure it would be General Cos, but by your uniform I feared you might've joined the Mexican Army." Calder eyed the foot soldiers as they withdrew. The two horsemen also retreated, to the Alamo.

Tomas moaned and shook his head. His eyes fluttered open.

"We made it, Tomas," Rubio said. "You're safe."

"I wouldn't say that just yet," Calder interrupted. "We've got to get back to camp."

"Tomas can ride with me."

"Damn right he will. I'll be keeping my hands on my rifle so I can put a hole in any Mexican that tries to stop us."

"What are we waiting for?"

"It'll be harder for them to see us when the full sun is up." Calder coughed. "What'd you find in town, other than your brother?"

"There are cannons on the corners of the plazas, but there weren't many soldiers on the street, at least that I saw."

Calder jerked his thumb at the Alamo. "Most must be in the mission, and most ain't real soldiers if they let you steal your brother out of prison." Calder glanced at Tomas. "You think you can get him on your horse?"

"That's easy. It was getting him here that was hard."

"Get to moving, then. Sun'll be risen shortly."

Rubio helped Tomas to his feet and half carried him to his horse. Calder kept watch on Bexar.

"We're ready," Rubio called shortly.

Calder nodded. "Follow the river a spell." Calder heard Rubio nudge his horse downstream. He looked at Bexar a final time, then slipped back down the slope to his horse, untied the gelding and climbed stiffly into the saddle. He followed Rubio's path and quickly caught up with him. They rode silently until they were certain they were out of range, then angled away from the riverbank onto the prairie, toward the Texian camp. As they neared the encampment, they were challenged by sentries, but one of the guards noticed Calder's lionskin cap and waved them on.

"Damned, if he didn't catch a Mexican soldier," the man said.

Calder touched his finger to his cap in salute. He was proud of his reputation as a fighting man. As they rode through the camp, men were rising. Calder caught the aroma of frying meat and coffee. He licked his lips, wishing Mary were around to fix his meals and boil his coffee. He aimed his horse toward his bedroll. As he drew up to his blankets, he dismounted, dropped his horse's reins, and placed his rifle on his bedroll. Then he helped lower Tomas to Rubio's bedding.

Rubio, who had drawn the attention of several soldiers, dismounted and quickly ripped off the Mexican uniform. He reclaimed his hat from Tomas's fevered head.

"I'll have a fire going shortly to warm him," Calder announced. "Then we can get some coffee and food in him." He placed kindling over a base of straw, sprinkled some powder from his horn on the straw, and struck his flint against his steel until the powder flashed and tiny flames began to lick at the straw. As he added wood to the flames, Calder built a roaring fire.

Rubio pulled his brother closer to the heat. "He needs food."

Calder looked at Tomas. "I can get him food," he answered, "but I can't get him well." Calder hadn't seen enough of white man's medicine to be certain it could save Tomas. He had more faith in the Apache medicine his wife had known and passed on to their daughter.

Calder looked up at the soldiers circling the fire and staring at Tomas. His gaze hardened and a few retreated, though a handful stayed close enough to enjoy the fire's heat. One of the spectators, a grizzled man with stained teeth and a scraggly beard, pointed at the discarded uniform, then Tomas. "Is he a soldier?"

"No," Calder answered coldly. "He's one of us."

The man scratched his beard. "Can't be. He's a Meskin."

"He's kin to Rubio Portillo, and that's good enough for me." Calder stood up and placed his hand on his skinning knife. "Anyone care to debate the issue?"

"Okay, he's one of us," the grizzled man replied, "just a little darker and a little punier."

"You'd be a little puny yourself if you'd been in a Mexican prison as long as he had." Calder circled the fire and the observers backed up a step, all save one, an officer who stared at Calder as he approached.

"You the one that caused the commotion at Bexar this morning?"

Calder wadded up his fists. "I had a hand in it."

"Then Commander Austin wants to see you and anybody else involved in the skirmish."

Rubio straightened up from beside Tomas. "I caused the trouble."

The officer stared at Rubio. "Then you come along as well."

"After I tend my brother and feed him."

The officer shook his head. "I will see that a doctor visits him and that he gets soup from the commander's pot. Austin's sickly too." The officer pointed toward Austin's tent. "Let's go now."

Calder nodded at Rubio. "Let's not keep the general waiting."

Two Texians with rifles lifted the flaps on the end of the tent. Rubio removed his hat and followed Calder inside. Austin lay on a bed of straw. He lifted his hand from beneath his blankets and pointed listlessly at two stools.

"It's Donley Calder and Rubio Portillo, isn't it." His voice was a raspy whisper. Austin coughed into his fist and shook his head. He took quick, shallow breaths. His eyes seemed tired and his skin was pasty. "I must know about the skirmish at sunrise. Who authorized you to go Bexar?"

Rubio wadded the brim of his hat. "I went to spy on Bexar and free my brother. The army had imprisoned him. His health is bad and he would have died if I hadn't rescued him."

Austin nodded weakly. "I know much of Mexican prisons, but I can't have men going off on their own. It could start an attack we would be unprepared to repulse. We cannot risk the future of Texas."

"Sir," Calder said, "his bravery has brought us details of Bexar's defenses."

"And, sir," Rubio added, "morale is bad among the enemy. I heard many gripes."

Calder waved his arm toward the tent flap. "Sir, if we wait to fight the Mexicans, our morale will be worse than theirs, what with the early cold and men separated from their families. Rubio has helped, not harmed, our cause."

"I know the cannon locations," Rubio said. "Only a few troops seem posted in the town. We can take Bexar."

Austin grimaced. "Tell my officers what you know, but neither of you are to approach Bexar in the future."

Calder shook his head. "Sir, the Texian army's just sitting on its haunches, like a hunting dog chained to a tree. It ain't gonna do nobody any good until it gets in the hunt. If we're afraid to fight, we might just as well cross the Sabine and live in Louisiana."

"I'll make the decisions for this army," Austin answered coldly.

"Sir, if you don't fight soon, you won't have an army."

Rubio grabbed Calder's arm and stood up. "Come let's let him rest," he said. "It will do us no good to argue with the general."

When they were outside, Calder cursed. "He's a good man and Texas owes him a lot, but he's not a good general."

Rubio saw a ring of Austin's officers squatting around a fire and urged Calder toward them, saying, "Let's tell them what we know." He recognized the man who had summoned him and Calder to Austin's tent.

The man nodded. "I have sent the doctor and soup to your brother."

"*Gracias,*" Rubio replied, and spent the next half hour explaining what he had seen in Bexar, where the cannon were placed, how thinly the guards were spread, and that morale there was terrible. The officers listened, but showed no inclination to fight.

Calder didn't hide his disgust. "The Texian army is commanded by girls who'd rather sit around and talk than fight. If Andy Jackson had commanded the same way, we'd be drinking tea in the afternoon and bowing down to a king instead of whipping them at New Orleans."

When the officers dismissed Rubio and Calder, the frontiersman spat in disgust, then fell in step with Rubio and grumbled all the way back to his fire.

"Maybe I should pull out, leave it to these girls to fight among themselves, because they damn sure ain't brave enough to fight any damned Mexicans." Calder grimaced and looked at his companion. "No offense, Rubio, I don't consider you a Mexican."

"Then what am I?"

Calder cocked his head and thought for a moment. He finally grinned. "You're a Texican is what you are."

Rubio grinned back, but the smile slipped away when he reached camp and saw the doctor beside Tomas. The physician was a thin reed topped with red hair and a pale face. His taut lips were grim as he nodded at Rubio.

"Keep him warm, keep him fed, and keep him dry," the doctor said. "He's awfully weak. There's not much more we can do." The doctor turned and walked away.

Rubio squatted by his brother and squeezed his hand. "You hold on, Tomas. I'll take care of you."

Tomas answered with a weak smile.

Rubio felt Calder's hand upon his shoulder. "You need someone who can care for him."

"I'll tend him."

"But you can't save him. I know someone who can."

"Who?"

"Mary. Her mother was Apache and knew much about curing illness. She taught Mary all that she knew about medicines, herbs, and cures."

Rubio liked the idea of someone who would tend solely to Tomas, and he wanted to see Mary again. He nodded at Calder. "I'll go for Mary, if the attack doesn't come soon."

"It'll take them four or five days to get up the courage to consider attacking Bexar," Calder said, "and by then the information you provided them will be old and they'll get nervous and decide they need to reconsider."

Calder was right, Rubio thought. He had spied on Bexar for nothing, though he had earned his brother's freedom. Maybe he should just get Tomas well and then abandon the army, as so many others had. Calder left them in early afternoon, to spend time around the officers, eavesdropping on their discussions. He returned about dark.

Rubio was waiting. "They're not attacking, are they?"

"No, sir."

"You think they'll attack before I can return with Mary?"

"Hell may freeze over before they attack, Rubio. Texas'll be in a sorry state, unless we find someone to lead. Mary could do better."

Rubio stared over the fire at Calder. The flickering light exposed the anger in the frontiersman's eyes. "Is our cause lost?"

"Come spring, Santa Anna is certain to send soldiers to Texas. We'll be outnumbered. Come morning, Rubio, you ride out, and take my horse. Head to Gonzales to fetch Mary."

At dawn Rubio saddled his and Calder's horses and headed east. He moved cautiously, taking three days to reach the Guadalupe outside the community where all the trouble began. Twice he saw Mexican troops, including one line with pack mules. Once, he saw Texian cavalry. He avoided both the Mexicans and the Texians. Though he shared the skin of the Mexican soldiers, he did not share their politics. Though he fought for what the Texians believed, he did not share their skin.

After he crossed the Guadalupe River outside town, he dismounted and washed the dust off his face to look presentable for Mary. Then he rode into a town now populated by women, children, feeble old men, and a few deserters. Most men were either in Austin's army outside Bexar, or Sam Houston's at San Felipe on the Brazos.

Rubio rode around the square, drawing the fearful stares of several women. Beyond the square and past the last buildings, he saw a collection of huts and even a wickiup. Knowing Mary Calder would be among the makeshift shelters, he aimed his horse toward them, heading first to the wickiup that abutted a thick grove of trees.

He reined up his horse and stopped. As he did, a woman with an armload of firewood emerged from the trees. When Rubio recognized Mary, he felt his spirits lift, but for only an instant.

Before he could say a thing, Mary dropped her firewood, screamed and charged toward him.

Rubio was dumbfounded, having no idea why she'd turned on him.

Mary saw the rider, but her gaze fell on her

211

father's riderless mount. She shouted, then flung the firewood aside and bolted for the gelding. Her fear overpowered her pleasure at seeing Rubio. "Papa, is he okay?" she gasped, grabbing Rubio's leg and shaking it.

"*Sí, sí,*" Rubio answered. "He sent me for you."

As her worry drained away, she bit her lip to fight back the tears. "I feared something terrible had happened." She released his leg and backed away. "I am sorry."

Rubio dismounted. "He's alive and as mean as ever, but he misses you. Said he's gonna starve eating his own cooking."

Mary smiled. That was like her father, to say such things.

"And," Rubio said, "I need you."

Mary was taken aback, not knowing what he meant. Before she could ask, he took off his hat and stepped toward her.

"It's my brother. He's been in prison and is terribly frail. Your father says you know many cures. Would you care for him?"

Mary smiled. "*Sí.*"

"*Gracias,*" Rubio replied.

He put his arms around her, pulling her briefly to him. She nestled against his chest, enjoying the strength of his arms. All too quickly, he released her.

"Tomas is weak. I fear if I wait to return, he might die."

"My belongings are few, Rubio." Mary scurried

inside the wickiup. From where he stood, Rubio watched her roll up her bedding, then gather the pot and skillet she used for cooking. She tossed her butcher knife, spoon, and tin utensils into the pot, then slid it and the skillet into a parfleche. Mary gathered a few more belongings that Rubio couldn't see, then emerged outside. She called to a neighbor and offered her the firewood she'd dropped.

Within five minutes Mary was astride her father's horse and ready to return to Bexar.

Rubio was quiet as they left town, not saying anything until they crossed the Guadalupe. Then he spoke, "We must avoid the roads. The Mexican Army has been using them to scout the territory."

"I will follow you."

At dusk they made a cold camp in a thicket of trees that screened their mounts from any one who might happen by. Come morning, they drank cold water from Mary's goatskin, rolled up their bedding, and resumed their journey toward Bexar.

Rubio didn't have much to say during the morning, even when Mary tried to start conversations. Maybe he was uncomfortable around her, he thought, or maybe he was just on edge that his brother might be dead or Mexican troops might keep him from returning with Mary.

"You've been quiet," Mary said.

He gave her a slight smile. "I am worried for my brother and for Texas."

"I shall save the first, and my father and men like you shall save the second."

"But nothing of Texas may be left to save if we do nothing."

"Father fought with Andy Jackson against the British and won."

Rubio grabbed her reins suddenly and jerked them so savagely that Mary thought she might have angered him. "Why did you do that?"

Rubio pointed to a hilltop not a hundred yards away.

Mary gasped, seeing a half-dozen Mexican dragoons on horses.

"We've got company," Rubio said.

14

Rubio jerked the reins of both horses. "We must run."

"*Alto, alto!*" cried the soldiers.

The horses whirled around. Rubio released Mary's reins and slapped the horse's neck. The animal bolted forward. Seeing the soldiers lift their muskets, Rubio spurred his horse and quickly caught Mary. He eased his stallion with its long powerful strides beside her. Mary's gelding ran with uneven strides, and Rubio realized it could not outrun the dragoons' mounts and he couldn't hold the soldiers off long enough for her to escape.

He cursed his luck and the pursuing soldiers. Stealing a glance over his shoulder, he wondered why the dragoons hadn't fired at them. Then Mary screamed and Rubio saw the reason why. He slowed his stallion. A hundred yards ahead, six more Mexican dragoons — their muskets aimed — blocked their escape route.

Rubio cursed. There would be no escape. He wondered if he would end up as sick as Tomas, and he feared what they might do to Mary. "I'm sorry," he said to her.

"You have nothing to be sorry for."

With guns pointed, the soldiers surrounded them. One soldier drew his sword and shoved the blade toward Rubio. Mary screamed.

The soldier laughed as he slid the sword beneath the bottom of Rubio's serape and lifted it to expose his pistols and knife. "Take his weapons," the soldier ordered.

Two more men edged their horses toward Rubio. One took his rifle and the second grabbed his pistols and knife. The man with the sword scowled. "Who are you?"

"I am a rancher."

"Then why did you run?"

"Your men drew their muskets."

"You are lying." The soldier shoved his sword back in its scabbard. He turned to Mary. "Isn't he lying?"

"No, he is a good man."

The soldier sneered. "You are lying too. A good man does not run from soldiers sent to protect him." He turned to Rubio. "You had no reason to run unless you were a traitor. We will take you to camp for our commander to see, then to Bexar."

Rubio grimaced. He knew he would be identified in Bexar.

The soldier turned to his men. "Bind them." Instantly, two more soldiers rode on either side of Rubio and Mary. They used lengths of rawhide to tie their wrists. "If you try to escape, you will be shot."

Soldiers grabbed the reins of their horses and steered them amid the line of dragoons. The commanding soldier pointed roughly toward Bexar and the soldiers advanced.

They had ridden but half an hour when they came upon a camp with more soldiers and dozens of mules in a field of tall yellow grass. Rubio bit his lip. He recognized several of the muleteers as Juan Paz's men. Most men — muleteers and soldiers alike — were using scythes to cut and bundle grass. By their work, Rubio realized Bexar was running out of fodder for its horses, and he wondered if he was running out of time.

The line of mounted soldiers advanced to a tent in the middle of camp. A soldier ordered the prisoners to dismount, but Rubio hesitated. The dragoon at his side lifted his musket and slammed the butt into his ribs. Rubio gritted his teeth as pain shot up his side. He slid off the horse, then helped Mary dismount.

A soldier grabbed Rubio's arm and jerked him toward the tent just as two men emerged. Rubio caught his breath. One was the captain in charge of the troops. The other was Juan Paz.

"Sir," a dragoon said. "We have returned with two prisoners."

As the captain eyed them. Rubio stared at Juan Paz, who looked slowly up, then licked his lips and stepped toward him. Paz laughed. "This is Rubio Portillo. He is a traitor bastard."

"You know him?"

"Know him? I'm marrying his betrothed on

what was to be his wedding day. And when the difficulties are over, I plan to claim his ranch for myself."

Rubio clenched his jaw in anger.

The captain turned to the dragoons. "Good work, men. Now help us cut grass so we can return to Bexar tomorrow."

The soldiers saluted and retreated.

"Rubio Portillo," Paz said, "is brother of another traitor in prison in Bexar for killing a soldier."

Rubio grinned at Paz, proud that he had freed his brother, even if the act would lead to his own death.

"This one is the worst of the two," Paz went on. "If he should try to escape, do not kill him, for I want that privilege."

"That shall be General Cos's decision when we return to Bexar."

Juan Paz marched around Rubio and Mary, eyeing them. "Angelita will know she made the right choice when I tell her you have been consorting with half-breeds."

"I don't consort with snakes like you do, Juan Paz."

Paz slapped Rubio, who flinched, then thrust his jaw out, as if daring Paz to hit him again.

Mary screamed, and the captain grabbed Paz's hand before he could strike. "If what you say is true of this man, then many will want to kill him in Bexar, but we will not get to Bexar until your mules are loaded, Juan Paz."

"They're carrying all that they can, save for the grass for the livestock. We can leave in the morning. I am anxious to return to Bexar now." He looked at Rubio. "With Rubio Portillo, I have a better load than I could have wished."

The officer instructed Juan Paz to tell his men to be ready to leave by sunrise, then sent him off. He studied Rubio for a moment and shook his head. The captain turned and ordered a soldier to bind Rubio and Mary together, back-to-back, and maintain a guard over them. A soldier led them away, found a lariat and tied them together near one of the fire pits the soldiers used for warmth and cooking.

The day dragged by slowly, and the night passed even slower because of the cold. They received no food, nothing to drink, and not even a blanket. Back-to-back, they shivered.

The soldiers clustered near them as they came to warm themselves by the fire or to eat their meager rations. Mostly, Rubio heard them complaining of the cold and about heading back to Bexar. Several said they would certainly die if they went back, either starving or freezing, if they weren't killed in battle.

Though Mary seemed to pass out in exhaustion, Rubio never managed to fall fully asleep. The camp began to waken an hour before dawn as the muleteers loaded their animals. The soldiers rose next, spelling those on guard, picking up their gear and saddling their horses.

Hunger gnawed at Rubio's belly like a rat. His

muscles were so stiff from the cold that his legs had little feeling. Though he and Mary were ordered to get up, they could not. Mary groaned, but Rubio tried to show no sign of weakness, not with Juan Paz around.

Two soldiers eventually helped them to their feet and unbound them from each other. Rubio stomped the ground, to restore feeling to his legs. Mary stood still, trying not to fall.

They received neither food nor water. A soldier brought them their horses and helped each into the saddle. Rubio was so sleepy and cold, he fought to stay in the saddle. He glanced at Mary, and she seemed little better.

By sunrise the supply train was moving southwest before angling toward Bexar. Rubio cursed Juan Paz, General Cos, Colonel Ugartechea, and everyone else who had turned his life upside down. The day passed slowly, the agony growing with each step of his stallion. He twisted his hands, hoping he could escape the grasp of the leather bindings around his wrists, but merely rubbed the skin raw. By mid-afternoon the sun felt good on his back, but he remained hungry and thirsty. By sundown he was so confused by his cravings that the sound he heard did not register at first — gunfire.

All around him soldiers panicked. Then Rubio realized the sound of gunshots was accompanied by the pounding of hooves. He twisted in his saddle and saw about twenty mounted Texians charging at the train.

A soldier grabbed his reins and jerked his horse forward, another soldier took control of Mary's horse, and they beat their own horses into a lope. The muleteers put their animals into a trot as well, and soldiers fell behind the mules to answer Texian guns.

The hard ride jogged Rubio back to his senses. "Mary!" he cried.

"Silencio," the soldier beside him shouted.

"Fall off your horse!" Rubio cried. "It's our only chance!"

The soldier at Mary's side tried to pin her in, but she jerked on her reins enough to slow her mount. She lifted her leg over the saddle and slid off, hitting the ground on both feet, collapsing and tumbling side over side.

The soldier running Rubio's horse edged in closer, trying to pin him in. Rubio stood in his stirrups and leaped for him, managing to get his bound hands around the soldier's neck. As the stallion rode out from under him, Rubio fell with his full weight on the dragoon's neck and shoulders. The soldier cried out and fell backward, holding desperately onto the reins. The horse reared and the soldier slid out of his saddle, Rubio riding the soldier to the ground, breaking his own fall. The soldier gasped as air was pressed from his lungs.

Rubio rolled away as the line of charging horses and mules galloped past, kicking clods and dirt and pebbles at him. One passing soldier fired his musket at him as he kept rolling and crawling away from the last of the stampeding column.

At last the Mexicans passed, and the Texians, a dozen of them, charged by. A couple peeled away from the others and rode straight to Rubio, pointing a pistol at him. Rubio rose to his knees and lifted his bound hands over his head. "I am Tejano," he rasped. "They had taken me prisoner."

The Texian eyed him from beneath the brim of his broad hat. "We'll see about that," he growled.

A second Texian checked out the Mexican soldier Rubio had knocked out of the saddle. "He's still breathing," he said.

Rubio grimaced. "The woman back there, she was a captive too."

"We'll get to her in a spell," the Texian replied.

"Can you spare me a sip of water?"

"Not until I know if you're Tejano or Mexican."

Rubio lifted his bound hands again, as if that should be explanation enough. He looked back down the trail and saw Mary get to her feet. She dusted herself off and plodded toward him, shaking her head.

The gun-wielding Texian eyed her warily as she approached.

Mary stepped up to Rubio and kissed him on the cheek.

"Are you okay?" he asked.

She nodded. "Bruised, but nothing worse."

At the sound of galloping horses, Rubio turned

to see the Texians returning. They were leading three riderless horses. Rubio grinned. One was his and another was Mary's. The leader of the Texians halted in front of Rubio and eyed him and Mary, his gaze seeming to linger on Mary a good bit.

Once more Rubio lifted his bound hands. "I'm Tejano."

"I'm Ben Milam," he announced.

"Ben Milam of Kentucky?" Mary said. "Ben Milam who fought with Andy Jackson at New Orleans?"

"The one and only. Who are you?"

"Mary Calder."

"Well, I'll be damned, little one. Last time I saw you, you wasn't much more than knee-high to a grasshopper. Where's your pa?"

"With Austin."

Milam bounded out of the saddle and jerked his knife. He stepped to Mary and slit the leather thongs that bound her wrist.

Mary pointed at Rubio. "Him too."

Milam extended his knife to Rubio's out-stretched wrists. "Put away your pistols, boys. If Mary Calder vouches for him, that's good enough for me. Not a more honest man or a better fighter in all of Texas than Donley Calder." Milam cut Rubio's bindings.

"We are hungry and thirsty," Mary announced.

"We ain't got much, but you're welcome to what we got," Milam announced. He ordered one of his men to give them some jerked beef and hard crackers. He undid his own canteen and offered it to them.

Mary and Rubio shared the canteen, drinking greedily.

Milam squatted beside Rubio. "That wasn't Colonel Ugartechea's men, was it? He left Bexar for somewhere, and we haven't seen him for a couple weeks."

Rubio shook his head. "It wasn't Ugartechea. Just a supply train. Their morale is bad and their supplies are low."

Milam smiled. "Tell me what you know, then we'll ride to Bexar tomorrow. I expect we'll be walking around in Bexar in a few days."

Donley Calder hit his fist with his palm. "This is nothing but a damned knitting circle. I've seen women with one foot in the grave that had more spunk than this bunch of so-called men. Armies are meant to fight, not sit around and cook all winter."

For the second time since Rubio had departed for Gonzales, an attack had been planned on Bexar. The first time, it was canceled because the army had lost faith in Austin. In the wake of the near mutiny, Austin resigned and Edward Burleson, a man with no military experience whatsoever, was elected to replace him.

Then Burleson planned an attack, but it too had been called off. The army was boiling mad and ready to claw out eyeballs — if not the Mexicans', then their own leaders'.

Calder sat down beside Tomas, who had gained some strength and color, but little else. "Once my daughter gets here, we might as well pull out. We'll be debating instead of fighting."

"When we fight, I'm with you."

"There won't be a fight, dammit. There's enough chicken in this army to feed all of Texas, including the Indians, for a century. You destroy the soul of an army by sitting around and doing nothing."

Hearing a troop of soldiers approaching the camp, Calder stood and shaded his eyes against the glare of the late afternoon sun. "Well, speak of the devil, it's your brother. He done brought back Mary and some more soldiers."

Tomas propped himself up on his elbow.

Calder did a little jig, glad to see his daughter. Mary smiled when she saw him. She jumped out of the saddle and threw her arms around him.

"I was worried about you," he said.

"Afraid you'd have to keep cooking your own meals."

Calder laughed. "No, afraid I'd have to keep eating 'em."

Rubio dismounted and stepped to his brother's side.

"Ran into an old friend of yours, Papa." She pointed to a man on a trailing horse.

Calder followed her arm, then slapped his knee. "Well, I'll be an alligator's mama, if it ain't Ben Milam. I heard you was about, but I wasn't going

225

to believe it unless I laid my eyes on you."

Grinning, Milam jumped off his horse. He strode to Calder and they wrapped each other in a bear hug.

"Donley, I wished I'd known you was around. We'd set off and taken a few Mexican scalps, wouldn't we?"

Calder broke Milam's grasp and pumped his hand warmly. "Seems you and me might be the only two around with any grit in our craw."

"We'll get them, Donley. I just rode in from a scout, and a good thing I did, as the Mexicans had your daughter and that Tejano there." Milam pointed at Rubio.

"Things've changed."

"I heard Austin's resigned."

"His replacement's got no more vinegar than Austin had."

"Can't be true."

"If I'm lying, you can skin my hide and nail it to a tree."

Milam's jaw dropped. "You're speaking the gospel, aren't you?"

Calder nodded. "Sure as I'm standing here. Fact is, he's passing word that the soldiers can leave for their homes and report back in the spring."

"In the spring? Hell, everybody knows Santa Anna'll invade in the spring. We might just as well line up and shoot ourselves. That's what it'll amount to if we let General Cos and his men winter here."

Calder threw open his arms and turned slowly around. "Look about the camp. Men are picking up and leaving."

"Dammit," Milam yelled, "if we abandon Bexar now, we'll die in Mexican prisons."

Several men around the camp stared at Milam. Calder watched him retreat to his horse. He untied his rifle and hoisted it over his head. He puckered his lips and cut loose a shrill whistle. "Who'll follow old Ben Milam into Bexar?" he shouted.

Calder clapped his hands and stomped his feet. His heart raced. It was good to see some fight and fire in someone. "I'll go with you, Ben." Calder jerked his lionskin cap from his head, grabbed the bottom of it and twirled it over his head. "You and me, Ben, the two of us will take Bexar. You other fellows, just go on home. We wouldn't want you to get your dresses dirty or torn." Calder laughed and whistled, then stepped in behind Milam. "Let's go right now."

Milam lifted his rifle to his shoulder and fired it toward Bexar. Throughout the camp men stopped what they were doing and turned to watch. "Who else'll follow me into Bexar? Donley Calder is the first. Who'll be next?"

"I will," came a cry from behind them. Calder turned to see Rubio Portillo stand up and be counted.

Milam glanced around and shouted, "Even their own kind is willing to fight them! Is it just the three of us, or will more of you stand up for Texas?"

A couple men nearby cried out they'd join. They raised their rifles in the air and fell in behind Milam. Slowly, the growing line snaked through the camp, picking up volunteers like a magnet picks up metal filings. Gradually, more and more men joined, until more paraded around the camp than watched.

Calder tapped Milam on the shoulder and pointed toward Edward Burleson, the newly elected commander who had yet to attack anything. Burleson stood in front of his tent watching. "See if our commander wants to join our battle or not."

With a wave of his arm, Milam started the parade toward Burleson, whose aide-de-camp and a half dozen other officers strode to him. Milam stopped not five paces from Burleson, removed his slouch hat and bowed. "Commander, these men don't want to go home with their tails between their legs."

Slowly, behind Milam, the men fanned out until they formed a thick crescent. Burleson stood silent for a moment, then turned to his aide-de-camp. "Take a count," he commanded. The aide saluted, then marched among Milam's volunteers. "The enemy's strong and fortified. They have a dozen cannon or more. We have two. Many of you will die if you charge the town," Burleson warned.

Milam shook his head. "More of us will die

later if we don't."

Burleson crossed his arms over his chest. "Is this a mutiny?"

Again Milam shook his head. "It's men ready to put the fighting behind us so we can go home and live in peace."

The aide-de-camp returned to Burleson's side and whispered in his ear. Burleson nodded and pointed to Milam. "Join me in my tent," he said.

Milam handed Calder his rifle and followed Burleson inside. The murmur of the men fell silent. The only noise was the sound of Milam and Burleson exchanging heated words. The minutes dragged by. Finally, the tent flap flew open and Burleson stepped outside, followed by Milam, a broad grin on his face.

"Once more," he cried, "who'll follow old Ben Milam into Bexar?"

The men cheered and almost four hundred took a step forward.

Burleson nodded. "You men be prepared to advance before sunrise. Those of you who don't wish to accompany Milam will stay here in reserve. Now, return to duties while Milam and I plan the attack."

Milam nodded. "Sharpen your knives and hatchets and oil your guns. Tomorrow you'll need them."

The ragtag army of soldiers dispersed, their spirits high. Calder whistled gaily as he carried Milam's rifle back to his fire. When he arrived, he found Mary had put more wood on and was boiling some roots in her pot.

She smiled at her father. "I'll get Tomas better, but it'll take time."

Calder grinned.

Mary shook her head. "There'll be fighting tomorrow, yes?"

Calder laughed. "Time to repay those Mexicans."

"You ever think you might be getting too old to fight?" Mary asked.

"When you're too old to fight, you get killed."

Mary shook her head and turned her attention back to Tomas.

Rubio joined them moments later.

"Where's your weapons?" Calder asked him.

"They were taken when I was captured."

"We'll get you a rifle and a blade or two. There's always a few men in any army who don't want to fight."

In an hour Ben Milam returned to Calder and reclaimed his rifle. He whispered to Calder that a cannon and a handful of soldiers would create a diversion toward the Alamo. Then the volunteers would be divided into two divisions, one charging down Acequia Street in front of the church and the other down Soledad Street at the opposite end of the Main Plaza. The soldiers were to be in position by five in the morning.

Calder accompanied Milam to inform others of the plan, then returned with a rifle, pistol, and an old hatchet and handed the weapons to Rubio.

"Get an early start on your sleep, Rubio. We've got to be in position by five."

Tomas coughed. "I wish I could fight with you," he said.

15

Juan Paz cursed the soldiers all the way to Bexar. How could they have let Rubio Portillo escape? With both Tomas and Rubio Portillo in prison, Rancho de Espiritu Toro would become his, a fine wedding present for Angelita Sanchez. Luckily, the sudden attack on the mule train had not cost him any mules or men. Gradually, the low-slung buildings of Bexar and the stone walls of the Alamo, which flew the Mexican flag, came into view. As the caravan neared the Alamo, it was greeted by the cheers of Mexican soldiers standing on walls, waving their hats and weapons. Paz knew they were expecting more and better food than his men had brought, but if they fought no better than the dragoons, he thought, they deserved to starve.

The gates of the Alamo swung open as the line of mules neared. Paz spurred his horse and dashed through the gate ahead of the captain and the troops. He wanted to be the first to see General Cos so he could announce the incompetence of the dragoons for letting Rubio Portillo escape. But then, how could he expect anything more from the dragoons than from their leader?

he asked himself. General Cos was incompetent too.

Paz halted his horse in front of the first officer he saw.

"Is the general here or in Bexar? I must see him."

The officer jerked his finger over his shoulder. "In the tall barracks." He gestured to a line of two-story quarters that fronted the open plaza. Beyond the general's quarters, the roofless church with its crumbling facade faced Bexar. It was a sad structure. Paz looked at it as he angled across the grounds surrounded by adobe and limestone walls, except for a breach in the north wall that had been filled with logs and dirt, and for a low wall that jutted out of the side of the tall quarters and paralleled the front of the chapel. A stockade wall packed with dirt had been built from the southern corner of the chapel to the corner of the south wall to close the other gap.

Paz spat and dismounted at the door guarded by two sentries. The guards blocked his path. "I'm Juan Paz to see the general."

One soldier nodded, cracked the door and stuck his head inside to announce Paz's presence. Paz heard the general's muffled voice through the door. The soldier swung the door all the way open.

Paz grumbled as he stepped inside. The room, with one small, low window, was warm, with a fire in a corner fireplace. The only other light was from a single candle on a crude table General Cos was using for a desk. As Paz entered, the general picked up a sheet of crumpled paper and stood up.

Not waiting for the general to speak, Paz shook his head and clenched his fist. "If it hadn't been for your men's incompetence, General, I would have had the traitor Rubio Portillo as a captive in prison with his brother."

Cos glared at Paz, a narrow, sinister smile crawling across his lips. He said, "Tell me more, Juan Paz."

"We captured Rubio and some half-breed he was riding with. Then a handful of traitors surprised us, and your soldiers let him escape."

Cos smirked. "Why didn't you stop him from escaping?"

"It is not my job."

The general waved the crumpled page at Paz, who leaned forward and took it from him. "What is this?"

"You've seen it before, Juan Paz. You had Colonel Ugartechea write it for you."

Paz looked at the page. He held it toward the candle and quickly recognized it. It was the note he'd requested so he and Angelita could visit Tomas's prison cell whenever they liked. "Where did you get this?"

"The soldiers found it on the floor of the guard-house."

He shrugged. "So?"

Cos licked his lips. "The morning that Tomas

234

Portillo escaped."

"What?"

"A man, perhaps Rubio, tricked the guard with this note."

"Your men are stupid."

"How did Rubio Portillo — if that's who it was — get that note?"

Paz shook his head. "I do not know, but I will find out."

"See that you do, Juan Paz, if you want to get paid for your work come spring."

Paz turned, his fingers tightly gripping the paper as he strode to the door. "I will find out everything, General."

He cursed Angelita as he left the general's office. Seeing one of his muleteers handling his horse, Paz strode over to him and jerked the reins from the man's hand. He jumped astride the animal and rode to the gate.

The guards let him pass. His anger flared within him. He knew what had happened. He didn't have to ask. Rubio had slipped into town to visit Angelita, and she had given him the pass. Perhaps she'd changed her mind about the both of them. Juan Paz cursed.

His horse thundered across the wooden bridge and down the street toward the Main Plaza. The sun was setting toward the west, and the streets would soon have to be clear for the night. As he reached Bexar's low-slung houses, Paz slowed his horse so he would not approach the plaza and the jittery guards too suddenly.

He stopped in front of the cannon guarding the plaza corner. A soldier recognized and admonished him. "You must not be on the street after dark."

Paz answered, "I intend to stay at the home of my betrothed."

The soldier nodded knowingly.

"She lives on the square. I will tie my horse out front. My horse doesn't have to be off the street, does he?" he asked sarcastically.

The soldier waved him on.

Juan Paz rode past the shivering soldiers. He drew up outside the stone house of Angelita and her parents, quickly dismounted and tied his horse. Clearing his throat, he stepped to the door and knocked.

—At the angry knock, Angelita Sanchez flinched and looked at her parents, who were sharing a bowl of beans in the dim candlelight. Food was scarce, and she'd taken only a few bites herself, leaving the rest for her parents. They seemed so frail and scared now. She was scared too. She rose from the high-back chair and started for the front door, fearing it was Juan Paz but praying she was wrong. Lifting the handle, she pulled the door open.

Before her stood Juan Paz, a scowl upon his face.

Angelita tried to hide the fear in her eyes. "You have returned safely," she cried, hoping her mock tears masked her feelings. She threw her arms

236

around him. "I've been so worried."

He pushed her inside. "You saw him, didn't you?"

"Who?"

"Rubio, that's who."

"No, I swear I have not seen him since you left, Juan."

He swung his hand at her face so fast that she couldn't deflect the blow. Real tears flooded her eyes at the sting of his palm. Turning around, she saw her parents.

"No, no, please leave or he might hurt you." She knew Juan carried a brace of pistols under his serape, and she knew the vicious look in his eyes.

"Do what she says or she will be hurt!" Paz yelled.

Angelita was relieved when her parents left the room, but fearful as Paz grabbed her neck. She could feel his callused hands tightening upon her flesh. "Have you seen him?"

She remained mute, fearing any response might anger him more.

He reached into a pocket with his other hand, withdrew a crumpled page and held it before her eyes. "How do you explain this? It was found in the prison after Rubio helped his brother escape."

She knew what it was. "Yes, he came here and said if I did not give it to him, he would kill my parents."

His hand tightened around her throat. "There's an army outside your door, and all you had to do was get them the word. They would've taken him to prison, where he could have died with his brother."

Angelita tried to speak, but Paz's grip was too tight. He relaxed his fingers. She inhaled deeply. "I sent him away. I told him never to return." She lifted her head defiantly. "It was my final gift to him. We were once betrothed."

"Now you are betrothed to me."

She shrugged.

"Shall we be wed tonight?"

"No!" Angelita cried.

He grinned wickedly. "No matter." He shoved her toward her bedroom, then pushed her again as he followed.

Angelita wanted to scream, but it would only terrify her parents even more. In her room, she clenched her jaw as he shoved her upon her blankets. He lifted her skirt and fell upon her, wrestling to unbutton the flap on the front of his britches. And then he took her, savagely.

She gritted her teeth against the pain of his lust and the pistols still snug in his waist sash, which banged against her as he moved atop her. Trying to push him off, Angelita's hand brushed against the handle of a knife in a scabbard at his side. She relented and quit fighting, hoping to slip the knife from his side and kill him. His breathing was heavy with desire. He seemed oblivious to everything as he moved wildly over her.

Though it was a lie she could barely muster the breath to express, Angelita let out a little moan, hoping it might distract him. She rubbed his back with her free hand, then lifted the knife over her head, ready to plunge it into Juan's back.

As her hand started down, his hand flew up and caught her wrist. His fingers squeezed tight around her flesh and the knife fell harmlessly to the floor, as he kept raping her.

She moaned in defeat, then began to cry silently, tears streaming down her cheeks. She wanted her mother to comfort her and her father to protect her, but they were too old and feeble to save her. She was humiliated when Juan Paz finished the act.

But he was not done. He undressed himself and then her. Three more times during the night he forced himself upon her, and Angelita could no longer fight him. It was futile to resist. Even when he seemed to be sleeping, he roused whenever she moved. She knew he might kill her if she tried to get his knife again. Tears streamed down her cheeks all night, and she was grateful when she heard cannon fire.

Juan Paz stirred from his slumber, then sat up suddenly in bed. "Texians," he cried and sat up. He swatted at Angelita as he flung back the blankets. "What have you done?"

Angelita sobbed. She had done nothing.

"The Texians are attacking Bexar," he cried, grabbing his clothes and pistols. He dressed hurriedly and darted out of the room and out the front door. Angelita grabbed the blanket from the bed, wrapped it around her and started for the door, but her foot slipped upon something. It was Juan Paz's knife. She bent and grabbed it by the handle. For a moment she lifted it to her head, wondering if she should slice her wrist or plunge the blade into her stomach so that Juan Paz's evil seed would not beget a bastard child. Then she lowered the knife and ran into the front room, the floor beneath her bare feet colder than Juan Paz's heart. She slammed the door and slid to the ground, sobbing.

She did not hear her mother walk in. "I'm sorry my child. Your father is frail, but he wanted to help you. I knew Juan Paz would kill him."

Angelita nodded. "There was nothing you could do."

"I'm sorry," he mother repeated sadly.

"You were right, Juan Paz is an evil man."

"It is better that you know now."

"But he has taken so much from me."

Her mother nodded. "But he could have taken even more."

Mary Calder spent the night beside Tomas Portillo, keeping him warm and forcing him to drink her herbal medicines four times before dawn. Even had she tried, she could not have slept, not with her father and Rubio readying in the darkness to attack Bexar.

She sat by the burning embers of her fire, drinking coffee for warmth. The night had been a restless one, with men moving about, quietly preparing for battle. Two-thirds of the men, her father and Rubio included, had left with Ben Milam. A cannon crew and a handful of infantry had crossed the San Antonio River and set up within range of the Alamo to act as a diversion. The remaining men, those who had not volunteered to go with old Ben Milam, remained in camp as reserves, ready to cover a retreat or repulse a counterattack.

The acting commander, Edward Burleson, had appropriated all the extra horses in the camp, including her father's and Rubio's, to mount patrols to scour the perimeter of Bexar so that the town might not be reinforced by troops from the Alamo or elsewhere. Burleson, who had not supported the attack, stopped by Mary's fire earlier in the evening to warm himself.

"You must be prepared to escape if the attack fails and the Mexicans attack us," he told her. "There's a cart behind my tent you can use to carry him." Burleson pointed at Tomas.

"I cannot outrun them without a horse, and I cannot leave Tomas."

"Then I cannot offer you protection."

"I need none."

Burleson had walked on.

Mary knew if the Texians did not take Bexar, Tomas would likely die, for he needed to be in a place where it was warm and she could better minister to him. She looked to the east for a sign of the sunrise, knowing it couldn't be much more than an hour before the start of a new day. She waited and worried. Then the sound of a single

241

cannon split the night. She gritted her teeth. The diversion had begun. Tomas, startled, twisted in his blankets. Mary gently stroked his forehead, which simmered with fever.

For a moment after the cannon shot, she heard only the sound of Tomas's breathing, and she feared the Mexicans realized it was a ploy. Then she heard a bugle and the distant role of drums. Another cannon shot sliced through the night, and Mary saw a brief flash of light in the direction of the diversion. Shortly, Mexican cannon answered back. She gave thanks. Answering cannon fire indicated the soldiers in the fort thought the attack was real.

Around the darkened camp several men cheered, but Burleson commanded them to be quiet. The noise awoke Tomas. He stirred and mumbled. Mary spoke softly to him, soothing his fears until he drifted back to sleep. There was nothing else she could do, except pray. She beseeched God to smile upon the Texians and their cause. As the skirmish died toward the Alamo, shooting began in Bexar and Mary saw brief flashes of light and heard the sound of muskets or cannon. As the sun rose, she saw gun smoke floating over the town like a widow's veil caught in the breeze.

With dawn, Mary began to fix breakfast for Tomas. Knowing it would be a long day, she wanted to stay busy.

The men shivered, waiting for the diversion. In

the cold of the night, sound traveled far. Ben Milam had ordered silence. He had divided his volunteers into two groups. The first division would charge south down Acequia Street to take the west end of the Main Plaza before turning west to take control of Military Plaza. The second division would race south down Soledad Street to capture the east side of the Main Plaza before turning eastward to take the houses toward the San Antonio River and the Alamo.

Rubio Portillo nervously awaited the order to advance. Donley Calder put a hand on his shoulder to reassure him. Around them other men stood, some stomping their feet against the cold and their anxiety. Others coughed quietly into their sleeves or the blankets they had wrapped themselves in to fight the cold. When the cannon across the San Antonio River finally fired, the men listened for the enemy's response. Not a man stomped his feet or coughed. Each waited as silently as the dead.

Then a bugle blared in the distance. A roll of drums followed, then came shouted orders and the rattle of muskets. Rubio stared toward the Alamo and saw a second flash of the Texian cannon. In short time it was answered by Mexican cannon and musket. The Mexicans were pouring lead into the dark at an imagined threat.

Calder elbowed him and whispered, "Stick close to me."

Rubio nodded. Around him the other men began to move forward, first at a walk, then at a trot, trying to balance swiftness with silence. Their footfalls were serenaded by the rattle of their weapons.

They reached the edge of town unnoticed. Around Rubio, men ran down the street, past the first house and the second. And still the Mexicans had not spotted them. The sound of the cannon fire and musketry to the east was working as a diversion. Rubio charged ahead, knowing they were racing toward a cannon that could easily spew canister at them.

Still the men advanced undetected, coming within two hundred paces of the Main Plaza before one of the soldiers tripped, his gun flying from his hand and clattering on the street.

Instantly, a Mexican sentry shouted, *"Alto!"*

A flash of exploding powder briefly exposed the sentinel at the corner barricade. Donley Calder lifted his weapon and fired. Rubio heard the scream of a soldier, and in the darkness saw a small flame behind the barricade.

Suddenly, Calder dove into him, knocking him to the ground. Rubio cursed, furious at being tackled.

"To the ground, men!" Ben Milam screamed.

"Fall down!" Calder yelled.

Rubio tried to get up, but Calder grabbed his head and pushed it to the ground. The belch of the cannon flung hot iron down the narrow street, drawing a solitary scream from an injured Texian. The soldiers jumped to their feet before the Mexicans could reload.

"Get inside, men!" Milam yelled.

The Texians began to break down doors and barge into the stone houses. Calder jerked Rubio up and dragged him to the closest dwelling, then kicked the door open. A man and woman in nightclothes screamed and tried to barge past them out into the street. Calder grabbed them. "Stay or the cannon will kill you."

Rubio repeated Calder's message in Spanish, then assured the couple they would not be harmed.

Several other Texians squeezed through the door.

The cannon roared again, the spray of lead splattering on the walls bordering the street.

Before the echo of the cannon had faded, several men jumped out the door and fired toward the plaza, then retreated back inside.

Calder turned to Rubio. "We got farther than we had any right to expect, but not as far as we needed to go. Come good light, the going'll be tougher. Don't expose yourself except to shoot."

Rubio nodded.

From outside came a call for Donley Calder, and Rubio recognized Ben Milam's voice. Calder stepped to the door. "Yeah, Ben."

"It's house to house, street to street, come dawn," Milam cried.

16

The day had been long and cold, the wind from the north whipping up grit and dust, flinging it in Mary Calder's face. Sometimes the winds howled so loudly that Mary could not hear the sounds of battle in Bexar, and at other times the breeze seemed to carry the mournful noise of fighting more strongly to her. She fretted and kept the fire going to warm Tomas, who tossed and shivered continually. Mary made a thin soup by boiling dried beef in water and adding dried beans and corn to the mix. She added what little salt she had and stirred it regularly, staying close to the fire to soak up what warmth the wind didn't blow away.

"Where's Rubio?" Tomas called out occasionally.

"In Bexar," Mary reminded him, "fighting."

Tomas cursed the Mexican soldiers before slipping back into the haze of delirium. While she waited on him, Mary could do little more than keep the fire going and the soup hot.

At nightfall the firing in Bexar died away. She heard that Burleson had sent men into town to check on the progress of the battle, and hoped she might overhear some report on the state of things. But by midnight, as Mary continued to tend the fire, she gave up on learning anything. With the wind howling at her from the north, she slipped under her blankets.

As she dozed off, she wished Rubio Portillo was beside her to keep her warm.

Angelita Sanchez had cried many tears of shame since Juan Paz had raped her, but now she cried from fear. Six Mexican soldiers had occupied her house, overturning furniture for barricades, eating what food she'd saved for her parents, and stealing their belongings.

And she could do nothing about it. She hadn't been able to fend off Juan Paz, much less an entire army. She'd been a fool not to listen to her parents, she knew now. Rubio Portillo was a better man than Paz. She hoped the Texians caught Paz and killed him, as he deserved.

For a full day the Mexican soldiers occupied her house, and come the cold dawn of the second day, when the shooting resumed, Angelita wondered if she would survive. Even though she was scared, she had to do something. She rose from the corner where she cowered with her parents and strode to the nearest soldier. "Get out!" she screamed. "This is our house, not yours, and you're destroying it."

The soldier regarded her with a vacant stare and shrugged. His indifference enraged Angelita. She raised her fists and pummeled his chest. "Get out. Leave us alone."

Perplexed, the soldier looked around the room for an ally among the other men, but they snickered at him. Angering, he lifted his rifle and shoved her away. She screamed and attacked him again, her hands flailing at him, her nails digging into the flesh of his cheeks. Cursing, he lifted his weapon and hit her jaw. Angelita staggered backward, her teeth rattling, her senses aswim. She felt the feeble hold of her parents on her arms as they pulled her back to their corner.

The gunfire outside seemed distant until a cannon was fired from the plaza. Angelita flinched at the explosion, then began to sob. She felt her parents ease her down onto their blankets.

"I'm sorry," she kept repeating, "I'm sorry." She did not know what she was apologizing for, because she had so many regrets. All she knew for sure was that she needed to apologize for something.

Donley Calder knew they had to break the stalemate. After their initial success before dawn, the Texian surge had stalled for the rest of the day. They forted up in some houses and behind walls, shooting at Mexicans hiding in adjacent buildings. As the new dawn approached, Calder listened to the sound of gunfire along the street, then called to Ben Milam and the other Texians in the house across the street. "Ben, me and Rubio are coming in. Open the door."

"Come on, then," Milam answered.

Calder motioned for Rubio to lead, then jumped in behind him. A couple of quick shots exploded from a house at the corner as the door across the street swung open. Rubio flew inside, followed by Calder, who dove in as more enemy shots exploded.

Milam flung the door shut behind them, grabbed Calder by the shoulders and helped him up. "The Mexicans've got us pinned down, don't they?"

Calder nodded. "But we've got them pinned down as well. The advantage is ours unless they reinforce the town from the Alamo."

Milam shook his head. "I hope Burleson posts cavalry patrols like he said he would. If he didn't, we'll all die. What do you propose, Donley?"

"It's simple, Ben, we either keep moving or start dying."

Milam nodded. "I asked for men to follow ol' Ben Milam into Bexar, and it's time for me to lead again."

Milam passed the orders for men to prepare to advance. The sun was just clearing the horizon when he led his men out of the house and onto the street, among them Calder and Rubio Portillo. The Texians split into two groups, attacking Mexican strongholds on both sides of the street.

The Mexicans manning the cannon at street's end were surprised by the sudden attack, and their slow reactions gave the Texians valuable time. Rubio followed Calder to the door of the nearest house and they battered it with their shoulders. It flinched but did not give. They backed out of the way as another Texian attacked the thick plank door with an ax. Between the blows of the ax, Rubio heard the excited chatter of Mexican soldiers inside. As soon as the door gave way, the Texians rushed in, Rubio in the lead.

Rubio fired his rifle at a Mexican retreating into the next room, then dove to the ground so the Texians behind him would have a clear shot. A cloud of spent powder enveloped the room, its stench burning Rubio's nose and eyes. Through the cloud he saw Donley Calder fire his rifle, then jerk his hatchet from his belt and charge into the next room, screaming like a wild man.

"That's for burning my home!" he cried.

Rubio loaded his musket while lying on his back, stood up and bolted into the next room. He saw two bloodied Mexicans on the floor, Calder standing over them with his tomahawk. Beyond Calder he saw an open door that had provided escape out back.

As Calder turned to face the Texians crowding into the room, Rubio saw the wild eyes of an enraged panther in the old man's face. It occurred to him the lionskin cap was a suitable headdress.

"Were's Milam?" Calder cried as the cannon roared outside.

"He's taking the house across the street," someone answered.

"Put a rifleman at each door," Calder yelled.

"Warn us if the Mexicans return. We won't be surprising the boys on the cannon again, so we can't attack from the street."

"Then how'll we get the Mexicans next door?" a Texian shouted.

"We'll knock a hole in the wall and attack them like rats," Calder answered.

A soldier with an ax began to chip away at the mortar between the stones. The ax clanged against the hard limestone rock, throwing occasional sparks. Other men chipped at the mortar with knives and hatchets, gradually loosening stones and prying one free. Then Calder dropped to his knees, shoved his rifle barrel through the hole and fired.

Terrified Mexican soldiers in the abutting house screamed as other Texians thrust their barrels into the room and fired as well. Some of the men continued loosening rocks from the stone wall until a hole had been opened broad enough for a man to squirm through. A Texian propped his rifle by the hole, pulled two pistols from his belt, primed them, then fell to the stone floor and wormed his way into the adjoining dwelling. Rubio heard the discharge of one pistol and the excited calls of soldiers shouting their surrender in Spanish.

"They're giving up," Rubio cried.

Shoving his rifle through the hole, he squeezed his way into the next dwelling. As he stood up he saw the Texian pointing his single loaded pistol at five soldiers with upraised arms. "What do we do with the prisoners?" the man yelled.

Calder stuck his head through the hole in the wall. "See that they have no weapons, then take their shoes and parole them upon their word of honor they won't take up arms against us again."

"The bastards have no honor," the Texian replied.

"We can't spare the men to guard them," Calder answered, glancing at Rubio. "Tell them, Rubio, what I said. If they agree to our terms, they can leave here when the fighting's done."

"What if they don't?"

"Kill them," Calder growled.

Rubio offered the men parole, and to his relief, each accepted. As they took off their shoes, he watched Calder crawl into the room, to be followed by the rest of the men in his contingent.

"Why take their shoes in such cold weather?" Rubio asked.

Calder grumbled, "If we find barefoot men fighting against us later, we know they didn't abide by the parole, so we shoot them. When you've got their shoes, throw them up on the roof where they can't get to them."

Rubio shoved the shoes back into the first dwelling they had taken and told one of the riflemen to toss them onto the house across the street.

One by one the soldiers squirmed into the newly taken dwelling. They stared contemptuously at the Mexican parolees while they reloaded their guns and caught their breath. Then they attacked the next wall, using axes, knives, and hatchets. Some of the Texians busted the captured Mexican rifles and used the barrels as crowbars against the stone and mortar between them and the next enemy den.

The attack proceeded building by building, room by room, until dark. The work was so hard and the fighting so bitter, Rubio was grateful for the darkness. When the fighting subsided, he collapsed in a corner and fell asleep until his turn to stand guard.

Infuriated, Juan Paz stormed past the guard and into General Cos's quarters within the Alamo. The room was lit by two candles, and General Cos sat on his bed, his head in his hands. He looked up and scowled. "Who gave you permission to enter?"

"You're doing nothing for the men of Bexar."

"You fear you won't get paid for your work, don't you, Juan Paz? You care not for these men, just yourself."

"If Bexar falls, so will this fortress. If you do not drive the enemy from Bexar, we are doomed to die."

Cos rose and threw his arms in the air. "My men are hungry, their powder is poor. They lack warm clothes. And where are my reinforcements? What can I do?"

"You can attack the traitors' camp. Destroy the camp, and the enemy cannot stay in Bexar. You can put snipers in the trees along the river. They can kill many of the enemy in town. There is much you can do, but you can't do it from behind these walls."

Cos strode back and forth in front of Paz. "My men are fighting for nothing. Officers must follow them into battle with their swords drawn, not to fight the enemy, but to prod their own men to fight."

"They're fighting for their lives," Paz said. "What are you fighting for?"

Cos looked at him and shrugged. "With winter, more of my men will die from starvation than from the bullets of our enemies."

"If you do not fight, General, even more men will die."

Cos crossed his arms over his sunken chest and turned away. "Our couriers say morale is fine in Bexar. Our cannon still hold the plazas. The rebels cannot take them."

"And you can't take the rebels unless you attack."

Cos turned and gestured toward the door. "Go on before I call the guard to place you under arrest."

Paz stormed out, disgusted with Cos's impotence. *"Viva Mexico,"* he scowled as he exited into the cold.

Paz strode across the grounds to the barracks where he stayed with his muleteers. He crawled into bed and slept fretfully, waking up an hour before dawn and leaving the barracks for the cold outside. He was surprised to find two dozen or more men lining up by the gate. Climbing up a ladder atop the parapet, he watched as the gate opened and the men slipped outside. In the dim moonlight he watched them advance toward the river, then hide among the trees. He grinned. Perhaps his talk with the general had helped after all. He hoped so. He was anxious to return to Bexar and have his way with Angelita Sanchez again.

Just before dawn, Donley Calder shook Rubio Portillo's shoulder. "It is time to fight, Rubio. Today we will take Bexar."

Rubio moaned. "I just got off guard."

"Four hours ago." Calder straightened, his joints stiff with the cold. "I'm getting too old for this."

"I'm too young." Rubio rubbed his hands to warm them.

Calder watched the shadowy figures move about the room as the men woke up and grabbed their weapons. They grumbled that they were cold, hungry, and thirsty. Calder was just as cold, hungry, and thirsty, but he would never let the others know. "Rally, men," he called. "Today Bexar and Texas will be ours. Grab your rifles and fight for your sweethearts, your wives, and your children. Old Ben Milam's led us this far, let's don't let him down."

Calder jumped for the door at the sound of a shot. "The dance is beginning again." He jerked his hatchet from his belt. "I'm tired of hacking through stone walls, men, let's take the next house by the front door. Come with me."

Calder charged out the door and toward the neighboring house. He saw a gun barrel sliding out through a crack in an unlatched shutter. He was so close to the musket, he struck it with his hatchet. The gun discharged into the street. Calder darted to the door and began to pound on it with his hatchet. For a moment he feared none of the men had followed him, then saw a dark profile dart from the house and recognized Rubio.

The door began to give and he heard excited Mexican voices behind it. Just as he shoved it open, Rubio appeared beside him. Both men charged into the house, Calder swinging his ax at the nearest man and jumping as Rubio's gun discharged. Others crowded in behind them. All was confusion, smoke, and the excited shouts of Mexican soldiers.

"No mas! No mas!" they cried.

"Stop firing. They've no will to fight," Calder said. For an instant all was quiet in the room, save for the heaving breath of the Texians and the clink of ramrods against gun barrels as men reloaded.

Rubio told the soldiers the conditions of parole and they quickly accepted, dropping their weapons and cartridge pouches, then removing their shoes.

Calder knew it would be a good day for Texas. He went around the room, patting each soldier on the back and commending him for his valor, and stopped at Rubio's side. "You

256

were the first to follow me."

"But not the last." Before Rubio could say more, a cannon blast thundered down the street, its baritone voice rumbling.

By the sound of the explosion, Calder knew whose cannon it was. "That's Texian powder, not Mexican," he shouted gleefully. He jumped to the door and laughed. Ben Milam was in the street, pointing to where the Texians had set up a cannon behind a low stone wall. They were shooting at the barricade on the corner of the plaza.

Slowly, the cannon drove the Mexicans back, and inch by inch the Texians advanced, Calder abandoning the paroled Mexicans and leading his own men to the final dwelling facing the corner of the plaza. The advance was slow because Mexican snipers still fired from the church tower and a handful still clung to the roofs of the low-slung houses. But by mid-afternoon the Texian cannon and the steady aim of Milam's sharpshooters had driven the soldiers to the far end of the plaza, where they clustered behind barricades, occasionally answering the Texian cannon, though without much effect. In Military Plaza, behind the church, the Mexican flag flew defiantly in the stiff breeze.

Calder had taken up a position in a window, and he alternated with Ben Milam, sniping at any Mexican soldier who raised his head above the far barricades. Across the plaza, Calder saw the fine house of the rich merchant Sanchez; it was the house he had always hoped to provide his daughter. Occasionally, he saw a soldier poke a rifle out the door, and he would fire at the stone facing, hoping the ricochet might hit a soldier.

Milam swatted Calder on the shoulder. "I told you ol' Ben Milam would take Bexar."

Calder grinned as he pulled away from the window. "You're right."

"I can't understand why the troops in the mission haven't tried to reinforce the troops in town."

"Maybe we should step out back and take a look-see," he offered. He led Milam out a back door into a small garden with a chest-high stone fence. Both men bent low, so the stone wall would screen them from the river and the Alamo beyond. Squatting at the base of the wall, Calder grinned at Milam, whose powder-stained face streaked with the tracks of dried sweat. "You're a damn poor sight, Ben, but damn, don't you like to fight."

"When the cause is right, I do. And the cause is always right when I'm fighting for it."

Calder grinned at his friend's remarks.

"I'm thinking we can end it soon, at least in Bexar," Milam rose slowly and looked over the stone fence. "I don't know about taking the mission. There's nothing to be gained by them staying there. Only a fool of a commander would hold onto the —"

Calder heard a thud that left Milam's sentence incomplete, then heard the retort of the rifle. Calder stood up and saw Milam slide down the wall, staining it with blood. He glanced toward the river and saw a puff of smoke floating beside a tree.

"Ben! Ben!" Calder screamed, falling on his knees beside his friend. He flinched when he saw the neat hole in Milam's forehead.

Several men bolted from the house, their guns at the ready.

Calder released Milam and stood up, swinging his rifle toward the suspicious tree. He thought he could make out the form of a sniper. He took quick but certain aim and fired. He heard a cry, but the man did not fall.

"In the trees, boys, in the trees! Snipers, shoot them all!"

As his men took their first shots, Calder frantically reloaded, glancing at Milam's body at his feet. He felt tears running down his cheeks. "Bastards," he yelled as he threw his rifle to his shoulder and aimed again at the form in the tree. He fired, and knew by the thud that he'd hit his target. A rifle fell to the ground and the sniper tumbled down as well. "Bastard!"

Around him a chorus of gunshots rang out and a half-dozen soldiers jumped from the trees and raced back toward the mission.

Calder dropped to his knees and cradled Ben's bloody head in his hands. He felt himself crying like a hungry newborn.

"Wake up, Ben! Wake up, Ben!"

Rubio squatted beside Calder and patted him

on the shoulder. "He's dead, Donley."

Calder looked up, seeming to stare through Rubio and the stone wall behind him. Rubio had never seen such a crazed look in any man's eyes. His eyes were caldrons seething with hate.

"We've got to bury him." He dropped Milam's head, scrambled on his hands and knees to the patch of garden where the soil was soft and began to dig like a dog in the dirt. Soon, other men were beside him, digging with their hands, their knives, and their hatchets, carving out what would be the last resting place of Ben Milam.

When the hole was the depth of his arm, Calder pushed himself away from the grave and grabbed Milam's limp arms. He dragged his friend into the hole, mumbling incoherently. Two men helped cover Milam, but the rest just stared.

No sooner was the dirt mounded over the grave than Calder grabbed his rifle and started reloading. A soldier offered him Milam's rifle, and he said, "Give it to Rubio, then ready your weapons, men."

Rubio took Milam's long rifle and looked at Calder.

"It belonged to one good man," Calder said, "now it belongs to another." He barely paused after reloading. "Follow me." Calder retreated through the house and out onto the street. "Who'll avenge Ben Milam's death with me?" he screamed.

Rubio heard his own shout and the shouts of the men around him, as if they had caught Calder's madness. They raced toward the plaza, several men coming out of adjacent houses or jumping up from behind fences to join the headlong charge. Suddenly, the plaza became a swirling vortex of screaming men, angry lead, and exploding powder. Rubio glimpsed Calder leading the stampede across the plaza, ten paces ahead of his nearest ally, and he saw fear in the faces of Mexican soldiers loading a cannon not thirty paces ahead of Calder. They threw up their arms and ran without firing, retreating behind the church, pouring onto Military Plaza.

The men cheered their demon leader as Rubio saw a gun barrel slide out of the door at Angelita's house, aimed at Calder. Quickly, he shouldered Milam's rifle and fired. His bullet splintered the edge of the door and the gun barrel jerked back inside.

Hearing the screams of women, hoping Angelita and her mother had not been hurt, he dashed toward the Sanchez house. He was desperate to keep any Texian from beating him and perhaps killing Angelita or her family, but no one followed him.

Rubio burst in the door and found six soldiers holding their hands in the air. He took their weapons and their shoes, then spotted Angelita cowering in the corner with her parents. In his disheveled state, and perhaps in her own poor condition, she did not recognize him, and he did not linger once he'd disarmed the soldiers. He told them to go out the back to avoid being shot.

261

When they left, he took the guns he'd collected and beat them against the floor until they shattered.

Rubio moved back onto the plaza to rejoin the Texians. Darkness was settling in. It was clear there would be no victory today. Mexican soldiers still held the Military Plaza, but victory was certain the next day, he told himself.

Rubio slept outside the church, anxious to finish the battle and return to Mary Calder and Tomas. Come morning, he awoke early and awaited word to renew the attack, but what he saw surprised and angered him. He had caught Calder's madness and was ready to kill more, but over the Military Plaza flew a white flag of surrender.

17

Mary Calder was startled from her sleep by the shouts of men. Fearing Mexican soldiers had attacked the camp, she flung back the covers and scurried to Tomas Portillo, ready to help him escape. The cold wind snapped at Mary with icy fangs. She shivered, partly from the cold and partly from fear. What she saw confused her even more. Men were jumping about and some were even dancing with each other. "What is it? What's wrong?"

A celebrating Texian leaped beside her. "Bexar has surrendered." The soldier aimed his index finger like a pistol toward the tower of the San Fernando Church. "A white flag flies from Military Plaza. It means the enemy has surrendered the town."

"Then I must find Tomas shelter in town."

"You cannot do that," the Texian told her. "You could be hurt."

Mary stopped beside the white ash of her last fire and pointed to Tomas. "He may die without shelter. Any man who tries to stop me will wish he was still fighting the Mexicans."

The Texian backed away.

Mary bent over Tomas and placed her hand against his forehead. He shivered at her touch. "I must hurry." She quickly gathered her modest belongings. Then she went to the remuda, where men guarded the horses. She picked out her father's and Rubio's mounts and moved to saddle them, but a guard stopped her until a sympathetic officer gave his permission, then saddled them for her.

Her hands were stiff with cold as she took the reins. She knew Tomas was too sick to stay in a saddle for even the short trip into Bexar. "Has anyone a cart?"

"Check behind the commander's tent," the guard told her.

She thanked him and led the horses toward Edward Burleson's canvas headquarters. Burleson was outside, wrapped in a coat, gesturing to three mounted men. The men nodded, then galloped past a Mexican cart beyond the tent. Mary felt Burleson's hard gaze upon her.

"Where are you going with those horses?"

"To Bexar."

"You have the brave heart of your father. My couriers say he turned the battle for Texas after Ben Milam was killed."

"Then he is alive, yet?"

Burleson nodded.

"And Rubio Portillo, do you know of his fate?"

"I do not, but only a handful of Texians have died."

She prayed Rubio was not among them.

"I will have men help you. Then you can go to Bexar."

"I am grateful,"

"And we are grateful to your father."

Angelita hated the soldiers for surrendering Bexar almost as much as she despised Juan Paz, not only for humiliating her, but also for abandoning her when the Texians attacked. Paz had run at the first sound of battle and left her and her parents trapped. She had feared the Texians would kill her, but when they captured her home, they abandoned it without touching her. She'd been too scared even to look at the Texian intruders, but one of them had sounded like Rubio.

She hoped Rubio was safe and that she could find him. With time, she believed she could win him back, but he must never learn of what Juan Paz had done to her. Angelita did not know if the Texians could run Bexar. Living on the rancho with Rubio might be preferable to living in a town with so many Anglos. And surely the Anglos would come, like locusts, unless the Mexican Army returned to drive them away.

The room was cold, and Angelita looked in the corner where her parents huddled under blankets. Hunger had dulled their eyes. She wondered when it would be safe to gather wood for warmth and for cooking. Stepping to the shattered door, she looked out across the plaza. Where Mexican soldiers had been posted the day before, Texians stood or squatted around the same fires. She hoped to spot Rubio and ask for help. He would not refuse her. How could he? She had loved him once and could love him again, if he would let her.

Then she spotted him, running across the plaza ahead of a man in a lionskin cap. Angelita stepped outside and lifted her hand to wave. "Ruu-bee . . ." she started to cry, but his name died on her lips. She saw a smile on his face and cursed softly as she watched him dash toward a rider leading a horse and cart.

The rider was a woman.

The woman dismounted as Rubio reached her.

Angelita bit her lip when Rubio threw his arms around her. She stared for a moment, then retreated into the house so she would not have to watch. It would be tough to win back Rubio, she feared.

Like all the Texians, Rubio Portillo awaited word on the terms of surrender. He stood by one of the fires, stomping his feet and rubbing his hands for warmth. Donley Calder squatted beside the fire, his face still grim from the loss of Ben Milam. The soldiers said little, just watched the fire and waited for news, all hoping they wouldn't have to fight the troops in the Alamo.

"Hey, Calder, ain't that your girl a-coming?" one asked.

Rubio spun around and saw Mary Calder atop her father's mount.

266

"Yep," Calder answered, rising stiffly from beside the fire.

Rubio bolted toward Mary. He was anxious to see her and learn of Tomas's health. When he realized his own horse pulled a cart, he feared its load might be his brother's body.

Mary waved and jumped from her horse. As he neared, he saw her face was long and drawn, her eyes tired, but still she was prettier than ever. He threw his arms around her and hugged her tightly.

"I am glad you're well," Mary cried, "but I cannot say the same for your brother. He is sick. He needs shelter, warmth, and food."

Rubio released her and rushed to his brother. "Tomas, Tomas," he cried, "everything will be okay." He pulled back the blanket and ran his fingers along Tomas's hot cheek. "The soldiers have been defeated. They'll never hold you in prison again. Don't give up."

Tomas's eyelids cracked open. He nodded weakly and struggled to shove his hand out of the blanket. He patted Rubio's fingers, but the meager effort sapped his energy and he closed his eyes.

Rubio felt Mary's hand upon his shoulder. "We must get him shelter and warmth."

"My rancho is too far, and Colonel Ugartechea roams somewhere. We must find a place here."

"Quickly," Mary said.

Rubio turned toward Angelita's home. He would not ask for a night under her roof for himself, but he would beg her to allow Tomas to stay in her home. He pointed at the house. "Bring Tomas. I can arrange shelter." Without awaiting an answer, he dashed across the plaza to Angelita's house and pounded on the door. "Angelita, Angelita?" he cried. "It is Rubio. I must ask a favor of you."

The door opened slowly, revealing the woman he had once planned to marry. Theirs was a marriage many had awaited, a marriage that now would never be. As she stood before him, he could not remember seeing her so awkward and ashamed. "Tomas is sick. He needs shelter. Can he stay here awhile?"

Angelita seemed not to hear his question. "In less than three weeks we would have been married, Rubio, man and wife."

"About Tomas?"

"We can still make it work, the marriage."

"Can Tomas stay?"

Angelita just stared, but her mother stepped to the doorway.

"*Si,* Tomas can stay. You too, Rubio. We have missed you. You are a good man and would make a fine son-in-law, unlike Juan Paz."

"*Gracias, senora.* I do not need room, but my friend Mary Calder has cared for Tomas. Might she stay with him as well?"

"*Si,* most certainly, Rubio," the woman replied.

"*Gracias, gracias, senora.* And I shall chop wood for your fire and hunt food for Tomas and all of you." He glanced at Angelita and realized she was staring beyond him.

He turned and saw Mary approaching with the cart. Abandoning the door, he stepped to the cart. Together with Donley Calder, he lifted his brother and carried him to the door. Angelita seemed rooted in the doorway, staring malevolently at Mary, until her mother pulled her away. The old woman led Rubio and Calder to the bed she shared with her husband.

"No, no," Rubio said, "he cannot sleep in your bed."

"We are honored to have decent men in our house, unlike Juan Paz."

Rubio and Calder lowered Tomas onto the bed. Rubio turned to the woman. "And where is Juan Paz?" Rubio asked.

The old woman bit her lip for a moment and trembled. "Once he was done with Angelita the night your army entered town, he ran like a coward to the old mission. We have not seen him since. But we do not have to see him again to know he is evil."

Mary entered the room and Rubio reached for her hand, pulling her gently between the senora and himself. "This is Mary Calder and her father, Donley. Mary will tend Tomas so he is not a burden to you."

Angelita scowled. "She'll be another mouth to feed."

"Angelita, no," her mother scolded. "Mary is welcome."

"Please," Rubio said to Angelita, "do not let

your anger at me make you think less of Mary or my brother."

Angelita stormed out of the room.

Calder whistled, then looked around the room. "Mary, I always promised you you'd live in this house one day."

Mary seemed embarrassed by his comment. "I'm just a guest, Papa. It is not my home."

"Not now, but one day," he replied.

Rubio Portillo started unloading the cart of firewood and carrying it into Angelita's house. The noonday air was cold, but the house was warm, and Rubio soaked up the warmth with each trip. He would cut every tree in Texas to keep the house warm so his brother could recover. He placed an armload of firewood on the floor beside the corner fireplace and lingered for a moment, enjoying the warmth before heading back outside. As he reached the cart, he saw Donley Calder angling for him.

Calder nodded as he reached Rubio. "So many men've left, I don't know that we've got enough to hold out should the Mexicans decide they don't want to leave after all."

"You think that's possible?"

Calder nodded toward the patch of ground where he'd buried Ben Milam, then he lifted his hand in front of Rubio's face and held his forefinger but a hair from his thumb. "That's how close we came to giving up and returning to our farms. Burleson and the others were set to abandon Bexar until the spring. Everyone but Ben Milam was."

Rubio saw Calder's eyes moisten.

"If it hadn't been for ol' Ben Milam, us Texians would've given up. Come spring, the Mexicans would've marched on us and stomped us like bugs. But ol' Ben Milam made us stand toe-to-toe with them. Without him, we'd been in sad shape."

"You think the Mexicans will return in the spring?"

The frontiersman pondered the question. He glanced toward Military Plaza, where the white flag of surrender hung limply from the flagpole. "They'll be back, these same soldiers and more. They're cold and hungry, but come spring, when they don't need warm clothes and their bellies are full, they'll be back, maybe even with Santa Anna himself in the lead. They'll be of fighting mettle then, and there'll be more of them than us."

"How will we beat them back again?"

"We won't stand a chance unless another leader rises to the top," Calder replied, "a man who can keep this stubborn band of men together and fighting against the Mexicans instead of among themselves. But we'll have the winter to prepare ourselves. Maybe that man will emerge. It ain't Ed Burleson."

Rubio shrugged. "I'll just feel better when the Mexicans leave. Have you heard the terms of surrender? When will they be going?"

"The soldiers and officers will receive paroles.

They will have to leave within six days. They will be given one cannon to protect them from Indians. Each man will keep one firearm, ten rounds, and adequate powder. We'll keep all other weapons and supplies. This afternoon, all armed Mexicans in Bexar are to march to the mission and stay there until they and the soldiers in the Alamo start back for Mexico. All armed Texians are to remain in Bexar until their departure."

Rubio remembered Calder's threat of taking over the Sanchez dwelling. "What about property?"

Calder shook his head. "All private property is to be returned to its rightful owners."

"So you won't claim Angelita's house for Mary?"

"Not yet, but maybe before I pass on."

"You're too tough to die, Donley."

"So was Ben Milam, but that's enough about the past. Some of the fellows are talking about a fandango tonight to celebrate the surrender. It might be you could take Mary. She would like that."

Rubio cocked his head and eyed Calder suspiciously. "You're the one that didn't want her seeing a Mexican, weren't you?"

Calder nodded.

"My blood's still the same."

"Yeah, but my mind's not. You're good stock unlike most of your kind, and you would do Mary proud."

Rubio stood taller.

Calder pointed at the cart still filled with wood. "We've flapped our jaws long enough. We need to get this wood inside, return the cart to Burleson, and get ready for the fandango."

The Texians piled firewood in the center of the plaza and lit the huge bonfire when darkness began to seep across the sky. The flames licked at the logs, then began to climb toward the wooden pinnacle. The fire roared and devoured the wood, casting flickering light and deformed shadows across the plaza. A couple Texians with fiddles, another with a banjo, and one with a harmonica were joined by an old Mexican man with a mandolin and started playing music. The jaunty strains of the melody drifted across the plaza and lured more men to the fire. Many of them alternated slugs of whiskey from jugs and bottles they passed around, and some danced with each other to the music.

Mary Calder stood outside the Sanchez dwelling, waiting for Rubio. She smiled when she saw him approaching after returning the cart to Burleson. When Rubio joined her, he put his hand around her waist and she snuggled to him. "Tomas ate some supper. I believe he will be fine, it will just take some time," she assured him.

"You have done plenty for Tomas. Now I hope you can enjoy the fandango." He nodded and pointed toward the bonfire. "The men are many and the women few. . . ."

"More senorita's will come as they see the fun."

"Even then, many men will want to dance with you."

"I will dance only with you, though I have never danced before."

"Then I shall teach you what I know."

As they neared the fire Mary could feel its heat reaching out with invisible arms. As a jaunty jig began, Rubio explained how to dance to it. As the night lengthened, they danced together many times, laughing and giggling at her frequent missteps. Finally, after midnight, Rubio tired.

"It is time to rest, Mary," Rubio said. "I must take guard duty until the Mexicans leave."

"And I should check on Tomas."

Rubio put his arm around her shoulder.

As they stepped away from the ring of warmth, Mary shivered, then thrilled as Rubio pulled her closer to him. He held her tightly until they reached the door of the home. Then he turned her around and kissed her on the lips. She was suddenly warmer than she had been moments before around the fire.

Her pleasure was broken, though, by Angelita's approach. The young woman bumped into them, then growled a low word of Spanish as she stepped inside the house and slammed the door behind her.

Rubio responded by kissing Mary harder on the lips. *"Gracias,* Mary, for all you've done. I should like to stay, but I must do a soldier's work since so many of our men have gone home." He released her. *"Adios,"* he called softly.

Mary stood watching him until he disappeared into the darkness, then she went inside the house and straight to Tomas's bed. As she looked at him in the yellow glow of a single candle, she placed her hand upon his forehead. By the cool touch, she knew the fever had finally broken. Tomas stirred gently at her touch, and she bent to tuck the covers tighter around him. As she did, she heard someone entering the room. She turned to see Angelita, her eyes brimming with hate.

"*Puta,*" Angelita spat.

Mary straightened. "You have no reason to call me a whore. What have I done to you?"

"You have taken my man."

"Rubio?"

Angelita nodded. "We were to be married this month until you came between us."

Mary bit her lip and felt her eyes water. Rubio had said nothing of this. Had he deceived her?

"*Puta,*" Angelita repeated. then spun around.

Mary saw her stop in her tracks, and watched Angelita's mother slap her on the cheek.

"You do not speak to a guest that way. You left Rubio for the evil Juan Paz."

Angelita stormed past her mother, crying angry tears.

The senora took a step into the room. "You are welcome here as long as you like to stay. I am ashamed of my daughter and express my sorrow to you now."

Mary nodded. "*Gracias.*" As she watched the old woman shuffle from the room, Mary's own tears slid down her cheek.

"She is an evil woman, Angelita is," came a raspy voice.

Angelita turned and saw Tomas looking up at her. She bent and kissed him on the forehead. "You are better."

He smiled.

The Mexican soldiers lined up outside the Alamo. Few had coats, many lacked shoes. Their uniforms were tattered if they even matched at all. They were a ragged army, though General Cos rode before them in a glittering uniform, like a strutting peacock.

Rubio Portillo stood among the Texians watching the ragged troops who had been their enemy form up for their final retreat. The weather had been cold, but the brunt of winter had not yet struck. Rubio wondered if the pitiful soldiers would make it back to Mexico.

Rubio watched a rider emerge from the Alamo and ride straight for General Cos. Though he wasn't in uniform, the rider seemed to be an important person among the troops. Rubio's lips tightened as he realized it was Juan Paz.

How different the events of the last four months might have been had not Juan Paz stepped between him and Angelita. Even so, Rubio wondered whether he ever really cared for Angelita, especially since he had met Mary Calder. She seemed a much finer a woman than Angelita. Rubio knew that Angelita would never have tended Tomas as well as Mary had, that he owed his brother's life to Mary.

Rubio stood silently as the troops took the first step on the road to Mexico. Come spring, when Tomas was better and he'd gotten the ranch back in shape, he would ask Mary Calder to marry him. He knew Mary would not be too proud to live on the ranch.

He longed for the arrival of spring.

18

The winter winds howled through the rancho compound. In the two months since the fall of Bexar, Rubio Portillo had done what work he could, but his cattle had virtually disappeared. Only a handful remained of the hundreds that had roamed his ranch. He wondered if the Mexican soldiers — or the ghostly bull — had led the animals away. With so few cattle to attend, he had time for periodic trips to Bexar to check on Tomas. On the last trip, Tomas had seemed strong enough to return, but Rubio insisted that he stay another week and rest further.

And too, with Tomas in Bexar, Rubio had an excuse to visit him — and Mary — frequently. Mary was a good woman, Rubio thought, and one who would make a good wife, one who would stand beside a man and make his life and his soul better. When the weather warmed and the countryside was blanketed with spring flowers, he would ask her to marry him. He knew he had Donley Calder's blessing. That pleased him.

Rubio planned to take Mary away from Bexar in early spring so she would be out of danger if the Mexican Army returned. Some among the

Texians believed the war had been won, though Sam Houston maintained an army to the east, around San Felipe. Others thought the Mexicans would return with Santa Anna himself in the lead. Whatever happened, Rubio wanted to keep the ones he loved away from the fray.

Came the day when he decided he must finally pull Tomas away from Bexar, Rubio saddled up his horse and two others, then started for Bexar. Except for a few old cows and steers too lame to stray from water, he saw no sign of his once vast herd. He nudged his horse into a lope and continued to town, nearing Bexar shortly after noon. Outside town, he ran into several Mexican families leaving Bexar, their belongings stacked high in ox-drawn carts.

"What's wrong?" Rubio asked one young man with a wife and three small children. "Have the Texians treated you so unfairly that you must give up your home in such cold weather?"

"It is better to lose your home than your family's lives."

"Are the Texians threatening you?"

"No, no," the man answered, without slowing the cart. "Santa Anna is coming."

"He will not return until spring."

The man looked over his shoulder. "Believe what you will."

Rubio rattled the reins and set his horse to a lope. Surely Santa Anna would not march upon Bexar in the cold. He recalled the ragged and coatless troops who had left Bexar in December and did not believe Santa Anna could have found replacements or reequipped those soldiers in so short a time.

Reaching the plaza, he saw Texians talking and gesturing wildly. They seemed to be confused. He glanced up at the tower of the San Fernando Church and saw several soldiers scanning the horizon. Rubio cut across the plaza to Angelita's house and dismounted, tying the horses and knocking on the door.

He was disappointed when Angelita answered. "Have you come to take these leeches from my home?"

Rubio studied her a moment. Her cheeks and waist seemed fuller than he remembered. "*Buenas dias,* Angelita."

She spat at him. "Your brother has slept with your new woman many times while you were gone, Rubio."

Until then, Rubio had never realized the blackness of Angelita's soul. Tomas had been right. He knew now he must take Tomas and Mary away from the house of so vindictive a woman.

Angelita stormed away. "It is Rubio," she called with disdain.

Almost instantly, Mary came into the front room, patting her hair with her hand and smiling. Rubio held out his arms and she ran into them. She tugged him into the house and pushed the door shut.

In the corner Rubio saw Donley adding wood to the fireplace. Calder looked up and grinned.

"You bring me any firewood?"

Before he could answer, he felt a strong slap on the back. Pulling himself from Mary's grasp, he spun around and looked fully upon Tomas. His brother had never looked better. His color was back and the hollowness of his cheeks had been filled by good and plentiful food.

"You are well, Tomas?"

"Mary has taken good care of me, and she makes fine tortillas. You are right to be fond of her."

Rubio nodded.

"But I am ready to leave here," Tomas said. "Mary and Donley have been fine, as have the senor and senora, but Angelita has been mean to us all, as she would have been to you had you married her."

Rubio looked to Mary, embarrassed that she should hear that.

She smiled. "Tomas has told me everything, and I have seen for myself that he is right."

"I have come to invite you to join me at the rancho," Rubio said. "Some say Santa Anna is marching upon Bexar."

Calder laughed. "They're just trying to scare us Texians away, nothing more."

"But it is the Mexicans who are leaving town."

Calder shook his head again. "Just rumors. We whipped them once, we can whip them again, if us Texians find us another leader with the fire of Ben Milam."

"I want in the fight this time," Tomas said. "I

281

owe the Mexican government for a few months in prison."

"Who's in charge of the Texians here, Donley?" Rubio asked.

The frontiersman shrugged. "Hard to say. William Travis may be, or Jim Bowie. Travis is a strutting cock better at giving speeches than giving orders. Bowie's been ailing and been drinking some. Old Davy Crockett even arrived a few days ago, so I've been told. You ever heard of him?"

Rubio shook his head.

"He's been a frontiersman, a bear hunter, and a congressman, though you shouldn't hold that against him. He can tell bigger stories than any man alive and can fight with the best of them. I hear Sam Houston's ordered them to destroy the Alamo and to join his army, but Travis is ignoring him."

"Gather your belongings, all of you, and we'll leave Bexar for them to fight over."

Tomas laughed. "I'm ready. I didn't carry much out of prison."

Rubio nodded. "I must see the *senor* and *senora* to thank them for their hospitality and your health." Rubio stepped into the adjoining room, where the elderly couple stood with their heads drooping.

"*Gracias,*" Rubio said, "for letting my brother recover in your home and giving shelter to the Calders."

They could not hide the shame in their eyes. "Angelita has not been kind to your people. We regret that deeply."

Rubio hugged the old woman. "Much has happened to Angelita."

"And much that you do not know about, nor anyone else."

Releasing the old woman, Rubio stepped to Angelita's father, grasped and shook his feeble hand. "Good luck to you. Maybe the difficulties are over and Angelita will forget what was to be."

The old man smiled weakly and patted Rubio's hand. "You are a good man."

"Gracias." Rubio nodded, then turned away. Just as he reached the front room, he heard the church bells peal.

"What's that?" Tomas asked.

Calder grabbed his gun and burst out the door onto the plaza. Rubio and Tomas ran after him.

"Mexicans! Mexicans!" the lookout cried, pointing to the west. "It's the whole Mexican Army. Cavalry's circling the town."

Calder shook his head at Rubio. "Reckon I was wrong, dammit."

All around the plaza soldiers gesticulated wildly. The rumors had been true and panic had set in like a cold winter wind.

Calder cried to Rubio, "I must get my horse." He dashed away.

Mary ran out of the house, carrying bedrolls and an armful of her possessions.

"Is this all?" Rubio asked.

"No, there is one more load." She shoved the

possessions into Rubio's arms and raced back inside the house.

Tomas took the bedrolls and both men stepped to the horses and began to tie things down. Mary returned with a final load, and Rubio secured the remainder to the horses. Then Rubio helped Mary onto the horse he had brought for her.

As Tomas was mounting, Donley Calder returned on his horse. "All the Texians are being ordered to the Alamo."

"Can't we make a run for the rancho?"

Calder growled. "No! We're surrounded. Our commanders didn't send out cavalry patrols. They were as dumb as me, thinking the Mexicans wouldn't return til spring."

Across the plaza men grabbed supplies, weapons, and horses and started toward the Alamo. From the west Rubio could hear the low sound of the army's drums. He jerked himself atop his horse and turned the animal about. As the horse circled, he saw Angelita standing in the doorway. She spat at the hooves of his horse. Rubio ignored her.

"If we leave town, they'll just send their lancers after us," Calder said. "We have no choice but to retreat to the Alamo."

Juan Paz smirked as he rode up on the rise and saw Bexar before him. The Anglos were scurrying like rats from town to the Alamo. He had left with a humiliated army and was returning with Antonio de Lopez de Santa Anna, his excellency the president of Mexico. Paz was not returning a rich man, for he had yet to be paid for his services to General Cos. But he would be paid even more for carrying supplies for Santa Anna's army of some six thousand strong.

When the rebellion was crushed, Paz mused, he would be the wealthiest man in Bexar and would receive appointments to governmental posts from Santa Anna. Though he found the general a vain and self-important man, he could put aside those feelings because his acquaintance with his excellency would make him a monied and important man in Texas.

The general rode beside him on a white horse as they topped the rise. Santa Anna reined his stallion and gazed toward Bexar. "Now tell me, Juan Paz, you have spoken of the most beautiful woman in Bexar and that you can bring her to my bed."

"Her name is Angelita and you will find her most pleasing."

"I shall look forward to spreading her loins, but I should like her saved for tomorrow. I shall want to attend to the siege today. I will kill all the traitors who stand before me."

"You will be remembered as a great leader of Mexico."

"After victory here I shall hunt down the remainder of the rebel army and destroy it. Anglos will never again hear my name without thinking of the spilled blood of their sons, husbands, and fathers."

Paz smiled. The Anglos could not stop Santa Anna.

It didn't matter how many Texians there were, Donley Calder knew there were too few to defend the mission and its walls. Contrary to orders by Sam Houston to destroy the mission, William Travis had actually fortified it. But with less than two hundred men to defend its expansive walls, the Alamo was doomed to fall and those within it to die. Calder did count seven women in addition to Mary, and five children. He saw Travis dispatch one rider out the gate, and word went among the men that Travis had sent the man to Goliad to seek reinforcements.

Calder cursed himself for getting caught in this trap. Yes, he had doubted the Mexican Army would return before spring, but he had also enjoyed staying in the house on the plaza. It was warm and the beds were soft, and he'd always promised Mary she would one day live in such a house. That promise might wind up killing them both. He did not care that he might die, for he had lived many years and seen many things. But Mary was still young and had a future before her, especially if she married Rubio. Now, though, even that was in doubt, because even if she survived — surely the Mexican Army wouldn't kill the women and children — Rubio would likely not.

He walked to the west wall and climbed a crude ladder onto the roof of a low-slung barracks. He slipped across the roof to the wall and watched a river of soldiers pour into Bexar. From afar their uniforms looked perfect and their weapons deadly, but Calder knew up close they would be ragged, their powder would be bad, and their commanders would have to prod them into battle. They were not the best fighting men Calder had ever faced, but they weren't cowards either, they had pompous officers. Then he heard Travis issuing commands and shook his head. Some things were the same for all armies.

The enemy troops lined up facing the Alamo, then the artillerymen wheeled ten pieces of light artillery in front of the soldiers. The light artillery could do little damage unless they moved within range of Texian rifles. If they did, those rifles would exact a heavy toll upon the cannoneers. Ultimately, the Mexicans didn't need cannons, just time to starve the Texians out.

Travis stepped to the wall and looked at Calder, then at the enemy. Calder looked at the dozen men on the roof with him.

One of them pointed toward the tower of San Fernando Church. "Look, a red flag has been raised. What's it mean?"

"No quarter," Calder answered matter-of-factly. "We will all be killed."

Travis stepped over to Calder and grabbed his arm.

Calder jerked his arm free and turned to stare at him.

"Soldier," Travis said, "we will have no talk

like that. You must have backbone. When Texians hear of our peril, they will rush to our aid. We will triumph like we did on the streets of Bexar."

Calder shook his head. "I fought in the streets of Bexar. Did you?"

Ignoring the question, Travis drew his sword and waved it at the Mexicans. "This is the most important ground in Texas because we are here. We will win this battle and this war."

Calder scoffed. "This is a mission, not a fortress. We're on an open plain defending nothing except our lives. We're useless to all of Texas beyond the reach of our guns, and then only as long as we have powder, lead, and food."

"You are not the commander, sir."

"And I am not a fool either." Calder saw anger flare in Travis's eyes.

"Colonel," one of his adjutants said, pointing toward Bexar. "The enemy is sending a soldier under the flag of truce."

Travis turned from Calder and looked toward town. "Send a soldier to see what he wants, a soldier who can speak Spanish."

The command was relayed from the roof to the grounds below. Men yelled to open the gate, and a single rider started toward the single Mexican officer. Calder watched and realized the Texian courier was Rubio Portillo. The horsemen met midway between the two armies. The Mexican officer handed Rubio a sheet of paper, saluted, then turned around for Bexar. Rubio returned at a gallop, barely slowing as he rode through the gate and then across the plaza toward the barracks where Travis awaited. Rubio jerked the reins, halted his mount, jumped from the saddle and scooted up the ladder to offer the message to Travis.

"Is it Spanish?"

Rubio nodded.

"Then read it."

Taking a deep breath, Rubio translated the letter. "The Mexican Army cannot come to terms under any conditions with rebellious foreigners. They have no other recourse left, if they wish to save their lives, than to place themselves immediately at the disposal of the Supreme Government from whom alone they may expect clemency after some considerations are taken up."

Travis shoved his sword back in its scabbard. "The Mexican Army shall have its answer." He spun around from the wall and strutted across the roof to the ladder. Standing with his hands on his hips, he addressed the men below. "Gentlemen," he cried, "we have been offered the opportunity to surrender to the Mexican Army and place our lives in the hands of our enemies. It is a course of dishonor I choose not to follow. Are you men with me?"

A cheer arose from the men.

Travis answered their hurrahs. "Could I spit fire, I would answer this with my own mouth, but since they would never hear me, I will answer with a mouth they cannot help but hear. Gentle-men, fire the eighteen-pounder toward the en-emy."

The men cheered, waving their hats and guns over their heads. When their shouts died away, the cannon barked the colonel's reply.

As the reverberation died away, Travis drew his sword. "Gentlemen, we will hold this ground until reinforcements arrive."

Calder was amused by the little bantam's per-formance. He knew it would take more than the-atrics to whip the Mexican Army. As he watched the enemy deploy, he estimated between three and four thousand troops were arrayed before them. Even at the lower estimate, the Alamo was outnumbered at least ten to one.

He turned to Rubio. "The enemy are too many, we are too few, and the wall is too long." With his index finger he followed the perimeter of the fort. "It's a quarter of a mile or better around the walls. We do not have the men to man that much wall."

"What about Mary?"

"She will not leave without me. Now you, Ru-bio, you could escape. You are Mexican."

"No, I'm Texican. You said so yourself."

Calder put his hand on Rubio's shoulder. "I knew you wouldn't run."

"My father never ran from what was right, and neither will I."

Calder nodded, then retreated back down the ladder, Rubio coming down after him. They fetched their rifles and powder as Tomas approached, holding a long rifle, a powder horn, and a bullet pouch.

"Where'd you get the rifle?" Rubio asked.

"I traded my horse for it. I doubt I'll be going anywhere for a few days, and I wanted to repay the soldiers for my time in prison."

"Then come on, boys, let's climb up on the roof and start the killing," Calder said.

One at a time they started back up the ladder. They knelt behind the high walls and rested their rifles on the top. Calder adjusted the lionskin cap on his head and loaded his rifle. Tomas lifted his rifle to fire, but Calder tapped his arm. "Don't shoot yet. Let them fire the first shot, maybe get a little closer than is safe, then we can knock off several of them before they can retreat. That's the way we whipped the British at New Orleans."

It took five minutes before the cannoneers had positioned their guns and readied them to fire. Then puffs of smoke shot from the ten cannons one right after the other. The explosions and balls followed.

"Now you can kiss them with some lead of your own." Calder fired at an artilleryman on the cannon farthest north. He fell. "I got mine," he said.

"I missed," Rubio said.

"Me too," Tomas said.

"Pick them off from each end. If you shoot a man in the middle of the battery, you scare his friends on both sides. If you work from the ends to the middle it takes them longer to realize how many fellows are getting popped."

After a few shots a couple more men climbed atop the barracks. One of them, a lanky fellow in buckskins, squatted beside Calder. "Mind if we join you?"

"Suit yourself," Calder said, "there's enough targets to go around."

The fellow loaded his rifle calmly. When he was done, he took aim and knocked down a cannoneer on the south end of the line. Calder nodded his compliments. "Good shooting."

The stranger returned the compliment when Calder winged another cannoneer. The artillerymen had had enough and started pulling their cannon back.

The man beside Calder howled with glee. "A victory for us Tennesseans."

"I'm from Kentucky," Calder noted as he looked at the man. He had leathery skin and lively eyes and he wore a coonskin hat.

The lanky fellow offered Calder his hand. "I'm Davy Crockett."

Calder grinned. "I've heard the name."

"I hope it's good what you've heard."

"It is, though I heard you strayed a bit and got into politics for a while."

Crockett nodded. "It's a venture that's no good for the reputation or the soul." Then he grinned. "I like your cap."

"I killed him with my knife."

The Tennessean seemed impressed. "Remind

me never to leave my hat alone in a room with yours."

Both men laughed.

As Santa Anna ordered the raising of the red flag and the deployment of his soldiers around the Alamo, Juan Paz left the general and rode to the Main Plaza. He angled for Angelita's house, dismounted and tied his horse. He planned on having Angelita once more before he loaned her to Santa Anna. Paz stepped to the door and flung it open. He startled Angelita's parents, who sat on a bench by the fireplace. They rose feebly, terror in their eyes.

"No, no," the old man cried. "You animal, you evil man."

Paz grinned and stepped up to the old man, who swung at him with his feeble fists, the blows falling harmlessly upon Paz's chest. Paz laughed, then slapped the man savagely.

His wife screamed as her husband tumbled to the floor.

Angelita ran from the adjacent room. "What's . . . ?" The question died on her lips. "Juan Paz," she said.

Paz felt the hatred in her voice.

"You have returned? Why?"

"To claim my fortune. When this is done, I will be the richest man in Bexar and a power in all of Texas."

"Leave. I want nothing to do with you."

Paz grabbed her jaw between his thumb and

fingers. "You will do what I say," he whispered, "or I will kill your parents."

The defiance melted from her eyes.

He shoved her toward her room. "You know what I want."

She sobbed.

Paz turned to her parents. "Interfere with me and I will kill her."

He stepped in behind her, not even closing the door. He ripped her blouse from her, then shoved her down upon the ground and lifted her skirt.

"You have turned fat," he scowled as he prepared to take her.

"I am with child."

Bending down over her, he slapped her.

"Whose bastard is it?"

"Yours, Juan Paz."

"Such a pity. I had promised his excellency the president the prettiest woman in San Antonio for his bed, and now you look like a pig. He will think me a liar. I must make amends. I will offer him you and your house for his quarters."

Paz laughed, then raped Angelita.

19

The morning broke cold and clear, with a blood-red sun casting long shadows behind the Alamo walls. With early light Rubio Portillo rose and walked to the edge of the roof overlooking the old mission compound. He stood above a rectangular plaza, which covered three acres. Barracks lined the west wall beneath him, and ran a parallel wall opposite him about two-thirds the length of the west wall. More rooms and barracks abutted the east wall, which opened into a courtyard in front of the old chapel, its roof collapsed and the upper reaches of its facade crumbling. A palisaded wall had been built from the chapel's outer corner to the south adobe wall, enclosing the chapel courtyard, and it was the weakest section of the fort's perimeter.

Behind the east wall and north of the chapel were two adobe-walled corrals, one with the thirty head of cattle the Texians had managed to get inside the fort for food, the other for their horses. Rubio could see Calder was right. There were too few Texians to cover the wall, much less man with full crews the sixteen or so cannons he counted. There was little food for the defenders and even less fodder for the livestock.

Retreating to the west wall, he glanced toward Bexar and saw more Mexican troops approaching the town. He wondered if Texas would send any men to aid the Alamo. Rubio walked to his brother, squatted beside him and gently shook Tomas's shoulder.

Tomas awakened with a start, his wild eyes calming only when he saw Rubio. "I dreamed they were coming to take me back to prison. . . . I'll never let that happen again."

Rubio sat down beside him. "I don't think they'll be taking prisoners this time," he said. "Things went bad for us after I saw the ghostly bull."

"I was the one thrown in prison."

"I keep hoping I'll see it again and it will bring good luck, like it did the second time for father."

"It's coincidence."

Maybe Tomas was right. Rubio said nothing more, just sat with his back to the wall, watching the sky turn bronze as the sun rose. With good light, Rubio heard Colonel Travis issuing orders in the plaza below and assigning men positions around the fortress.

Shortly, Rubio heard someone climbing the ladder and saw a head peek up over the barrack roofline. "You men get down here so Colonel Travis can position you."

Rubio grabbed his rifle and rose, then bent to give Tomas a hand. Tomas waved him away and stood up on his own. They climbed down the ladder one at a time. Calder was leaning against the wall, and he stepped to greet Rubio when he heard the voice of Davy Crockett.

"Calder, I've been looking for you." Crockett pointed at the palisaded section of wall outside the chapel. "Colonel Travis assigned me and my Tennesseans the weakest section of the fort. He wants the best shots in the outfit there. I told him I wouldn't accept unless he assigned you to the same spot, even if you are from Kentucky and even if your cap might eat mine."

Calder grinned and nodded. "If I can't eat, at least my cap can."

Crockett bellowed with laughter.

"Let me take a couple men with me," Calder said. "Rubio and Tomas Portillo."

Crockett turned to Travis, who had joined them. "I need two more men and we can hold that wall until summer."

"I'll give you one more," Travis answered.

"You go, Rubio," Tomas said. "With the women staying near that wall, in the chapel, maybe you can see Mary some."

"*Gracias*, Tomas."

Travis looked at Tomas, then pointed to the north wall. "I want you up there on the gun emplacement. You know how to man a cannon?"

"I'll learn."

"Good," Travis said, and moved on, issuing commands to others.

Rubio grabbed Tomas's hand and shook it vigorously. "Take care of yourself, brother."

Tomas nodded. "Good luck to you and to Mary."

Rubio smiled. "I'd planned to ask her to marry me come spring."

"She's much better for you than Angelita."

"You were right all along about Angelita."

"And you were right about Mexico. We're better off with Texas."

Rubio hugged Tomas before each went to his assigned post.

Mary Calder pushed open the chapel door and stepped out. She was pleased to see her father and Rubio standing behind the cut log, palisaded wall. She eased over to her father.

"Mary, what are you doing here?"

"I came to see you and Rubio."

"Stay away from the wall," he scolded. "You could get hurt."

"So could you."

"It's my job." He looked to Rubio. "Take her to the chapel."

With his rifle in one hand, Rubio took Mary's arm by the other and escorted her away from the palisade.

"I want you to see where I stay," she said, "so you can visit me." She led him to the back of the chapel, then cut to her left. She opened a door and slipped into a darkened room lit by a single candle. Several women and children huddled there, including one white woman nursing a baby.

"My apologies," Rubio said and backed out. He turned to Mary. "It is a solid room and it should protect you well, but you should leave the fortress."

"I cannot abandon father and you."

"We cannot protect you, and I would not want to see you hurt." He gently kissed her cheek. "Come spring, I'd planned to ask you to marry me."

Tears began to roll down her cheeks. "I would have said yes."

He put his arm around her waist. "I must return to my post."

As Mary returned to her shelter, she wondered how much remaining time they had together.

Rubio marched with the others from their posts to the center of the plaza, or parade ground, as Colonel Travis had named it. Travis called for quiet as he strutted back and forth in front of the defenders of the Alamo. He turned to face his troops and stood akimbo, a sheet of paper in his right hand. "Men, Colonel Bowie has taken ill. He is bedridden and unable to share in this command, and he has given sole command of this fortress to me. I have sent calls for reinforcements to Goliad, and I have received word by courier that Texians are to gather at Washington-on-the-Brazos to consider declaring independence from Mexico."

The men nodded their approval.

Travis lifted his right hand and waved the paper. "I have written a call for help that reflects my belief in our destiny. Any man who does not believe as I do is free to try to escape through enemy lines."

The men fell silent as Travis shook the letter in his hand. With a strong voice, he began to read:

"To the People of Texas and all Americans in the World —
Fellow citizens and compatriots:
I am besieged by a thousand or more of the Mexicans under Santa Anna . . . I have sustained a continual Bombardment and cannonade for twenty-four hours and have not lost a man . . . The enemy has demanded a surrender at discretion, otherwise, the garrison are to be put to the sword, if the fort is taken . . . I have answered the demand with a cannon shot, and our flag still waves proudly from the walls . . . I shall never surrender or retreat. Then, I call on you in the name of Liberty, of patriotism, and every thing dear to the American character, to come to our aid, with all dispatch . . . The enemy is receiving reinforcements daily and will no doubt increase to three or four thousand in four or five days. If this call is neglected, I am determined to sustain myself as long as possible and die like a soldier who never forgets what is due to his own honor and that of his country —

VICTORY OR DEATH
William Barrett Travis
Lt. Col. Comdt."

The men cheered, and Travis smiled for the first time. He carefully folded his paper. "I have sent for reinforcements, and all of Texas will rally to fight the iniquity of a government that gives us no say in our own destiny.

"A promotion is in order for the first soldier to see the stream of Texians who will come to join us," he said. "Now return to your posts and fight for yourselves and Texas."

Many of the men ran back to their positions, but Donley Calder walked. Rubio walked beside him.

"We are alone, Rubio," Calder said. "A few may come, but never enough. If words were bullets, then Travis and Texas would carry the day."

For eleven more days the Texians held out, fighting off each attack the Mexicans threw at them. But each morning when daylight cracked the darkness, the Texians found the Mexicans and their cannons dug in closer. Additional cannons arrived, all larger than the light cannons they had first brought, and began to pummel the walls.

The Texians Colonel Travis expected to come never arrived. Save for a handful of men who came from Gonzales and a lone courier who arrived from Goliad to say Colonel Fannin would not be sending reinforcements, no one answered the rallying cry of William Barrett Travis.

In the cold of a late dusk, he had called all his men together a final time. There, in the packed dirt of the parade ground, Travis jerked his sword from his scabbard and etched a line in the ground. He said the situation was grim, but he was determined to buy time for Texas with his life. Stepping across the line, he turned to face his men. He asked those who would fight with him to cross the line and those who preferred to try to escape during the night to stay on the other side. All but one man crossed. Even the bedridden Jim Bowie asked to be carried across the line.

The men returned to their posts, most sleeping and eating at the wall, holding their guns at the ready, grim and determined. Since powder had dwindled, Travis ordered the cannons to shoot no more than three or four times a day, to save powder for the assault that was certain to come. By morning, the lone man not to side with Travis was not to be found.

Like all the others, Rubio stayed at his post. He was glad Donley Calder was nearby. They talked some, but mostly they just waited, like the others, some sharpening knives and hatchets, others counting and recounting their bullets.

Crockett paced about, reassuring his men while admitting to Calder that he didn't like being hemmed in. Just after sunset on the night of the twelfth day of the siege, Crockett was summoned to Travis's quarters. Shortly, Donley Calder was summoned as well. Rubio was curious, and even more so when he too was called to see Travis.

The colonel sat at a rough-hewn wooden table, a single candle lighting the room a sickly yellow. Crockett and Calder, lips tight and eyes narrow, leaned against the wall. Rubio stood in front of Travis, who said nothing. Rubio saluted awkwardly.

Travis nodded, then rose from his stool and studied him. "I am told you are loyal to Texas, a man who can be trusted."

"I am."

"We are in a desperate spot," Travis said. "The enemy each day grows stronger and closer. Our pleas have gone unanswered except for a few brave men." He picked up an envelope and handed it to Rubio.

Rubio saw the name *Sam Houston* written upon the paper.

"I am beseeching the commander of the Texas Army to come to our aid before it is too late. You are the man I want to deliver this message."

"I cannot abandon my brother and my betrothed."

"You will be abandoning Texas if you don't."

Rubio turned to Calder.

The frontiersman nodded. "I promised Mary a fine house."

Though he said nothing more, Rubio knew Calder wanted him to marry Mary and care for her after his death. By volunteering Rubio to deliver the message, Calder was giving him a reprieve and Mary a chance at a decent future

— if he made it.

Travis asked, "Do you have any questions or requests?"

"See that my horse and another good one are saddled."

Travis looked confused. "Why two?"

"I can alternate mounts and cover more ground without tiring my mounts. I will leave immediately."

Calder stepped away from the wall. "No, Rubio. Wait until a couple hours before dawn. That's when the sentinels are sleepiest and your chances of escaping are best. It will give you time to rest as well."

Rubio nodded. And time to say good-bye to Tomas and Mary.

Angelita Sanchez grimaced at the sound of Santa Anna's voice. He had taken over the house, evicted her parents, and kept her for his personal pleasure. She had cried many tears over the humiliation Juan Paz and Santa Anna had forced upon her.

She hoped the president would die in the battle. She hated herself for what she had done to Rubio, hated Paz for what he had done to her, and hated Santa Anna for what he was doing to her and to Bexar. Her anger rose when she heard Paz speaking in the next room with the president.

"After tonight," Santa Anna said, "I will not need the hospitality of this place."

"And why is that, *el presidente?*"

"I have ordered the final assault. All will be put to the sword as traitors."

"As well they deserve."

"And when I have put down this rebellion, you will be handsomely rewarded."

"I hope you found Angelita's charms a worthy reward for all you have done for Texas. Should I see that she accompanies you?"

Angelita almost screamed her hatred, but somehow managed to control her venom.

"No," Santa Anna said. "I shall have her early tonight, so I can sleep, then be awakened to direct the final assault. After tonight, I will be done with her."

Angelita began to cry.

Tomas shook Rubio's hand, then flung his arms around his brother. "God be with you, Rubio. If I die, at least it will not be in prison."

"I will return to this place to find you, Tomas."

"All you may find are my bones."

"Then I will give you a final burial in a place of honor on the ranch."

Tomas laughed. "I'll do about as much ranch work that way as I did before."

In the darkness Rubio wished he could see his brother's eyes, because he knew he would never see Tomas again.

Tomas seemed to read Rubio's thoughts. "It is good that one of us will survive and that that one is you. You'll work the ranch. Me, I'd always find too many distractions."

Rubio hugged his brother again. "I must go."

"And I must stay." Tomas picked up his rifle and stepped past the cannon to the wall.

Rubio looked at Tomas, a dark silhouette against the glow of distant enemy fires. Then he turned and started down the ramparts and toward the chapel. He passed the fires of several men and walked by the palisade. He saw Crockett pacing back and forth like a caged animal.

The massive chapel door was cracked wide enough for him to get in. The roofless chapel was lit by a fire in the middle of the floor. A couple of men looked up as he headed for Mary's refuge. He caught his breath, then rapped lightly on the door. "Mary, Mary Calder," he said softly, so as not to wake any children who might be sleeping. "It's Rubio."

The door eased open and Mary slipped out, tugging a blanket around her shoulders. "Is everything okay?"

He nodded. "I'm leaving. They want me to take a message to Sam Houston."

Mary threw her arms around him, her blanket sliding down her back to the ground. "Be careful, Rubio, please. I don't know what I would do without you." She began to cry softly and to nuzzle against his chest.

"I will be safer out there than you will be in here."

"When will you leave?"

"A couple hours before dawn. I came to say good-bye before I get some sleep. I've a long ride ahead of me."

"Where will you sleep?"

"At my post."

Mary pushed herself away from him and bent to pick up her blanket. "I will go with you."

"Your father said you should stay away from the palisades."

"He will not stop me. This could be my last night with you ever."

Taking the blanket, she grabbed his hand and tugged him to the door, leading him outside to his post. Rubio felt foolish but did not resist.

No sooner did he reach his position than Calder was beside them. "What are you doing here?" he asked.

"I'm staying with Rubio," Mary answered.

"I meant Rubio, Mary, not you."

"I'm taking my position," Rubio answered.

"Your responsibilities have changed. You need a good night's sleep. Take your bedding and throw you a bed inside the chapel, where the walls'll break the wind. Maybe it'll be a little warmer. I'll wake you up when the time's right."

"*Gracias.*" Rubio gathered his gear.

"It'll give you a chance to be alone with Mary," Calder said.

After he had corralled his belongings in his arms, Rubio returned to the chapel with Mary. She pushed the door open so he could get through with his armload of gear, then steered him toward the vacant room just inside the chapel door. Taking his bedding from his arms, Mary spread it out on the ground while he propped his weapons in the corner.

"I will keep you company," she said softly.

He turned around and did not see her. "Where are you?"

"Down here."

Rubio stepped toward the bed, then bent and patted the blankets. He felt Mary's leg beneath the covers, crawled beneath the blanket and reached for her. His hand brushed against a soft mound of flesh, and he realized she had removed her top. He fell against her, kneading the flesh and kissing her hard upon the lips. Mary answered his kiss with a smoldering passion. She climbed atop him and drained him of his desire. Then Rubio fell into a deep restful sleep.

It seemed like only moments before he'd been in her arms, and then he heard the gruff voice of Donley Calder. "Wake up, Rubio. It's time to ride."

Rubio roused, turned and brushed against Mary. He was embarrassed that her father had found them together, but the frontiersman made no note of it.

"The horses are ready, Rubio. You can have a couple moments more with Mary, then you must ride. The Mexican camp has been more active than usual."

He rolled over and kissed Mary. She answered lovingly. Then he began to fumble with his clothes. Mary dressed too, and rolled up his bedding.

"Be careful," she whimpered.

"I will return for you."

"I will await your return."

He picked up his pistol and shoved it in his belt, then his knife and scabbard. He draped the powder horn and bullet pouch over his shoulder and grabbed his rifle.

Mary offered him the blanket roll. He hugged her with one arm, kissed her again, then took the bedding.

"I slept well," he said.

"Me too."

They walked side by side out of the room, then out of the chapel. Calder was awaiting them, and behind him stood Crockett, holding the reins to two horses.

Rubio tied his bedroll to his stallion, turned and shook Calder's hand. "I've admired knowing you."

"You're a damn good Texican, Rubio."

Rubio kissed Mary. "Take care of your father and yourself," he said.

She began to cry.

Rubio took the reins from Crockett and tied the leathers of the spare horse to the rigging of his own. He mounted quickly.

He aimed his horses toward the gate. Mary grabbed his leg and walked with him. He wished he could take her with him, but it would be too dangerous, though staying behind was dangerous as well. At the gate he bent and kissed her hair.

When the gate swung open, she released his leg

and Rubio rode outside the walls for the first time in thirteen days. He said a silent prayer as the gates closed behind him, then turned his horse away from the Alamo.

20

Rubio Portillo advanced, ever slowly, always listening, ever hopeful he could make it through the Mexican lines. He heard his breath, he heard his pounding heart. His mount tossed its head and blew. The sound seemed to roll like thunder across the darkness. Rubio listened for the enemy, but at first he heard nothing except every breath of the two horses, every step of their hooves, every squeak of their saddle leather. He listened so hard he could almost hear his own thoughts. Then, above that, he heard a rattle.

Drawing gently back on the reins, he stopped and leaned low over the stallion's neck. He listened and heard nothing for a moment. Then his ears caught another rattle and the soft din of what could only be soldiers readying their weapons. Had they seen him? He didn't know. Were they about to attack the Alamo? He remained motionless, listening closely until he heard the rustle of shoes on dry grass. He strained in the darkness to make out the threat but could see nothing of what his ears could hear. He thought he might be imagining ghosts, then heard a whispered command.

"Advance, soldiers. We must take the fortress."

Rubio caught his breath. The soldiers were advancing. He could not see them. Were they advancing upon him? He did not know, but he realized he could not sit still long. Gently, he shook the reins and guided his horse away, hoping not to bump into the advancing troops.

A soft breeze stirred and he heard the sound of rustling grass but was uncertain if it was the feeble breath of night or the advance of Mexicans across the plain. His whole body tensed and his mount seemed to catch his nervousness. The animal tossed its head and the one behind whinnied.

Rubio grimaced. The animals would give him away. He tugged on the reins, then patted the stallion softly on the neck. He listened carefully, but heard nothing. Maybe they had passed. He slowly sat up in his saddle and nudged his stallion forward, but his mount flinched and lifted its head suddenly. Rubio heard a more threatening noise from another direction. It was the sound of soldiers snapping their bayonets in place.

A major attack was about to take place. The Texians had repelled all the others. Rubio just hoped they could fight off this one. He knew he must escape, but he could not leave without trying to warn the troops behind the Alamo's walls. He cocked the hammer and set a percussion cap. What he was about to do was foolish, it might mean his own death, but he felt he had to alert the men of the Alamo. He lifted his rifle and pulled the trigger. The rifle flashed and exploded.

It was a meager warning and all that he could do. He heard a shout in Spanish and spurred his horse, galloping away from the Alamo to find Sam Houston.

Rubio rode a league or more, then pulled up his horses to listen. He could detect no hoofbeats in pursuit, but he did hear the sound of battle. And in the distance he saw flashes of light. As he reloaded his rifle, he began to cry.

Tomas Portillo had stared at the darkness so long that he saw many things, and none were real. Then he spotted something that made him shiver. In the dark sky to the north he saw a cloud. Or was it a cloud? He could not be certain. Whatever it was resembled a great ghostly bull with burning eyes and snorting nostrils. The bull seemed to be charging straight for him. It had to be a dream, Tomas thought, because he did not believe the superstitions of a ghostly bull. It was said the bull brought bad luck until it reappeared. Tomas rubbed his eyes, but he still saw the bull. Chills ran down his spine. He grabbed his rifle.

Then, from the distant south, he heard the faint sound of a gun, almost unheard over the snores of the men who slept at their posts beside the three eight-pound cannons that crowned a dirt parapet abutting the north wall.

Tomas glanced south but saw nothing. He looked back to the north, relieved that the bull had disappeared. As his eyes focused, they seemed to be playing even crueler tricks upon him. He made out a wavering line of dark forms that could only be soldiers. Or his imagination. He blinked and thought the earth seemed to crawl with movement. He cursed himself and his eyesight, started to raise the alarm then paused.

Beyond the wall a ghost cried out. *"Viva la Republica!"*

Another answered, *"Viva Santa Anna!"*

Then in unison many added their voices to the cry. *"Viva la Republica! Viva Santa Anna!"*

"They're coming! They're coming!" Tomas cried. He lifted his rifle and fired. Around him startled men tossed back their blankets, grabbed their guns and took positions at the cannon.

"I'll get Colonel Travis," yelled one, who bolted down the cannon ramp and raced across the plaza to Travis's quarters.

As Tomas reloaded his rifle he said a quick prayer for Rubio's safety. He looked eastward, saw the first hint of a dawn like a stain of blood on the horizon and cursed the Mexicans before him. Now that he had seen the ghostly bull, Tomas knew he would die before the sun rose, but he vowed to walk to heaven or hell over the bodies of Mexican soldiers he took with him. As soon as he was reloaded, he lifted his rifle, pointed it over the wall and fired.

A line of flame answered from the Mexican line. Other Texians replied with shots of their own, and the hurrahs of the Mexicans gave way to screams and shouts and terror.

As Tomas loaded his rifle again, the artillerymen shouted hurried orders to each other, then curses at the enemy. They touched fire to a cannon beside Tomas. The cannon spit scrap metal and Tomas felt its hot breath upon his shoulder. He fired again and saw the enemy by the flame of their gunfire as they raced toward the walls, yelling, cursing, shooting, waving their arms, falling and dying. Two more cannons sprayed iron at the enemy, whose agonized screams followed as soon after the cannons' barks as a cart behind an oxen.

All along the line men fired, then dropped behind the protecting wall. Tomas saw by the flash of guns along the walls to the south and east that the enemy was attacking from several directions. As he reloaded yet again, Colonel Travis raced up the dirt ramp to the parapet.

"Give them the sword, men!" he yelled, lifted his shotgun and fired it over the wall. The gun flashed and bucked and Travis dropped it at Tomas's feet. Then he yanked his sword from his scabbard and waved it over his head.

Tomas scrambled to pour the powder for his rifle.

Travis glanced down at him. "Be quick or —"

Tomas bit his lip, he was loading as fast as he could. He waited for Travis to finish his command, but the commander's face suddenly contorted with surprise, his mouth gaping, his eyes widening. He tottered just a moment. Tomas saw a hole gushing blood in his forehead. The features of the colonel's face were suddenly masked in a veil of blood. Then he dropped his sword and tumbled backward, sliding down the dirt ramp.

"Colonel Travis is down!" Tomas screamed, jumping up and leaning over the wall to shoot at the enemy below. He fired at a faceless soldier, who fell. Beside him the cannon belched.

Tomas was staggered as he pulled himself behind the wall. At first he thought he was stunned by the blast of the cannon, but then he realized his left arm fell limp. It would not move. He could not load his rifle. He cursed and pulled his pistol from his belt. Another cannon in the battery fired.

"No, no," he shouted. "They are too close, depress the cannon."

"We can't," an artillerymen answered.

His left arm was wet and sticky with blood. He lifted his pistol and held it over the wall, shooting down into the swarming mass of soldiers, who managed to throw ladders up against the fort.

"The ladders, the ladders!" Tomas cried, pushing them away.

One landed against the wall in front of the cannons. Tomas shoved at it with his right arm just as a soldier scrambled up toward him. He pushed his pistol at the soldier, cocked the lock and pulled the trigger. The gun snapped and Tomas realized he'd forgotten to reload.

The Mexican kept climbing.

Panicked, Tomas spun around for a weapon. He saw Travis's sword at his feet and bent to grab it. As he did, the cannon behind him roared. He screamed as the shot came so close that it scorched his flesh. He spun around to the wall.

His wide-eyed enemy stood on a high rung of the ladder, his torso above the wall. He tried to swing his rifle at Tomas.

Tomas dodged, then thrust the sword at him, running the blade through the man's chest. The dead soldier fell backward, almost wrenching the sword from Tomas's hand. Like locusts, another soldier replaced the one who had fallen. Tomas hacked at the man's head and shoulder. The man screamed, then slid partially down the ladder, his uniform snagging and suspending him there until the next soldier pushed his body aside.

Tomas gasped for breath, but his lungs absorbed more burnt powder than air. He laughed crazily then, just waiting for the next soldier to come within reach of his sword. He lifted the blade, ready to strike, but something kicked him in the back and he staggered to the wall, then pushed himself back until he bumped into the scalding barrel of the cannon. He cried out in pain as the feeling left his legs and then crumpled onto the dirt, stunned. His senses were clouded, except for hearing. Around him all was noise, the sound of metal against metal, powder exploding, men screaming and battle roaring.

After a moment his mind cleared enough for him to know the noise was the sound of death. He knew he must arise and kill as many more of the enemy as he could. He tried to get up, but he couldn't.

His left arm was numb. Nothing could make it work.

He tried to push himself up with his right hand and hang onto the sword, but his legs had turned to mush. All he could manage was to sit up.

A Mexican topped the wall.

Tomas screamed.

A Texian swung the butt of his rifle at the enemy, catching him square in the teeth. The soldier flew back into the dark void on the other side of the wall.

But yet another Mexican sprang up from a new ladder just planted against the fortress. There were too many enemy and too few Texians. Where several men had been manning the guns, Tomas saw but one still standing. Other men lay around him at distorted angles, some crying for the battlefield trinity of God, Mother, and water.

Tomas lifted his sword. The lone Texian still standing swung his rifle at a soldier clearing the wall, but behind him another Mexican had landed inside the fort. "Watch out!" Tomas cried.

The soldier fired his gun not six inches from the Texian's back. The flash of powder set the Texian's shirt on fire. He dropped his rifle, swatted at the flames, then fell motionless.

Tomas raised his sword, but the Mexican did not see him. The soldier moved past him, and Tomas managed to stab him through the kidneys. The man fell on Tomas's numb legs, screaming and thrashing.

For a moment the dying man's gaze lingered on Tomas's, silently pleading for compassion. Tomas wriggled the sword, trying to yank it free from the soldier. The soldier turned his head to die.

Tomas glanced to the east. The sun had not risen, and he knew he was dying. He could not free the sword, no matter how hard he struggled. He looked to the north, hoping to see the ghostly bull returning to bring good luck. He saw nothing but the darkness of a malevolent sky and the enemy pouring over the walls. Several grabbed cannon carriages and wheeled the field pieces around to fire on the Texians. Tomas screamed at the pain pulsing madly through his body.

A soldier straddled him and the dead man in his lap. The soldier lifted a pistol. Tomas saw the black hole in the barrel, then closed his eyes and saw the black void of eternity.

Donley Calder heard a distant shot to the south and wondered if Rubio had encountered trouble. Then he heard cheers and more shots to the north. The Mexicans were attacking. He grabbed his rifle, pulled his lionskin cap in place and glanced between the logs of the stockade. His eyes adjusted to the darkness but he saw nothing. The shooting picked up to the north, then a cannon barked.

Davy Crockett strode past him. "I never did like being hemmed in," he grumbled as he raised his rifle. "Hope our boys at the other end can hold them off. Me and my Tennesseans can stand toe-to-toe with anything on two feet."

Calder squinted and made out dark shapes by the hundreds. "Looks like you're gonna get your chance, because here they come."

"I see 'em. Tennesseans, hold your fire," Crockett called. His men waited as the gunfire grew to a roar to the north. "Now!" Crockett yelled.

The line of Tennesseans exploded with gunshots. Calder aimed at the biggest soldier in the approaching line. With their shako hats, the Mexicans appeared to be giants emerging from the darkness. Calder squeezed the trigger. The gun flashed fire and smoke. Like the men around him, Calder dropped behind the protection of the log wall and reloaded calmly, quickly, and efficiently.

Only when it seemed that the Mexican soldiers were right upon the stockade did the Tennesseans fire the lone cannon along that stretch of the fortress. The cannon's growl pried screams from men ripped, cut, and gutted by shrapnel. Four Tennesseans reloaded the cannon and touched it off. Another gap appeared in the line.

Calder fired with the others, then dropped to load again. He worked quickly, stood up and shot another Mexican soldier. The enemy line wavered, then seemed to halt as if the soldiers were too scared to advance but too numb to retreat. Abruptly, the Mexican infantry broke to the west, running from the stockade and the southwest corner of the fortress.

The Tennesseans lifted their rifles and cheered briefly before calmly reloading again. "We're still hemmed in," Crockett said.

Calder glanced north, trying to see how the battle was going in that direction. He feared the worst.

"Men," Crockett cried, turning from the sound of battle and looking up and down the stockade wall. "You can jump the wall and make out the best you can on your own because there'll be no tomorrow for any of us if they breach the wall anywhere. As for me, I'll not turn my back on Texas."

"Neither are we," answered one. "We're Tennesseans."

"This Kentuckian is with you too," Calder said.

Crockett patted Calder on the shoulder. "If we could just bring your cap back to life, we could sic it on them."

The firing intensified to the north and west. Around Calder the Tennesseans waited, their weapons primed, their faces grim. They looked over the stockade toward the ground where the enemy had attacked. The ground writhed with wounded. The threat would not come from the south. The Tennesseans had driven the enemy elsewhere to probe for a weak spot, and when they found it, they would spill into the fortress like a thousand angry ants. One by one the Tennesseans turned about and looked toward the plaza where the dying embers of last night's fires left glowing pockmarks in the gloom. The sounds of gunfire, screaming men, and terrified horses and cattle in the nearby corrals ran together in a gigantic cacophony of fear and death.

Calder had always known he would die, but now he knew the day. "I'll fend for myself, God, but please take care of Mary," he said aloud.

He saw a couple Texians then, running past a glowing fire. They had to be retreating from the north wall. One of them threw up his arms before collapsing beside the fire. Calder cursed, knowing the Mexicans had breached the wall.

"They're inside, men," Crockett cried, "and we're hemmed in unless we push them back." He stepped away from the stockade and moved toward the plaza. His men started after him. They didn't run and neither did Crockett. They marched to the low wall separating the large plaza from the smaller chapel plaza. They were men walking to their death as calmly as if it were someone else's funeral.

Calder stepped with them. They were good men to die with.

First one, then two, three, four, ten, thirty, sixty, a hundred or more Mexican soldiers rushed across the plaza, stopping to shoot men off the wall. Nearer the south wall, two cannons that had been guarding the gate were wheeled around and the Texians fired upon the Mexicans. Many soldiers fell, but many more took their place, two hundred, three hundred, five hundred, seven hundred.

The Tennesseans fired, and Calder with them. Gunfire rang from all over. Calder could hardly shoot without hitting the enemy, but he could not reload in time to stop the tide of flesh, steel, powder, and bullet lead rolling toward him.

A Tennessean fell beside him. Calder fired again, then dropped his own weapon and jerked the one from the hands of his dead ally. He fumbled for a percussion cap in his pouch, set the cap, cocked the lock and fired. The gun convulsed in his hand. He bent, picked up his own rifle and retreated with both toward the chapel.

Mexicans burst through the small gate in the low wall and converged on Crockett. He fired his pistol, then flung it at one. Grabbing his rifle by the barrel, Crockett swung it at the nearest Mexican, all the time backing toward the chapel. He bashed the brains of one soldier, then stumbled over the body of a Tennessean before steadying himself with the butt of his rifle. A Mexican fired his rifle at Crockett, who cried out and charged like an enraged bull into the advancing tide. The Mexicans rammed his body with a dozen bayonets. Calder saw Crockett fall limply at their feet.

The remaining Tennesseans backed toward the chapel. A dozen enemy charged at Calder, but he flung the spare rifle at their feet and they tripped over it and each other. Dozens more were behind them, however, their eyes wide and the whites visible against their brown, powder-stained faces.

The Mexicans surrounded him and five other Tennesseans on three sides. Their only refuge was the chapel. The Texians bumped into each other as they scrambled for the door, their guns empty. Two men stumbled through the door ahead of Calder and raced to the end of the building. Calder darted into the first room on his left, tripping and hitting the ground. His cap fell across his eyes and he jerked it off and flung into the corner. Quickly, he reloaded his rifle. Two other Texians fell in the chapel doorway.

For a moment no enemy dared enter the chapel, but Calder knew they were only pausing to reload. Then they poured in, like angry hornets, all ignoring Calder's room, until a straggler rushed him.

Calder shot him, the man grabbing his chest as he fell. Calder jumped over him, wrenched the man's musket from his hands and shot the next soldier who came in. Several more tried to enter, but he used the Mexican musket as a club, swinging madly. He knocked down five or six, then swung so wildly that he hit the stone facing of the door and broke the musket.

Taking his knife from his belt, Calder stabbed a soldier who had stumbled over a compatriot. Calder tossed his knife to his left hand and jerked his hatchet from his belt with the other hand. He stood at the door, chopping and slashing at anyone who tried to enter. Out of the corner of his eye he caught movement and saw a soldier lift a musket. Calder jumped backward. The gun exploded, missing him.

In that instant, five soldiers charged through the door. One shot, then a second fired. Calder screamed as their bullets struck him in the gut and shoulder. He stumbled backward, tripping over his discarded rifle and falling into the corner atop his lionskin cap.

He swung his hatchet limply.

Another soldier fired into Calder's chest, driving his whole torso against the cold, hard wall. Calder looked down at his chest and saw splotches of blood on his shirt. As he looked up, he saw the glint of bayonets at his chest. For an instant he felt the burn of blades sliding into his flesh. Then he felt nothing more forever.

The noise started as a distant popping, muffled by the stone walls and roof of the room. At first Mary Calder ignored it as if it was the crackle of a large fire, but the sound grew and grew until it awoke the whole room. The women whimpered and the children cried. The roar could mean but one thing: the final assault had begun. Mary knew her father and Tomas were doomed and that Rubio could already be dead. She wondered if she would survive. The room was pitch-dark. She heard a woman sobbing softly, and she fought not to cry as well. She prayed that Rubio had gotten away, that her father would live, and that Tomas might survive.

The noise strengthened like a bad wind. She

knew the fighting was nearing the stockade, and found herself holding her breath several times. For a bit she thought the sound of battle had receded. It gave her hope, but hope for what? Then the roar returned as if the earth were hungry and grinding its teeth on the flesh of men. Mary whimpered. She could no longer stand it. She began to cry too.

A first she heard shouts in English. Then she heard occasional yells in Spanish. The fortress had fallen. Her cries became sobs.

The battle seemed to come from outside into the chapel itself. Men cursed in English. They discharged their guns and shouted at the enemy. They were answered by gunshots and curses in Spanish. Then the shouts were all in Spanish.

The women and children crawled to a corner where they huddled with their arms around each other, uncertain what was happening outside the door and fearful of what would happen once the door opened.

A child grabbed Mary, who pulled the little one to her breast. There was nothing else she could do but wait. And pray! For the first time, she prayed for herself.

And then the door was flung open. The room went silent. Even the children were terrified into absolute quiet. A figure like the devil stood in the doorway, a shadowy demon with fires ablaze behind him. Then another soldier thrust a torch into the doorway, illuminating both men. The whites of their eyes and their teeth shone eerily through their smudged faces.

Mary caught her breath. The bayonet of one soldier dripped blood. She wondered if her blood would soon stain the blade as well.

21

Mary bit her lip to keep from sobbing as the soldiers escorted the women and children from their hiding place and past the bodies of the Texians and their enemies. She could not count all the bodies inside the chapel. Through the collapsed roof overhead she looked at a bronzed sky, so she wouldn't have to see the dead. She fought her tears as savagely as the Texians had fought their enemies. She could not — would not — let her father's killers see her grief. Mary marched stiffly out the door and held her breath. The carnage outside was even more terrible.

Sunlight stabbed at the scene before her. Men were splayed across the courtyard like they had been dropped from the sky. Trails of blood snaked through small ruts earth. The faces of the dead, moist with blood and smudged with powder, stared with half-opened eyes at the dozen survivors who marched with Mary Calder to the south gate. The clothing of many dead still smoldered from the burning powder of point-blank gunshots. Though none of the Texians seemed alive, the ground before Mary writhed with the thrashing limbs of the wounded Mexicans. They moaned and cried out for help, slapping at the earth with their hands, kicking with their feet, tossing their heads back and forth. The cry was pitiful.

The path the survivors followed wove among the dead and wounded. One desperate Mexican soldier grabbed at Mary's ankle, held it a moment before Mary pulled herself free and then moved on, trying to stay out of reach of any other soldier, but the ground was too littered with the dead, wounded, and broken. Mary looked closely for her father, but the faces of nearly all the men were so contorted from desperation and so covered with burnt powder that she did not recognize a single one. There were bodies everywhere, scattered upon the ground, hanging from the walls like the devil's sordid wash hung out to dry. The parade of survivors turned toward the south gate, and Mary almost broke down when a line of officers removed their hats and held them over their hearts as the women and children passed.

"Your men were brave," one of them said.

The women marched through the gate and outside the fortress, away from the carnage. Even more Mexican soldiers stood outside the gate, staring at the pitiful band of women and children as they passed. The Mexican guards pointed the survivors toward Bexar and the wooden footbridge over the river. They covered the distance quickly, and Mary, so lost in her thoughts and her silent grief, was surprised when she realized they were in Bexar itself. The guards herded them into a small house where an old couple offered them blankets.

Mary felt the warmth of the house and realized that she'd been shivering, but she could not tell if it was from the cold or the grief. She stepped to the corner fireplace and tried to warm herself up. The old woman came over and patted her on the back, offering her condolences. Mary looked up into the woman's kindly eyes and recognized her as the mother of Angelita Sanchez. Mary looked around to confirm that this was not the same large house where she had stayed to nurse Tomas back to health.

"Your *casa?*" she asked.

The old woman grimaced. "*El presidente* took it for himself." Her face turned to shame. "And Angelita for himself as well."

Mary patted the woman on the shoulder. "I'm sorry."

The humiliated mother walked away. "I must find you food." She returned shortly with a platter of tortillas. "I have no more," she apologized as she offered the food to the children, then the women.

Mary quickly ate the food. It felt good on her stomach, but would have felt better had more been available. Then they sat quietly awaiting their fate. After three hours the guards called for one woman and took her away. Mary listened for the sound of gunfire but heard nothing. When a guard returned for another woman, Mary went with him.

The guard led her down the street to the Main Plaza and pointed her across the square to a low-slung dwelling that she recognized as the house of Angelita and her parents. She realized she was headed for an audience with Santa Anna. She gritted her teeth, for he was the butcher of her father and Tomas. Mary fought her emotions as she stepped inside the door.

In a corner she saw Angelita, wearing a fine dress and jewelry.

Angelita looked up, recognized her and exploded in anger, charging across the room. *"Puta!"* she cried, drawing back her arm to slap Mary, but the guard jumped in front of her and grabbed her hand.

"Let me at her!" Angelita screamed. "She stole my betrothed!"

The guard held her back. *"El presidente* ordered that the women and children were not to be harmed by anyone."

Angelita screamed again, then spat upon Mary's dress.

Another guard emerged from an adjacent room and shook his head. *"Muy loco,"* he said of Angelita. Then, gently taking Mary's hand, he led her into the next room.

There, behind a table he was using as a makeshift desk, sat the president himself. He was dressed in a full uniform with gold buttons and epaulets and rows of medals upon his chest. He wore a gaudy hat and a soft, disarming smile. He stood and saluted Mary.

Mary did not know how to respond, for she hated the man so. She nodded slightly, meanwhile noticing the four other officers standing by the wall behind him, as well as a civilian to his side.

"I am his excellency, El Presidente Antonio Lopez de Santa Anna." He took his seat. "You are?"

"Mary Calder," she announced, noting the particular interest the civilian exhibited in her name.

"Why were you with the enemies of Mexico?"

"I was with my father."

The civilian stepped to the table and placed both hands upon its surface. "And you were with the Portillo brothers?"

"Juan Paz," Santa Anna chided. "I shall do the questioning."

"But the Portillo brothers were worse than the Anglos because they were traitors to Mexico and to their own skin."

"*Silencio,* Juan Paz," he commanded, pointing to the wall.

Paz grumbled, but retreated to the wall.

"Now," Santa Anna said, "what happened to your father?"

She grimaced. "He died bravely."

Santa Anna nodded. "And these Portillo brothers that Juan Paz mentioned, what happened to them?"

Mary shook her head. "I can only guess they died too, though I did not see even my father's body."

"Neither of them escaped?" Paz interrupted.

Mary looked from the general to Juan Paz.

"*Silencio,*" Santa Anna commanded Paz. "Now, why did you know the Portillo brothers?"

Mary shook her head. "I had hoped to marry Rubio in the spring."

"It is a pity," Santa Anna said. "My condolences."

Santa Anna snapped his fingers, and one of the officers stepped forward, a pouch in his hand. The officer withdrew two pieces of silver and placed them on the table. A second officer approached with a blanket and left it on the table in front of Santa Anna.

The general picked up the coins, leaned across the table and dropped them on the blanket. "This is a small gift to you with my condolences. Please go forth from this room and tell others that you were treated kindly, but tell them also the fate that awaits their men if they continue to take up arms against Mexico."

Mary did no want the money, nor the blanket, but she gathered the coins in her hand and raised the blanket to her chest. "*Gracias,*" she said without sincerity.

"You are free to go wherever you must," Santa Anna said. "I have drawn up a paper that you can carry with you so that my army will know that you travel with my blessing." He handed her the paper. "Good luck."

Mary turned and walked out the door into the front room. Behind her, she heard Paz's loud voice in heated discussion with Santa Anna. Angelita jumped up from her bench and charged her. Mary lifted her arm and slapped Angelita as soon as she came within range.

Angelita screamed with rage and shock until a guard threw his arms around her. "Please leave, quickly," he instructed Mary.

Mary stepped outside, not knowing where to go. She had Apache blood in her, so she could survive. She walked back to the house where Angelita's parents were living, showed the guard Santa Anna's pass, and he let her back inside.

Seeing Angelita's mother, she smiled. "I have something for your kindness."

"You owe nothing but the thanks which you have offered many times."

Mary nodded, holding up the blanket. "You have asked for nothing, but you deserve much. This is a new blanket, which I will trade for an old one."

"That is not wise."

"It wasn't wise to give me tortillas when you had so few."

The old woman took the new blanket and picked up an old one from the corner. Mary accepted the blanket from her, then caught the old woman's feeble hand and turned it over. In the woman's open palm she placed the two pieces of Santa Anna's silver. She could never spend silver given to her by the man who killed her father.

"*Gracias,*" the senora said.

Mary turned. "I must go."

She stepped outside, uncertain where she should go, but wherever she went, she knew she would survive because she was Apache. She walked out of town and glanced toward the Alamo, where soldiers were removing Texian bodies and stacking them like firewood in great piles beyond the walls.

Mary kept walking until Bexar and the Alamo were no longer in sight. She glanced back once, saw a column of smoke and knew the Mexicans were burning the bodies of the Texians. She stopped beneath a tree and began to sob as the dam of her emotions burst. When she finally rose, she knew where she must go and what she must do.

Rubio Portillo did not have to wait for the outcome. He knew all the fort's defenders had died. He hoped and prayed that Mary Calder had lived, but he could not hold out hope for Tomas and Donley Calder. Rubio had to find Sam Houston's army and convey the fate of the Alamo. Rubio rode first to Gonzales, where it had all started in a contest over a small cannon. Houston, he learned, had just arrived from Washington-on-the-Brazos, where the constitutional convention had adjourned after declaring independence for Texas.

Rubio caught his breath upon hearing the word. The war was no longer being fought to restore the Mexican constitution of 1824, but for independence for all of Texas. Rubio felt that those who had died in the Alamo would have been honored to know of the declaration.

He was taken immediately to Sam Houston, a tall, craggy-faced man with a strong handshake and a booming voice.

"The news is bad?" Houston wanted to know.

"The worst. The Alamo has fallen."

"Were there survivors?"

"I cannot say for certain, but I think not. I had been sent out only minutes before the attack to deliver Colonel Travis's plea for reinforcements. I am too late."

Sam Houston nodded. "Son, it was too late from the moment Colonel Travis closed the gates on his men inside the Alamo. It had no value, and Travis had been ordered to destroy the fortress and abandon Bexar, but he chose to make a stand."

Rubio nodded. "A lot of good men died for Texas."

"And more will die yet, but when we are done with this war for independence, none will have died in vain. Though he disobeyed me, Colonel Travis has done Texas a favor. With his life and those of his men, he has bought time for Texas, and time is one of many things this army needs."

"If you need one more man, I'm here."

Houston smiled. "I have a brigade of Tejanos, and you are assigned to it. When the time comes for a fight, I know I can count on you."

Rubio nodded and was led away by an adjutant

and introduced to his new allies.

Over the next three days, Rubio drilled with the Tejanos. Then an Anglo woman who had survived the siege of the Alamo with her daughter reached Gonzales to tell of the horror of the battle. She reported all the men had died, but the women and children had survived and were permitted to leave Bexar and spread Santa Anna's warning about traitors.

The next day, Houston burned Gonzales and led the army east toward the Colorado River. Spring rains muddied the retreat, but the army got across the river before the floods hit and raised the waters so they could not be crossed. Word arrived, too, that Colonel Fannin's army near Goliad, almost twice the number killed at the Alamo, had been captured by an army commanded by General José Urrea. The full defense of Texas now fell upon the lean shoulders of Sam Houston, who started training his small army in the fundamentals of close order drill.

As the Colorado began to recede, Houston retreated again, even after learning from a captured Mexican soldier that Santa Anna had split his army into three groups. He moved his men to San Felipe, on the Brazos, promising them they would fight soon, as he'd done three times before. But then, after burning San Felipe, he ordered another retreat.

The soldiers began to complain cynically that Houston would destroy Texas and save Santa Anna the trouble. Then word came that Fannin's men, captured near Goliad, had been executed by order of Santa Anna. Upon learning of the slaughter, Houston retreated yet again. The soldiers joked that they'd soon have to swim the Mississippi River if they were to keep up with Houston's retreat. Many in the army pleaded with David G. Burnet, the president of the new-born Texas government, to replace Houston with Secretary of War Thomas Rusk. Rusk even visited the army, but Houston, ever persuasive, convinced the secretary that his retreat was the only hope for the young republic.

For six weeks they retreated and grumbled, wishing for a leader who would fight. And then one day the army stopped with its back to Buffalo Bayou near its confluence with the San Jacinto River. The land was a level, open plain bordered by intermittent groves of oak trees. The Texians camped in the trees to mask their numbers. Despite the dissatisfaction of the soldiers, the army had grown to almost a thousand soldiers, picking up men who had abandoned their homes before the advancing Mexican Army.

Tired of running, and itching for a fight, the soldiers of Houston's army watched the approach of the Mexican Army as it set up camp across the plain from them. Santa Anna himself was rumored to be in command of the Mexican force. Then, with the rivers still up from the spring rains, Houston ordered the bridge across the bayou burned and the ferry destroyed. The soldiers who had complained so hard about Houston's cowardice swallowed hard and waited nervously, especially after scouts estimated the Mexicans to number at least three hundred more than the Texians.

The Mexicans made a reconnaissance trip to get an idea of the size of the Texas Army, but Houston's men drove them back without exposing more than a handful of men. Then night settled over the camp. Houston prohibited fires, so the soldiers stared enviously across the plain at dozens of enemy fires. Dawn came and the Texas Army still sat, some saying Houston was yet asleep, almost until noon. And then he called his army officers together.

Rubio felt his pulse race as his captain returned from Houston's tent, a smile upon his face. "Today is the day we have long awaited," the captain announced. "We are to make battle."

"When?" Rubio asked.

"At four o'clock."

Rubio remembered Tomas and Donley Calder and how both had certainly died at the Alamo. He recalled how the soldiers had tried to capture him. He thought of his last night with Mary Calder and wondered if he would ever have another night with her. He loaded his rifle and pistol, sharpened his knife and hatchet, and waited.

Then the orders came to assemble for battle. Rubio and the brigade of Tejanos lined up as infantry. They were given pieces of paper to stick in their hatbands so the Texians would not mistake them for the enemy. Finally, Houston's two cannons fired at the Mexican camp and the line of infantry broke from the trees, racing double-quick toward the Mexicans. A line of cavalry emerged from the cover as well and attacked the left flank of the enemy line as the infantry raced across the open plain. When the line moved within range of the enemy, Houston commanded his army to fire. The line of Texian guns exploded in lead and smoke.

"Reload, reload!" Houston yelled.

Rubio screamed. He did not want to take time to reload. He sensed confusion in the enemy. He broke forward, anxious to get among the Mexicans so he could kill them with his bare hands. "Remember the Alamo!" he cried out.

He looked over his shoulder and saw that others had broken ranks as well. He could hear their cries as they took up his yell.

"Remember the Alamo, remember Goliad!" they screamed as they raced toward the barricades that screened the enemy.

Rubio saw the Mexicans retreating from the barricades, so complete was the surprise of the attack. He raced ahead, jumping over the earth and wood they had piled before their camp as breastworks. A Mexican turned to shoot at him, but Rubio clubbed him with his gun barrel, then grabbed the barrel and pounded his head. He saw another Mexican aim his rifle at Houston. Jerking his pistol from his belt, Rubio cocked the lock and fired. The soldier toppled over dead. All around him Texians swarmed like hornets, their cries of revenge colliding with the enemy's fearful shouts. Metal clanged, powder exploded. From somewhere behind the Texians a band played a song that Rubio did not recognize.

The Texians pushed forward like an unstoppable tide sweeping the enemy before them. Terrified Mexicans threw their guns aside and ran toward the river, their pitiful cries only increasing their panic. Only one pocket of enemy refused to retreat, and they manned a cannon that fired at the advancing Texians. Houston's men fell to the ground, reloaded their guns, and fired, knocking off most of the artillerymen. The rest turned and ran, save only a uniformed officer whom Rubio took for a general.

The man stood with his chest thrust forward, facing the charging Texians. "I have never shown my back in battle," he cried, "and will not do so now!"

He had barely finished his sentence before he was cut down with a dozen balls to the chest. Once the cannon was captured, there was no organized line of defense by the Mexicans. They ran in a panic through the camp and toward the river.

Hundreds of Houston's men followed, cursing and screaming for Mexican blood to avenge the Alamo and Goliad. Though some of the Mexican soldiers managed to slip around the Texian cavalry, most fled headlong toward the river, bogging down in the marsh that bordered it.

Rubio, running with the other Texians through

the abandoned Mexican camp, was surprised by the great number of discarded weapons. The Mexicans had carried little to defend themselves with. He ran past tents and Mexican bodies, then cleared the camp. He and hundreds of others followed the enemy into the marsh, clubbing, stabbing, kicking, slashing, and hitting the enemy.

Rubio swung his rifle by the barrel, clubbing dozens of enemy before the stock of his rifle broke. He flung it aside, then pulled his knife and hatchet. He cut, sliced, and hacked at the soldiers, knocking them unconscious into the marshy ground. Rubio fought with such a frenzy that he did not accept the pleas for surrender. He screamed, "Remember the Alamo! Remember Tomas and Donley Calder!"

He approached a Mexican captain who threw up his arms. "Please brother, do not kill me," the man begged. "I am Mexican like you."

"Damn you," Rubio cried, "I'm Texican." He lifted his hatchet and hammered the officer's neck with it. "You killed my brother."

The side of the man's head spurted blood, then he collapsed into the marsh, never to rise again.

All around him it was a frenzied flash of movement and death, the enemy soldiers shouting to Providence for deliverance and receiving no reply. The Mexicans who traversed the marsh found themselves at the edge of a small lake where water from the San Jacinto river pooled. They flung themselves into the water, but their awkward thrashing showed that most could not swim.

The Texians who followed them to the edge of the marsh simply stood their ground, calmly loading their weapons and shooting the soldiers or letting them drown. Soon the thrashing waters of the lake were splotched with blood and bodies.

As some of the Mexicans bobbed up and down in the water they yelled, "Me no Alamo, me no Goliad." The Texians, though, stood shooting them as they raised their heads out of the water for breath.

Rubio finally grew tired of the carnage and retreated from the marsh, collapsing on firm ground and sobbing for his dead brother and for Donley Calder. Their deaths had been avenged.

When Texian officers finally called a halt to the killing, Houston ordered the soldiers to round up all the captives they could. They must find Santa Anna if he were still alive, he said, because the victory meant nothing if the general did not surrender. Rubio realized then that if Santa Anna were among the dead, the wanton slaughter might have done more damage than good to the cause of Texas independence.

But the next day, Santa Anna was captured. He was taken before Sam Houston, who requested that the Tejano who had been the last man out of the Alamo translate Santa Anna's Spanish.

Rubio was summoned by his captain and escorted to a tall oak tree where Houston lay on an blanket after taking a musket ball in the ankle.

Rubio slipped through the crowd of murmuring soldiers lusting to lynch Santa Anna. When he moved into the circle, he was surprised to see how small a man Santa Anna was.

Houston looked up, saw Rubio and smiled. "Tell him that your brother was slaughtered at the Alamo."

Rubio made the translation and watched Santa Anna's dour expression sink even lower.

"You have whipped me and I am your prisoner," the general said simply.

Rubio translated his words for Houston.

"Ask him why I shouldn't execute him for the deaths of men at the Alamo and Goliad."

Nodding, Rubio repeated the question.

Santa Anna nodded. "My army is in many pieces, and my generals will continue to fight if you execute me. They will not surrender and you will have to fight and beat them too."

After translating his words for Houston, the Texian commander had another question.

"What does he propose?"

Rubio quizzed Santa Anna about what he was offering.

"Spare me," Santa Anna replied, "and I will give the orders for my armies to leave Texas."

Rubio made the translation.

Houston nodded. "Tell him he will be spared, provided his armies abandon Texas and the Mexican government recognizes Texas as a sovereign republic no longer under the rule of Mexico."

After listening to Rubio's translation, Santa Anna nodded. *"Sí, sí,"* he repeated.

Sam Houston nodded once again, then turned to the men encircling Santa Anna menancingly. "Not a hair on his head is to be harmed," he told them. "He is trading his life for the birth of a nation."

Several men grumbled.

"Perhaps he deserves to die," Houston cried out, "but Texas deserves to live even more. What you did yesterday was a great victory, but it will be an incomplete victory if Santa Anna dies, for then Texas may well die with him, and many more of us as well. That is my order. Any man who attempts to harm him will be put to the firing squad."

Rubio looked around. The men didn't like it, but they didn't argue. Houston oversaw the signing of orders that Santa Anna could send out to his other generals. When the general initialed the orders, Houston put him under the guard of a dozen trusted soldiers and sent him away.

"Men," Houston called out, "the war for Texas independence is over."

They cheered mightily.

"We will face many challenges as a nation, and our battles will be many, but Texas will be a fine nation with strong men like you."

They cheered again, then Houston dismissed them to return to their duties. The war had ended. Soon, Rubio knew, he could return to Bexar to find Mary Calder — if she was still alive.

22

The countryside was ablaze with the color of bluebonnets, Indian paintbrush, and the dozens of other flowers that bloomed in the meadows and along the sad trails that led back to Bexar. Rubio approached Bexar by the same route he had abandoned the Alamo. When he came within sight of the abandoned fortress, he felt his lip tremble. The adobe and limestone walls shone golden in the afternoon sunlight. Beyond the Alamo he saw Bexar, and found it hard to believe so much had happened since the celebration of Mexican independence in September. What had started as a movement to restore representation for Texas under the Mexican constitution of 1824 had turned into a movement for Texas's own independence.

He was tempted to bypass the Alamo and go straight to Bexar, but he could not. He must pay his respects where his brother and Donley Calder had perished. Too, he might find sign of Mary. Even if he never found her, he hoped she had survived to live a happy life.

As he entered the south gate to the fortress, he removed his hat. He looked around the fortress

346

and shook his head. The ground was still littered with broken and discarded guns, pieces of uniforms, broken swords and bayonets, hats and shoes. Rubio saw walls stained with powder and, in spots, blood, and peppered with pockmarks from bullets that missed flesh. He rode to the north wall where Tomas had been stationed on the rampart and eased his skittish horse up the ramp to the spot where cannons had awaited the assault. On the earthen embankment he saw dried splotches that could only have been caused by spilled blood.

He turned his horse and retreated down the embankment, then retraced his trail through the plaza toward the courtyard in front of the chapel. He saw the stockade where Donley Calder had joined with Crockett and his Tennesseans. Had he stayed in the fort a half hour longer, Rubio knew he too might have died nearby. In front of the chapel he dismounted and led his horse past the door that had been knocked from its hinges. He walked through the chapel to the back and the room where the women and children had stayed. The door lay on the ground. Through the dimness of the room Rubio looked for signs the women and children had been hurt. He saw no bullet marks on the walls nor splotches on the floor.

Rubio turned his horse about and led him back through the chapel. As he was about to exit he stopped at the door and looked inside the room to his right. There, Mary and he had spent their last night together in each other's arms. Dropping the reins, he stepped inside and looked around. Men had died in this room where he'd lain with Mary. The walls were chipped from bullet lead and the floor stained with blood, an especially large splotch in front of the door. Something caught his eye in the far corner. Rubio moved toward it, squatted and picked up the tawny skin. He shivered as he lifted Donley Calder's lionskin cap. He held it in his hand, studying the bloodstains. Donley Calder had made his last stand in this room. He hoped Mary had not stayed in this room too, for the blood on the ground could be hers as well as her father's. Had Calder retreated here to protect his daughter?

Rubio removed his hat, placed the lionskin hat on his head, then retreated from the room. Taking his horse's reins, he led the animal out of the chapel. After tying his hat to his saddle, he pulled himself atop the stallion and exited the fortress for Bexar.

The streets still showed signs of the battles that had been fought there, walls damaged by cannonballs or chipped by musket lead. Rubio guessed as many as half of the houses were deserted. The streets were quiet, with few pedestrians. Surely, he thought, Bexar had heard of Sam Houston's victory at San Jacinto.

"The war is over," he called. "Texas is now its own nation."

No one answered and no one came out to

greet him. As he reached the plaza, he pointed his horse at Angelita's house. He had no place better to start his search for Mary Calder. He dismounted and tied his horse. As he approached, the door opened and Angelita's mother came out.

She hugged him warmly. "You are safe."

"The war is over."

"We know. Juan Paz informed us."

Rubio detected hatred in the old woman's voice. He shared her disgust. "How did he know?"

"He was with Santa Anna and barely escaped capture. He returned to Bexar after he heard his excellency had surrendered. His dreams of becoming rich and important have withered."

"And your husband, is he well?"

The senora released her feeble hug and began to cry. "He died a week after the army left. The strain of Angelita's conduct was too much for his heart."

"I am sorry. And Angelita?"

"She has changed."

"Has Juan Paz taken her for his wife?"

The senora hung her head in shame. "Juan Paz has only taken her."

Rubio did not understand what she meant.

"Perhaps, Rubio, it would lift her spirit to see you. She is inside."

Before he could answer, she grabbed his hand and tugged him toward the door.

He did not want to see Angelita, because he

no longer cared for her and wondered why he ever had.

The senora opened the door. "Angelita, you have a visitor."

Rubio stepped inside, not bothering to remove his lionskin cap. When Angelita entered the room, her jaw dropped, her eyes widened and she caught her breath. She could have been no more shocked than he was, however. It was plain she was with child. Now Rubio understood what her mother had meant about Juan Paz taking her.

"I thought you were dead in the Alamo." Angelita rushed to him and threw her arms around him. "Now we can get married and live on your ranch, just as we planned, and have many children." She hugged him tightly. "I'm so happy you came back to me."

Rubio pried her arms from him. "I came for Mary Calder."

Angelita's anger flared. "Then you are breaking your vow to me!"

"You broke that vow yourself, Angelita," Rubio replied. He turned away from her and faced her mother. "Please, *senora,* believe me that this is true."

The old woman nodded. "You always treated Angelita with honor. Juan Paz never did."

"I am sorry," Rubio answered.

"Marry me as promised," Angelita cried, "or you'll regret it."

Rubio ignored her and spoke to the senora. "I

must go and find Mary Calder, if she survived the Alamo."

The senora nodded. "She did."

Rubio felt suddenly elated. That knowledge, though, was but one rung on the ladder to finding her.

"I saw her," the senora said, "after her audience with Santa Anna, but have not seen her since. I don't know what happened to her."

Angelita put her hands on her hips. "I know."

Rubio turned to her. "*Por favor*, where is she?"

Angelita turned her back to him. "I am too upset to tell you."

"*Por favor*," Rubio implored her, but she was as selfish as ever.

"When I am not so upset by your betrayal, I will tell you."

"And when will that be, Angelita?"

"In three hours, inside the Alamo, when I am recovered from the humiliation you have caused me."

Rubio shook his head. She had humiliated herself, but he did not speak his thoughts aloud, for all he wanted was to find Mary Calder. He turned to the senora. "May your luck improve."

The old woman dabbed at the tears falling down her cheek. "May God be with you."

He turned around and left the house, knowing he would never again set foot in it. With nothing to do but wait, Rubio mounted his horse and rode back to the Alamo. He entered the grounds, then turned his horse and retreated outside. Too many dreams had died within those walls and he did not care to recall them. So instead he rode around the outside of the fortress, winding in an ever widening circle as he waited for Angelita.

As he rode he saw three spots of scorched earth, each circle about twenty feet in diameter. They were too big to be campfires and too small to be much of anything else. His horse whinnied and tossed its head as he approached. Dismounting, Rubio studied one circle, then another.

He picked up what resembled a scorched branch broken in half, and realized it was a bone. By its size, it seemed a leg bone. It struck Rubio then that the rings of fire were all that remained of funeral pyres. The Mexicans would not have burned their own dead. The black charred circles and a few charred bones were all that remained of the brave defenders of the Alamo.

He walked around the circles, gathering what bones he could find. He had promised Tomas he would bury his bones on the ranch. The bones he picked up were likely not Tomas's, but he would bury them anyway. He stowed them in his bullet pouch, remounted, and rode back toward the Alamo as the time neared for Angelita's arrival. When he rode into the compound, he heard a cry and saw her standing near the chapel door. Rubio resented her presence so near the spot where Mary and he had lain.

She was crying as rode up. He dismounted and walked over to her, but she averted his gaze.

"I have come as you asked, Angelita. Now tell

me of Mary and where she is."

"You were once my betrothed and now you have scorned me. I will never forgive you."

"Where is she?" Rubio stepped toward her, anger rising in his voice.

Angelita laughed crazily. "She never left Bexar. Juan Paz found her, raped her, and killed her."

"You're lying." Rubio reached for her, but she backed away from him until the wall prevented her retreat.

"She's dead, Rubio, she's dead!" Angelita screamed.

"And now," came another voice, "you'll die too."

Rubio turned and saw Juan Paz emerging from the chapel. He held a cocked pistol in his hand.

"Mary," Rubio shouted, "what did you do with Mary, you bastard?"

Paz laughed. "Killed her like I'm about to kill you." He lifted the pistol for Rubio's chest. "I have taken your woman and now I plan to take your life. Angelita will be mine and you will be dead."

Angelita charged Rubio then, screaming and spitting and slashing at him with her nails. "You humiliated me!" she cried.

Rubio shoved her aside with one hand, and with the other jerked the lionskin cap from his head and flung it at Juan Paz. The pistol exploded, but the lionskin jarred Paz's aim and the bullet flew harmlessly past Rubio.

Enraged with the news of Mary's fate, he

charged Juan Paz and grabbed him around the chest before Paz could react. With all his might he squeezed, until Paz gasped for breath. Then, with the fury of a lion, Rubio lifted Paz and flung him into the stone wall of the chapel.

Paz screamed in pain before slumping to the ground, stunned.

Rubio kicked him in the stomach, then kicked him in the face, bloodying his nose and mouth. From somewhere, Paz mustered the strength to rise to his knees. He slugged Rubio in the gut, stunning him for a moment. Then, at a blow behind his knees, Rubio tumbled backward and realized Angelita had struck him. He hit the ground hard and clawed to get up, his fingers wrapping around the lionskin, but before he could get to his feet, the bloodied Paz jumped astride him and gripped his neck.

The rough hands clamped onto his throat and the fingers began to tighten. Rubio bent his knees to plant his feet on the ground, then with all of his might bucked upward, flinging Paz over him. He got to his hands and knees, his fingers still gripping the lionskin cap. He looked at the cap, then jerked the leather tie string loose. It was a good three feet long.

Leaping on Paz's back as he tried to get up, Rubio looped the leather thong around the man's neck and jerked it tight. Paz gasped and bucked, but Rubio held the leather strand tight, tighter, tightest, even as Angelita beat against his back with her hands and clawed at his face with her nails. Paz struggled, collapsed, fought to get up, then slumped down and lay motionless on the ground. But Rubio held him firm until the leather thong cut into his neck and sprouted blood. Only then did he loosen his grip, confident that Paz was dead.

Angelita screamed and called Rubio vile names, then collapsed beside Paz as if her tears could bring him back to life. Rubio had killed Paz for what he'd done, and he knew if he didn't leave quickly, he might kill Angelita for her part in Mary's death. He turned from her, retrieved the lionskin cap, retied the bloody thong, then mounted his horse and rode away from the Alamo, vowing never again to enter its walls.

He wondered where Mary might be buried so he could put spring flowers upon her grave. It would be a question without an answer, for the man who would know was now dead, and Angelita was so embittered she would never tell.

With no place else to turn, Rubio started for his rancho.

Storm clouds were building to the west as Rubio Portillo neared his ranch compound. Still stunned by word of Mary's death, he rode in a daze, uncertain if he cared to ranch anymore. It might not matter whether he did or not, because he had not seen a single cow with his brand upon it. Since the appearance of the ghostly bull, his cattle had disappeared, his brother had died, and the woman he planned to marry was gone.

When he came within view of the ranch compound, he was pleased to see that it still stood. As he drew closer he saw smoke coming from the chimney in his quarters. He hoped it was the senora who had done his cooking before the war. But with so many families displaced from their homes because of the hostilities, he would not have been surprised whoever was staying inside.

When he reached the walls, he found the gate open and called out, *"Hola!"* He rode inside and dismounted. *"Hola!"*

As he led his horse, he saw the door to his home open. He moved toward it, then stopped. It was Mary who stood in the doorway.

His knees turned soft, then he ran toward her. Was Mary like the ghostly bull? Was he seeing things? She didn't move for a moment, then ran out to meet him.

"Rubio! Rubio!" she cried, "I feared you were dead." Abruptly, she stopped in front of him, as if she'd seen a ghost herself.

"I thought you were dead," Rubio told her with wonderment. "Angelita said you were." He grabbed her and kissed her, and Mary strongly returned his embrace.

She broke from him and pointed to the hat, saying, "It is papa's."

Rubio removed it respectfully. "I found it in the Alamo, in the room we shared our final night together."

"I hope we will spend the rest of our nights together," Mary said.

In the distance, thunder rumbled.

"This can be your home too," Rubio said, "if you will marry me."

She nodded and began to cry. "Papa always promised me one day I would live in a fine house." She gazed around the compound. "He was right."

Rubio escorted her inside, where she had boiled a rabbit. "I fixed a meal every evening for you to share," Mary told him. "I hoped you would return."

They ate and spoke of all that had happened since the Alamo. Rubio told her of the bones he'd collected before killing Juan Paz.

"I will bury them tomorrow, and we will place a stone over them. To us they will always be Tomas and your father."

After dark they stepped outside and watched the storm clouds build, then flash with lightning and rumble with thunder.

"The clouds remind me of the first time I came here," Mary said, putting her arms around Rubio. "I was desperate then."

Rubio nodded, then caught his breath. There on the horizon, he saw it.

The ghostly bull!

"Do you see it, Mary, do you see it?"

"What?"

"The bull."

"No, what are you talking about?"

"The bull. On the horizon!"

"I don't understand."

Rubio said nothing more. He knew it sounded crazy. But he saw its broad shoulders churning as it ran, its nostrils flared, its eyes shining brightly. It had brought bad luck the first time his father had seen it and good luck the second time. Rubio had seen it after Independence Day, and then bad luck had come in cartloads.

And now the bull had returned.

It didn't matter if Mary never saw it.

Drops of rain began to fall, but Rubio didn't move until the bull ran out of sight. Only then did he steer Mary toward the house, where he and she shared a blanket for the second time.

Come morning, Rubio awoke late, dressed quickly and stepped outside. He was surprised at what he heard — the bellowing of cattle. He ran to the gate and looked across his ranch land. Stretched before him, as far as he could see, was his herd of cattle.

They were back, and with them, his luck had returned.

The luck of Texas, bought with blood, was just beginning.